TO THE MOON

BOOK THREE IN THE LOVE UNDER THE ARIZONA SKY SERIES

HILARY DARTT

ALSO BY HILARY DARTT

Love Under the Arizona Sky

All the Stars

The Whole Sky

Mint Creek Ranch

My Favorite Story

My Favorite View

My Favorite Place

Arizona Heat

Pure Luck

Sweet Luck

Terrific Luck

Christmas Luck

Seedling Homestead

A Summer of Wonder

A Dream of Home

A Promise of Forever

The Intervention Series

The Dating Intervention

The Marriage Intervention

The Motherhood Intervention

Garden Club

Jasmine's Pact

Studying Sequoia

Just Holly

TO THE MOON

BOOK THREE IN THE LOVE UNDER THE ARIZONA
SKY SERIES

HILARY DARTT

1

Shane West wasn't living his ideal life, but jumping out of airplanes every day helped take his mind off that. At least, most of the time. One Monday morning, at ten thousand feet altitude, he grinned at his business partner, Roman.

"Ready?" Shane asked, and Roman gave him a nod and offered his fist for a bump.

They had a busy schedule that day — six jumps between seven a.m. and five p.m. — which meant Shane was in his happy place. Their first client, Debbie McIntyre, was celebrating her fortieth birthday with Jump Zone. From the light in her eyes as they got her suited up, Shane was pretty sure she'd become a skydiving junkie. But this was her first time, and she'd become a junkie only if Shane and Roman made it really special.

Shane would jump first, solo, and document Debbie's experience with his high-speed camera. Roman and Debbie would jump second, tandem. The two men took turns photographing and jumping, and Shane loved both tasks equally. He pulled open the door of the airplane and the wind rushed in, whipping around the cabin, making it difficult to hear.

"Ready?" Shane asked Debbie.

She gave him a thumbs up, the smile she'd worn all morning

now stretching into a grimace. Suddenly giddy, Shane gave Roman the countdown and jumped out. For just a couple of seconds, he free fell, gravity pulling him toward the earth at a spine-tingling rate.

"Amazing," Shane murmured to himself. The experience *was* amazing, every time. Every single jump felt like the first: thrilling, scary, dangerous. Exhilarating. He rotated his body so he could see the plane and the silhouettes of Roman and Debbie in the doorway. Good. He was in perfect position. He pulled his cord, knowing that as Roman watched his parachute unfurl, he'd be preparing to jump. Sure enough, a couple of seconds later, the pair came gliding past him. Shane had his camera ready and used it to capture as much of their descent as he could. Roman and Debbie landed first and Shane selected a spot on the other side of the field for his own landing. By the time he made his way over to the pair, the birthday girl was on her feet, arms raised in triumph. Shane lifted his camera and snapped a few photos as Debbie let out a wild holler.

"This is why we do what we do," Roman said as he unhooked his harness from Debbie's. "Happy birthday, Debbie."

Still breathless, Debbie said, "What a thrill! I'm hooked. Some people buy convertibles during their midlife crisis, but I'm going to be a serial skydiver."

"I thought you had that look about you," Shane said.

She threw her arms around him in a giant bear hug.

Back in the office, Shane pulled the memory card from his camera and popped it into the computer. The images from the jump came up on the monitor, and Debbie gasped, jumping up and down. "Oh my gosh! These are great! I look like a complete maniac!"

Smiling, Shane said, "These *are* great. Some of the better images I've gotten. Listen, because it's your birthday, I'll give you one print and all the digital images for free. Consider it our birthday gift to you."

"Really? You would do that?"

"Absolutely," Shane said. "It's not every day someone turns forty and celebrates with us."

Debbie came around the corner and gave him another hug. "Thank you so much!"

Shane printed her favorite image, a snap of her flying past him, giving the camera a double thumbs up and a wild smile, and she practically floated out the shop door.

"That was fun," Roman came to stand beside Shane. "When do you think she'll be back?"

"A month, tops."

"That's what I was thinking. What do we have next?"

Shane clicked over to the scheduling software just as the shop door opened. "You must be Patrick."

The packed day, end to end with takeoffs, jumps, photos, and landings, kept Shane's mind busy. Just the way he liked it. Only at six p.m. as he and Roman prepped the parachutes for the next day, tidied up the shop, and locked the door, did Shane have the mental space to think about anything else. First, he thought about dinner. He had some leftovers in the fridge. That idea made him groan as he got in his truck. Maybe he'd pick something up. A hot, juicy burger and French fries right out of the fryer would really hit the spot. He'd just make an online order and grab the food on the way home.

He took out his phone and despite his best efforts to keep his mind off her, he was forced to think about Jessie Monroe. Because there, on his screen, was a notification she'd sent him a text. He thanked his past self for removing her profile picture. Simply seeing the letters that comprised her name conjured images of eyes with their dark lashes and her full, pouty lips. The last thing he needed was that visual reminder. He opened her message.

Hey, Shane Train. The throwback to his childhood nickname and the memories it dredged up of her cheering for him at track meets made a lump form in his throat. *Would you give me a call when you get a chance?*

Shane rested his head against the headrest, scrubbed his face with his hands, took a deep breath. When would he ever get over her? He had no idea. One thing he did know, though, was that he wasn't going to call her on an empty stomach. He opened the app for Burger Barn and ordered a double cheeseburger and fries. Then he texted her back. *Just about to eat. I'll call you after.*

Suddenly deciding he didn't want to eat alone, Shane updated his order, doubling it, then texted Roman: *Burgers and beer, my place?*

The response came through right away: *See you in 15.*

"I wouldn't say eating a burger from Burger Barn is a religious experience, exactly," Roman said after digging in, "but it's pretty much as close as it gets."

Mouth full, Shane nodded. He grabbed several fries and swiped them through the ketchup he'd squirted on his burger wrapper. "Definitely a religious experience."

Shane's phone dinged again. He turned it over, looked at the screen, and swore.

"What's wrong?" Roman asked. "Another girl asking for a second date you don't want to go on?"

Shane didn't want to have a whole conversation about Jessie, so, without taking a break between bites, he stuffed the burger into his mouth again.

"Ah," Roman said. "I see. You don't want to talk about it. I take it it's that girl. Your childhood best friend. What was it, Judy? June? Jennifer?"

Rolling his eyes, Shane swallowed. Took a swig of beer. "Jessie. Jessie Monroe."

"That's a good name. She sounds like a —"

Shane held up a hand. "Don't even say it."

"What's the deal with her, man? Whenever she comes up, you act all weird about her. You never want to talk about it, but she definitely seems to have an effect on you."

As much as Shane loved the way he and Roman worked together — intuitively in sync, complementary — he hated that that relationship came with Roman's ability to damn near read his mind. He made a dismissive gesture. "You're right. I never want to talk about her."

"What does she want?"

"Your burger's getting cold. You should probably do less talking and more eating."

Roman laughed. "Fine. But I want you to know that I know

something's going on. And not to be all mushy or anything, but if you want to talk about it, we can."

"Thanks." Shane stuffed the burger into his mouth. "I don't."

For the next couple of minutes, he felt content with the silence as the two of them ate and drank. The only problem: it was during those silent moments that thoughts about Jessie crept in. Since he'd left their small hometown a few years before, he'd relived his last summer there dozens of times, each time questioning himself. Asking himself what he could've done differently.

"I was in love with her," he blurted out.

Roman, who had his beer bottle to his lips, raised his eyebrows, took a gulp of his beer, and then said, "I suspected that might be the case."

Shane shook his head. "I was in love with her for years. And she never knew. To her, I was just Shane West, the chubby, nerdy best friend. The confidant." Bitterness edged his voice. "I heard about every one of her crushes, endured questions about whether I thought they liked her. Listened to her pine away after them. Sometimes even had to stop her talking about what great kissers they were."

"Got any ranch?"

Shane pointed at the fridge, and Roman stood up. "Did you say chubby?"

Shane leaned back in his chair and rubbed his six-pack. "I did. I definitely did not have this rockin' bod before I moved here."

Having retrieved the ranch, Roman sat down at the table. "You're, like, the most ripped guy I know."

Chuckling, Shane said, "Yeah, well, that's new. Relatively."

"So, if you guys were best friends, don't you keep in touch? I mean, seriously. If she saw you now, don't you think things would be different?"

If they were going there, Shane needed sustenance. He took two long swigs of beer. "Nah. We still text, pretty regularly, but to tell you the truth, I've avoided seeing her. When I go down to Prescott, I choose weekends I know she's gone. I invited her up here once or twice when I first moved, and we hung out, just like always." Because his voice threatened to crack, he grinned. "But that was before I got these guns." He pulled back his shirtsleeve and flexed his biceps. "But honestly, man, she never thought of me in that way."

His friend shook his head. "So, what did she text you about?"

Shane picked up his phone again and unlocked it. "Earlier, she asked me to call her. I told her I was about to eat and would call her back. Just now, let's see." He navigated to his texting app. "She says she knows I can inhale my dinner in about three-point-seven seconds. And wants to know why I haven't called yet. See? Still thinks of me as the chubby kid she knew back then."

Roman leaned back in his chair, mimicking Shane's posture. "Or, she has something important to tell you and doesn't want to stress you out."

Huh. Shane hadn't thought of that. "If it was that important, I guess she could call me, couldn't she?"

Roman shrugged. "I guess she could." A few beats of silence passed before Roman said, "Well, I guess I'll clear out. Leave you to it."

Shane took his time cleaning up. Not that procrastinating would change anything. In fact, procrastinating simply gave him more time to think about Jessie. He'd always loved her liquid brown eyes, too-big front teeth, and the dimples on the right side of her mouth. As a girl, and even a younger teen, she was cute. She wore bows in her hair and collared shirts with flowers on them. But then one day when they were fourteen something changed.

They ran into each other — literally almost collided — on the sidewalk in front of both of their houses. She laughed, the sound so familiar, the contrast between it and her new look shocked Shane. Her hair, typically in a high ponytail, curled gently around her face and over her shoulders. She wore a plain black v-neck shirt and high-cut jeans that accentuated her slender waist and generous hips. He was thinking, *You look different*, but he knew better than to say that — especially because of the way his body was responding to that difference. For the first time, he felt pure, unbridled lust for an actual girl. Not a movie star or a musician, but a real, actual girl. The girl next door. And because he didn't know what to do with that, he blurted out an apology, did an about-face, and hightailed it back to his house where he ran up the stairs and locked himself in his bedroom to sort out his thoughts. He'd always loved Jessie Monroe, but that was the day he fell *in* love with her.

Even though she looked different after that (she took a new interest in fashion and beauty magazines and implemented what she read), she was still the same, funny, sweet girl he'd grown up with. They still walked to school together, stopped by her house for snacks after school, and hung out on weekends, watching movies or doing science experiments. He knew he could never tell her how he felt. It would change things between them.

Then she started dating. *That* changed things between them, but she didn't even know. Completely oblivious to the things she did to him, she went about her life.

Sometimes, Shane would watch from his bedroom window — not in a creepy way, but in a sad, wistful way — as another guy picked her up for a date. His dad noticed (of course he did).

One night, just after Jessie climbed into Ranger Morrison's truck and the thing sped away with an earsplitting roar, Shane's dad, Alvin, knocked on his door. "Son? Why don't the two of us go out and do something fun?"

Even in his state, somewhat heartbroken, mad at himself for not being able to share his feelings with Jessie, Shane could see the value in his dad's idea and agreed to go. They wound up at the only arcade in town, just to find that Jessie and Ranger had come up with the same brilliant idea. For a little while, Shane and Alvin did their best to avoid Jessie and Ranger. They played a couple of rounds of Skee-ball and two games of miniature basketball. But when his dad saw him watching Jessie and Ranger compete in air hockey, he threw an arm around Shane's shoulders and said, "Come on. Let's go shoot some real hoops."

Back then, Shane wasn't athletic, but he and Alvin enjoyed shooting around at the park. After an hour, they were both sweaty and tired, and Shane admitted to his dad that he was feeling quite a bit better.

"Listen, son. I see the way you look at Jessie. And I'm sorry she doesn't look at you the same way — at least, not right now. I wish I could tell you she would come around, but it's possible she won't. There's just no way to tell the future. But I want you to know, she's the one who's missing out. You are a wonderful young man, and whoever you end up with will be a lucky woman."

Emotion clogging his throat, Shane said, "Thanks, Dad."

Although his dad spoke with authority, he'd never married — he adopted Shane when Shane was seven, and it was just the two of them after that.

As a teen, his heart aching for a young woman he couldn't have, Shane didn't give more than a passing thought to whether his dad might be speaking from experience. Instead, he wallowed in his own misery.

Fast forward to present day. He wasn't a teen anymore, but his emotions around Jessie still gripped him. The garbage from Burger Barn sat in the trashcan, along with Roman's empty beer bottle. Shane finished off his second beer while he scrubbed the kitchen counter, which gleamed, and the sink, which sparkled.

Having run out of things to do Shane picked up his phone, and sighing heavily, called Jessie.

"Took you long enough," she said, her voice coming through line with its normal playful tone. "What did you do, buy out the whole burger joint?"

Despite the memories he'd just relived, Shane found himself smiling. "How do you know I got burgers?"

"Something about the tone of your voice. Your text voice."

Shane couldn't help it. He pictured Jessie at home in her cute little craftsman-style bungalow, wearing baggy sweats and an even baggier t-shirt, her hair in that high ponytail he so loved. She'd probably already washed her face, which meant she was at her prettiest.

"For your information, I had just one burger. A double, but still."

"I knew it." Her tone had shifted, and Shane said, "So, what's up?"

The sound of her deep inhale and long exhale came through the earpiece. His stomach roiled with nerves.

"I don't want you to be worried," she said, and he said, "You know that by saying that, you've now made me worry."

Her laugh was just shy of authentic. "Sorry. Has your dad mentioned that he and I have been spending some time together?"

Weary all of a sudden, Shane sat down at the bar, his elbow on the counter and his hand rubbing his eyes. "He mentioned it." What Shane didn't mention was the sharp pang of jealousy he felt whenever his dad mentioned having lunch or shopping with Jessie, tasks he'd imagined doing with her.

"Shane — I'm just going to say it. I'm worried about your dad. I don't know that he should be living alone. Most of the time, his mind is there. Sharp as a tack. But he's been a bit forgetful. And he's gotten pretty frail. I do love hanging out with him, but the real reason we've been spending so much time together is because I'm checking up on him, and, to tell you the truth, helping him out quite a bit."

While she talked, Shane felt a tremor starting somewhere deep in his core. Alvin West couldn't get old. He couldn't be frail. He was the strongest man Shane knew. He gulped. "How bad is it?"

Another deep breath. "I mean, it's not too bad right now. But, for example, last week we got just the tiniest bit of snow, and the driveway was icy. He fell while he was going to get the mail." She chuckled. "I think he overestimates his abilities."

"He fell? Why didn't he call me? Why didn't *you*?"

"Everything was fine. And neither one of us wanted to bother you. You've made it pretty obvious that you're busy, and aside from a little bruising, he was none the worse for wear. We didn't want to worry you. But then, just yesterday, I went over there to bring him dinner and I noticed he'd left the stove on. No flame, just propane, leaking into the air. That's dangerous. I feel like it might be a good idea for you to come home, spend a little time, see what you think."

2

———————

Jessie Monroe made one more lap around Alvin West's house, checking that everything was in order. The walk-around had become part of her evening routine. She checked for tripping hazards, made sure the doors were locked, and did various chores, like taking out the trash can or bringing it in, carrying the laundry from the laundry room into the living room for Alvin to fold, and tucking his shoes under the entryway bench.

"Go on now, honey," Alvin said to her from his spot on the couch. "I know you've got plans tonight. You don't need to worry about me. I'll be just fine."

From her spot atop a step stool in the kitchen where she was putting away a vase, Jessie called back, "I know you can, but you know me. There are just certain things I can't leave undone."

She heard Alvin mumble something about her OCD and she smiled to herself. Of all the aspects of her life that unfolded over the past several years, her relationship with Alvin was probably her favorite. She loved her job at the high school, and her friendships with her best friends Rose Coffey and Taylor Cole. She loved living in her childhood home, having made it her own after her parents sold it to her and moved out. But most of all, she loved hanging out with Alvin.

He'd been her next door neighbor throughout her entire childhood, and the father of her best friend, Shane. Once Shane moved out, Jessie started checking up on him, and they found they had a lot in common: a penchant for crosswords, a love of ramen, and strong enthusiasm for the Arizona Cardinals.

"Hey, help me with this one before you go. A long time in a dungeon. Three letters." Alvin had done the newspaper's daily crossword puzzles since Jessie was a kid and he asked her for help whenever she came over. That hadn't changed. Jessie closed the cabinet and put away the step stool. She walked into the living room and sat down on the loveseat. "That's a tough one. How many letters did you say? And what's it start with?"

"Three, and ends with an *N*."

"Could it be eon?"

Grinning, Alvin touched his nose. "You got it." He wrote the letters into the crossword puzzle. "See? This is why I keep you around."

"That's sad," she said, pouting. "I thought you kept me around because I'm such great company."

He looked up at her and winked. "That, too."

They worked out a few more clues together and then he looked at the clock. "Don't you have somewhere to be? Get out of my hair."

"As much of it as you've got left."

Alvin guffawed. "Very funny. You sound like Shane."

"Well, we did grow up together."

"True."

"Speaking of Shane," Jessie said. "You heard from him lately?"

"He calls every Sunday. No more, no less."

Jessie frowned. She talked to her parents almost every day. Maybe men and women were different. Still, Alvin was getting older, and she didn't want Shane to regret his infrequent calls and even less frequent visits. She made a mental note to talk to him about that when he came.

"But," Alvin said, looking up from his crossword with a smile on his face, "he says he's coming this weekend. Should be here tomorrow."

Oh, good. "That's great. It'll be nice to see him."

"It will. And you'll get a couple of days off from keeping an eye on me."

Jessie shook her head. "I like keeping an eye on you. Besides, now that Taylor and Rose are both paired off, you're my social outlet most of the time."

"But not tonight." He used a hand to to shoo her. "Now go on. Get out of here."

Fifteen minutes later, Jessie, her friends Taylor and Rose, and Rose's five-year-old daughter Celeste sat in the round corner booth at Rita's diner. Rita, proprietress, stood in front of the table, a hand on her hip, a piece of gum in her mouth. "How are you ladies today?"

"We're great!" Celeste said. "I just beat Jessie at tic-tac-toe. That's only, like, my third time ever beating her."

"That's great, sweetheart," Rita said. She took a mint candy from her apron pocket and set it in front of Celeste. "I think you deserve this."

Celeste glanced at Rose, and without asking permission (she wasn't supposed to eat candy before her meal), she pulled on the ends of the plastic wrapper, plucked out the candy, and popped it into her mouth.

Rita looked at them over the top of her glasses. "The usual for you ladies?"

"The usual," Celeste said.

"The usual," Jessie, Rose, and Taylor said.

Rita jotted down their orders, snapped her notebook closed, and with one last wink at Celeste, went back to the kitchen.

"So what's new, ladies?" Jessie asked. With Taylor starting Sugar Pine Barn and her wedding just days away, and Rose newly engaged to their coworker, Johnny MacKinnon (and having moved onto his farm), the two of them had more going on than Jessie did. Sometimes she felt a little lonely and wished for a romantic partner. But she'd learned the hard way that romantic partners weren't all they were cracked up to be.

"Well," Celeste said. "It's almost Christmas. As you know."

Jessie chuckled. "I did know that, yes."

"What you don't know," Celeste said, "is that Mac and Mommy and I are going to go to the forest and cut down a Christmas tree."

"Wow," Jessie said. "That sounds like so much fun!"

Celeste nodded. "Way more fun than putting up our fake tree."

"When are you going to do that?"

"I think this weekend, right?" Celeste said to Rose, who nodded. "Yep. This weekend. I'm kind of excited about it. It's my first time."

Jessie felt a little stab of jealousy, but she tamped it down. One day, she would get to create her own new traditions with whoever was lucky enough to be her life partner. And hopefully, with their children. For now, she could live vicariously through her friends.

"And what about you, Taylor?" Jessie said.

"Well, nothing too exciting. Thanks to you guys, I have hardly anything to do before the wedding."

"I can't believe it's happening in a week," Jessie said. "It seems like just yesterday the two of you first met."

"I know," Taylor said. "And to think, before we met, I thought I was destined to be an invisible librarian, single and lonely, for the rest of eternity."

Jessie smiled, but Taylor's words hit close to home. Sometimes, she felt like she was destined to be single and lonely for the rest of eternity. Every time she thought she'd met someone — not even the one, but someone with whom she could share a real relationship — the universe threw her a curve ball.

Quite out of nowhere, a memory fell down out of the atmosphere and flooded her consciousness.

Her first "serious" date, with Ranger Tillman. She initially noticed him freshman year. His eyes were the most incredible light blue color, like the powers that be had doled out actual scoops of ocean water when they assigned them. Although he never looked her way unless he was looking past her, she somehow convinced herself that he knew she existed. They had a couple of classes together. She sat right behind him in math class, and once he asked her to borrow a pencil. That's when she noticed how straight his teeth were.

To her high school self, he was *everything*. Hung the moon and the stars and all that. When he asked her to the homecoming dance sophomore year, she managed to stop herself from jumping and pumping her fists for only as long as it took him to walk away, that cocky, smug (sexy) smile on his face. She spent the next week daydreaming about their time together. He said he had a commitment before the dance but would meet her there. He'd wait at the school entrance, beaming with anticipation. His eyes would widen in shock at how beautiful she looked in the dress she'd gotten to match his cummerbund (it was a weird pea-green color, but she didn't care; she'd lusted after Ranger the entire time she'd been in high school and would wear a trash bag if he asked her to).

He would smile, so warmly, and hold out his hand. She would slip hers into it and immediately notice how they fit together like two pieces of a puzzle. Her adult self rolled her eyes, internally, at her younger self's naiveté.

Neither Rose nor Taylor had dates for the dance, so they were going together and promised to find Jessie there. She spent the entire day primping and prepping, physically and mentally. She showered and shaved, curled her hair and followed an online makeup tutorial. And she looked *good*.

Just before she left the house, her mom said, "I love that you're dressing up so nicely, hon, but I hope you're doing it as much for yourself as you are for this Ranger boy."

"I am, Mom," Jessie said, grinning so big, her cheeks hurt. "I promise."

Even then, as she got into her car and drove to the school, she knew she hadn't told the whole truth. She was primping for Ranger … if she hadn't had a date, she wouldn't have done quite so much.

After parking, she touched up her lipstick and powder, and then checked her teeth, pinched her cheeks, and got out. So what if the heels were a little hard to walk in? So what if her dress pinched her rib cage on the right side? So what if the strapless bra wanted to slide down every time she moved? She was going to the homecoming dance with Ranger Tillman.

And there he was, standing right in the school entrance, just as she'd envisioned a hundred times since he asked her to the dance.

Only, he wasn't wearing a cummerbund to match her dress. He wasn't wearing one at all. He was wearing a bow tie, and it was pink. Hot pink. That's when Jessie realized: he was standing with his usual crowd, one of whom was a curvy, vivacious, and bitchy girl in their math class, Vikki Spitz. She was wearing a hot pink dress that matched Ranger's bow tie exactly, and she sneered — actually *sneered* — as Jessie approached.

"Nice dress," she said. "Did you spill split pea soup on it, or something?"

The sound of the rest of the gang snickering echoed in Jessie's consciousness, like she was in a spooky cave. It took only seconds for Jessie to nail down what happened: Ranger invited her to the dance as a joke. Surely he knew she'd fawned over him since freshman year, and, apparently, his cronies knew that, too. He'd wanted to see how far he could get her to go.

Pretty far.

She turned and ran back to her car, the sharp pain when she twisted her ankle nothing compared to the hurt she felt inside. Tearing off her heels, she threw them across the parking lot. She drove home barefoot repeating the mantra: "I will never fall for anyone, ever again."

She later told Rose and Jessie she'd gotten sick at the last minute and never revealed the truth. It was simply too humiliating.

Then there was Mitch Williams. Her fiancé ... at least, in her mind, for a week. They dated for several months their freshman year of college. More accurately, she thought now, they spent every spare moment in bed together their freshman year of college. He said all the pretty things to her.

Things like, "I can't wait until we graduate and start our lives together," and, "Making love to you is a spiritual experience," and "You're the only woman for me." She believed every single one of them. And although Mitch proclaimed he was the quiet type, Jessie shared every single one of her feelings with him: all her fears and insecurities, her hopes for the future, the names she'd already chosen for the children she'd have one day, which color she wanted to paint her first house, and which flowers she'd plant out front.

If he was less invested than she was, he didn't let on. Or she didn't notice.

Second semester, he met Taylor and Rose. The four of them hung out a few times. They went out to dinner, to the movies, and bowling. He asked for her friends' phone numbers. Because Valentine's Day was around the corner, she convinced herself he'd asked because he wanted to propose and was going to ask their advice on how best to do it.

One weekend in early February, she went home to do laundry and visit her parents. Mitch came to her parents' house to surprise her. At first, she was mortified — she was wearing her flying pig pajamas, which she normally wouldn't be caught dead in — but then she realized he'd probably come to propose. She greeted him with a series of deep, intense kisses and waited. But nothing. He didn't so much as ask her on a date, much less propose. Jessie told herself he couldn't live without her while she was away from college for the weekend; that was almost as good as proposing.

She'd later realize she was projecting her own feelings onto him; she would have loved to marry him, and she figured he felt the same way. Only, he didn't.

Rose came to her one day the second week of February and said, "Jessie, I've got to tell you something important and I don't know how to say it."

Jessie didn't even think to be nervous. "Just spit it out."

Rose took a deep breath. "Mitch asked me out."

Jessie was devastated. Crushed. Her soul was shattered. Mitch, of course, denied asking Rose out, but Jessie trusted her friend more than she trusted him. She played it off to Rose, acting like it didn't bother her, even though she was tempted to swear off men for good. She'd poured her very soul out to him ... just like she had with Ranger Tillman. And he'd stomped on it. Again, she vowed she'd never fall for anyone, ever again.

"Yoohoo, earth to Jessie," modern-day Rose was saying.

Jessie blinked, bringing herself back to Rita's Diner, where she sat safe and sound across from her two best friends. Two best friends who still had no idea what she'd gone through with

Ranger Tillman or how much she thought she loved Mitch Williams.

"Sorry," Jessie said. "I just zoned out for a minute. Tired, I guess. What were we talking about?"

"Anyway, to kill time while we wait for the wedding festivities, Judd and I are rearranging some of the rooms in the house so I can have a home office." She shrugged. "Not the most exciting stuff, but it'll be nice to have somewhere to put all my paperwork."

"And all the girly decorations Uncle Judd doesn't want in the living room," Celeste said.

Taylor's jaw dropped. "What makes you say that?" she asked.

Celeste immediately snapped her mouth shut and averted her gaze. "Nothing."

Knowing guilt when she saw it, Jessie said, "Did Uncle Judd say something about that to you?"

Celeste looked down at the table and drummed her fingers. "Maybe."

The four of them were still laughing when Rita brought their food.

They'd almost finished eating when the bell jingled over the diner's door. Jessie had her back to the door, and although she couldn't see who'd come in, she clearly saw her friends exchange a glance, eyebrows raised.

"Who is it?" Jessie asked, already craning her neck to see for herself.

"I don't know," Rose said, "and I know I'm recently attached, but I'd be remiss if I didn't say that's a very built young man."

She was right. Two of them had walked in and stood at the counter, their backs to the room. Jessie knew immediately which one Rose was referring to: the man on the right looked like any other guy, dressed in jeans and a sweatshirt, a beanie on his head. And then there was the guy on the left. Not only was he taller, but he also looked like he worked out for a living. Broad-shouldered, trim-waisted, and cut from actual marble, he filled out his jeans like they'd been made for him.

"You should close your mouth," Celeste whispered to Jessie.

After obeying, Jessie licked her lips and said, "Wow."

"I know," Taylor said. "I am also recently attached, but I'd also be remiss if I didn't say, *yummy*."

That threw Celeste into a fit of giggles, and Taylor rushed to explain. "That's probably not the most appropriate thing for a lady to say about a gentleman, and I'm not setting the best example, Celeste."

"I know," Celeste said, making a dismissive gesture with her pudgy little hand.

Momentarily distracted, Jessie looked back at the counter, where Rita stood facing the two guys, chatting them up like she knew them.

"I mean, I could just—"

"Careful," Rose said. "We have little ears at the table."

"Take a hike, Celeste," Jessie said, and when Celeste made an exaggerated pouting face, Jessie wrapped an arm around her. "I'm totally kidding." She covered Celeste's ears and whispered to Rose and Taylor, "I could really just grab that delicious ass."

That threw Rose and Taylor into a fit of giggles, and Jessie felt her face flushing.

"Wait," Taylor said. "There's something familiar about that guy, isn't there?"

By that time, they'd seen his profile a couple of times as he looked from Rita to his friend.

"Oh, trust me," Jessie said. "If I'd seen him before, I'd know."

At long last, Rita slid their to-go containers across the counter, and all three women (plus Celeste) sat up straight to get a better look as the men turned around. Jessie realized they were all poised to stare at the pair, and said, "This is so obvious," before quickly looking down at the table.

"Oh, my God," Rose hissed, and Taylor gripped Jessie's hand under the table and whispered, "Holy shit."

"What?" Jessie said.

She looked up just in time to see the two men reaching the door. And then she saw him: that sexy man she'd just been ogling like a cat ready to pounce or a dog drooling over a piece of steak ... it was Shane. Shane West, her very best friend from childhood.

Only, he didn't look like Shane West anymore.

"Well, he's certainly grown up," she choked. She swallowed. How was that possible? Why hadn't he told her?

What would he even say, dummy? she chided herself. *"I've become a total heartthrob since the last time we saw each other. I'm smokin' hot now. You're going to want to sleep with me on sight."*

His friend opened the diner door and just before they went out, Shane glanced in the direction of the corner booth. At first, his eyes roamed over their table as if he didn't realize he knew the people sitting there. But then he seemed to see Jessie, and his eyes came to rest on her.

Energy zipped across the room and hit her right in the heart, warming as it traveled through her body, tingling all the way to her fingers and toes. Shane's face lit up, and his smile was so full of affection and so genuine, she forgot that just a moment before, she'd been admiring his ass in his jeans, and found herself flying out of the booth and into his arms as he came to sweep her up into a giant hug.

Everything was the same and everything was different.

It was Shane, through and through. Her heart knew his, their connection built through a lifetime of shared experiences. But also, for the first time, she saw him as a *man*. He smelled so good and his arms felt so strong and she had to stop herself from wrapping her legs around his waist. His laugh sounded so deep and rumbly and it turned her on. Hers probably sounded maniacal, but she didn't care.

He set her down and the two of them stood there, staring at each other, grinning like a couple of idiots.

"It's good to see you," he said, and she said, "It's good to see you. I hardly recognize you."

If it were possible, his smile got even bigger. "It *has* been a while."

"Because you always come home when I'm out of town, you big lug!" She gave him a friendly punch on the shoulder, and then grimaced. "Geez, your shoulder is, like, rock hard!"

Fortunately, Taylor, Rose, and Celeste had made their way over to greet Shane, and saved both him and Jessie from bathing in the discomfort of her talking about rock-hard body parts.

"Wow," Rose gushed, "You're, like, built, Shane! Have you been hitting the gym, or what?"

Now he was blushing, and looking a lot more like the best friend Jessie grew up with. *Only, hotter.*

"I have," he said. "I guess since my hobby became my business, I had to get a new hobby."

"How's your business going?" Taylor wanted to know.

"Great," Josh said. "I'm loving it. We're real busy, which is good, and we have some great employees, which is why I was able to get away for the weekend."

He looked at Jessie again and she said, "I'm so glad you came. Your dad must have been happy to see you."

A shadow passed over Shane's face before he answered, while scratching the back of his head. "I haven't seen him yet. I'm spending the night at Mikey's house." He jerked his thumb at the friend he'd come in with, who lifted his chin in greeting. "I wanted to hang out before diving in to all the stuff you mentioned about Dad."

Jessie nodded. "I get that. But I don't want you to worry. It's not an emergency or anything."

Shane shifted his weight. "Good to know. Anyway, I'd better get going. We're meeting some friends at The Hideaway tonight for a few drinks after dinner."

After hugs all around, Shane and Mikey left, and the girls stood there, flabbergasted. Always picking up on a vibe, Rita hollered across the diner, "Why don't you sit down, ladies? You're blocking the doorway. That Shane West is a tall drink of water, isn't he?" She cackled as the girls returned to their booth.

Once Jessie was settled, she looked up to see both Rose and Taylor staring at her, their hands folded on the table in front of them. Celeste noticed, too, and copied their posture, her bright eyes focused on Jessie.

"What are you guys thinking?" Jessie asked, even though she already knew.

"I'm thinking, wow," Rose said. "Not just because Shane is now like, totally hot, but also because we all saw how you reacted to said transformation."

Again, Jessie felt her face heat with embarrassment.

Taylor jumped in. "Yeah. I mean, first of all —" she fanned her face with her hand. "And second of all, your reaction was … let's just say, not the reaction a best friend would have. It was carnal. Lustful. Dare I say, impure?"

"What's impure?" Celeste asked while Jessie's face continued to burn, and she looked anywhere but at Taylor and Rose.

"Um." Rose cleared her throat, and Taylor offered her an apologetic look. "Usually it means, like, something mixed into something else."

"Hmm," Celeste said. "I don't get it. So Aunt Jessie had mixed-up thoughts about that guy? Shane?"

"Exactly," Jessie said. "You nailed it."

They ordered dessert, and when Rita brought them the slices of apple pie with ice cream, she said to Jessie, "You know, your two friends here" (she pointed and Taylor and Rose) "they found romance at Rita's. After what I just saw, I'm thinking maybe you just found romance here, too."

"That's ridiculous," Jessie said, scooping a big hunk of pie onto her fork. "We grew up together. We're just friends. That's it."

Rita looked at Jessie over the top of her glasses. "Uh huh."

Because Jessie's mouth was full, Rita directed her attention to Taylor and Rose. "Mark my words," she said to them. "There's romance in the air … and it all started here at Rita's Diner."

Celeste held up her fork, using it to make a point. "Mark her words, ladies. Aunt Jessie's about to fall in love."

Rita floated off, calling out to her husband, "Sal, we have a new love story forming here, honey."

Obviously trying not to smile, Rose said, "Well, we've stayed late enough. It's almost Celeste's bedtime."

"But it's a weekend," Celeste said. "And we're having so much fun, aren't we?"

Jessie wrapped an arm around Celeste's shoulders, eager to ensure the conversation stayed on the topic of bedtime. "We *are* having so much fun. But aren't you going to cut your tree tomorrow?"

Celeste's eyes lit up. "Yes!"

"Well, that won't be as much fun if you're grumpy because you didn't get to bed on time. You know that."

Slumping, Celeste said, "True. Fine. I guess we can go, Mom."

Rose's eyes twinkled with humor when she said, "Fine. You calling me Mom now, instead of Mommy?"

From under grumpy eyebrows, Celeste looked up at Rose. "For tonight, anyway."

Everyone scooted out of the booth, exchanged hugs and good-byes, and went their separate ways, with Rose and Celeste promising to send pictures of their tree the next day.

Alone in her silent car, Jessie leaned her head against the head-rest. Was she attracted to Shane? How, after all these years, could she suddenly want to jump his bones? He was the same guy she'd spent the long days of summer with, fishing and catching tadpoles and frogs and climbing trees. They'd walked to the bus stop together every morning, and spent afternoons at one of their houses, doing homework and eating snacks and gossiping about their classmates. They were more like siblings than anything else.

Until now, a coy voice piped up in the back of her mind. *Until he walked into Rita's Diner looking like an absolute hunk.*

Picturing him again, Jessie felt herself wondering what he looked like without a shirt on. Undoubtedly his muscles were divine, and the idea of running her hands over his skin made her feel tingly all over.

What in the world is happening?

Certainly these feelings would pass after a good night's sleep. With that thought comforting her, she put her Jeep in gear and went home.

3

___

Shane's skull vibrated with each beat of his heart. This was the worst hangover he'd had in as long as he could remember. When he dared to open his eyes, the sunlight streaming through Mikey's living room window seared his eyeballs. He cringed, groaned, and closed his eyes again, rolling away from the light and burying his face in the space between the couch cushions and the back of the couch.

"Hurtin' pretty good this morning, eh?" Mikey said.

From what Shane could tell, his friend was somewhere in the house. His voice echoed, sending waves of nausea through Shane's body. He moaned in response and Mikey laughed, the son of a gun.

"Sit up, man. I have just what you need."

Shane obeyed. His head pounded even worse. Mikey handed him a glass and a plate.

"What is this?"

"In the glass, my man, is the best hangover cure I've found. If you can keep it down. And on the plate is my favorite post-night-out breakfast: a greasy breakfast burrito stuffed with bacon, eggs, cheese, and potatoes."

"Huh." Shane grunted and sniffed the contents of the glass. "Smells like orange soda."

"Tastes like orange soda," Mikey said.

"How are you so chipper, dude?"

"Sorry," Mikey said. "I think you had more to drink than I did. After we ran into Jessie at the diner, you got blitzed, man."

Apparently, Shane's language skills were limited to grunts and moans.

"Drink up," Mikey said, then winced. "I mean, go ahead and try the hangover cure. It'll help. Just take small sips. I'm gonna hit the shower."

After setting his plate on the coffee table, Shane did as Mikey instructed. He was surprised when, after a few minutes, his mind began to clear a bit, and his headache and nausea subsided a little.

Naturally, when those symptoms stopped inhabiting every cubic inch of his consciousness, he thought of the night before — and Jessie. God, she was still just as radiant as ever. There was just something about her, something almost ethereal. Seeing her was a surprise, although he knew she and the girls often hung out at Rita's. Because he'd been caught off guard, he hadn't had time to steel himself against his reaction to her.

His heart leapt — he could feel it in his chest. Then, when they hugged, his dick leapt. He could definitely feel that. And although he was probably reading her reaction wrong, it seemed like she found him *attractive*.

"You're definitely reading it wrong," he muttered before finishing off the drink Mikey made him. "You're her best friend. The only thing she wants to do in the bedroom is have a pillow fight."

Still, letting himself imagine, just for a minute, or maybe even for the day, that she found him attractive couldn't hurt, could it?

Feeling miraculously better, he picked up the breakfast burrito and took a giant bite. The salty food tasted heavenly. While he chewed, he let himself fantasize. What if Jessie really did think of him as more than a friend?

He'd imagined making love to her innumerable times, so that fantasy was nothing new. But what would it be like to date her? To spend evenings together, cuddled up on the couch? To ask her for advice or bounce ideas off her while they made coffee in the morning?

Mikey's return pulled Shane out of full-on fantasy mode, and he was at once grateful and resentful.

"Ah, I see you're feeling better."

"And you're smelling better," Shane quipped.

"Haha. Thanks, though. That burrito hit the spot. And I think that hangover cure stuff worked wonders."

"Every time, man. I'll send you a link so you can buy some."

"Thanks," Shane said, "but I don't plan on drinking that much in a sitting anytime soon. Maybe ever."

Mikey laughed. "All right, I've got to head to work. Stay as long as you like. I left the key on the entry table. Just lock up and leave it under the garden gnome."

"No problem. Thanks again for letting me stay."

"Any time, bro. You know that."

Driving up to his childhood home thirty minutes later, Shane exhaled. Coming home always felt like ... well, like coming home. It felt comfortable. Safe. But this time, it also felt nerve-wracking.

Jessie said his dad was getting older, Shane thought as he put his truck in park and turned off the ignition. Generally, children knew their parents would age, but Shane figured watching it happen was just about the worst experience. Maybe that was part of why he stayed away. Jessie being the other part.

The sound of his seatbelt unbuckling seemed loud in the silence of the cab, and so did the sound of him pulling the door handle. His feet crunched on the leaves blanketing the driveway and walkway.

Before he knocked on the door, Shane noticed that the trim on the house was peeling — just enough that he'd need to hire a painter to put on a fresh coat. He made a mental note to get some bids and schedule that before the summer monsoon season.

After he knocked, it seemed like forever before he heard the doorknob turn. The hinges creaked as Alvin opened the door. When Shane saw his dad, he felt overjoyed ... and he also noticed that he did, in fact, look quite a bit older. The lines in his face were deeper, and the bones in his shoulders and wrists protruded.

Grinning, Alvin opened his arms. "My boy!"

Shane stepped into his embrace. "Hi, Dad."

He may be getting older, but his hug still felt exactly the same. His arms were strong and he smelled like the cognac-and-musk cologne Shane bought him for every birthday.

Alvin gripped Shane's shoulders and held him at arms' length. "You been eatin' your spinach!"

Shane grinned. "You know I have."

"Come in, come in. It's so good to see you."

His dad stepped back to let him inside and Shane couldn't help but notice that he looked smaller and frailer as he shut and locked the door and then led Shane into the kitchen, where he started going through the fridge.

"I wasn't sure what time to expect you," he said, "so yesterday, I made your favorite soup. I figured we could eat it for dinner. And, I invited Jessie to join us." Shane's stomach lurched, and Alvin went on, "She's been feeding me near every day, so I figured I could repay the favor. And that you'd like to see her."

"Sure," Shane said, hoping his dad couldn't tell he was gritting his teeth. "Great!"

Alvin turned around, the giant soup pot in shaky hands. Shane was tempted to take the pot from him but refrained — it wouldn't do for him to come in here and start treating his dad like an invalid.

"I'll just put this on now," Alvin said. "I know it's only lunchtime, but the longer it simmers, the better it tastes."

He set the pot on the back burner and turned on the flame. Someone knocked on the door. Alvin looked at the clock, and then at Shane, a happy gleam in his eye. "I'll bet that's Jessie. She usually stops by at lunchtime on weekends, since she's not at work."

Again with the stomach lurching.

"Why don't you get it? She'll be so happy to see you."

Shane shrugged as if the idea of seeing her again didn't give him palpitations, walked to the front door, and pulled it open. And there she was, smiling so big, he figured she thought it was Christmas morning.

Her smile changed, just the tiniest bit, when she realized it was

Shane, not Alvin, who'd answered the door. He couldn't tell if it bordered on a grimace or an extra-excited smile, and decided not to dwell on it.

"Shane! Hi!" Jessie opened her arms for a hug, but before he could reciprocate, she stuck out her right hand for a shake. He'd already put a hug into motion, though, and when she realized that was his intention, she dropped her hand and opened her arms again.

And then they were embracing, and his heart responded, and his sensible inner voice was telling him it was just a hug and not to get excited over it.

She smelled so good, like vanilla and cinnamon and honey, and he had a hard time letting go of her.

"I wasn't sure what time you were coming," she said when he did, "so I was just stopping by with lunch." When Shane glanced down at her empty hands, she put one of them to her forehead. "Which I left in the car. Be right back."

"What happened?" Alvin asked, his voice coming from just behind Shane's shoulder.

"Left your lunch in the car," Shane said.

Alvin guffawed. "That girl."

There it was again: jealousy. Alvin talked about Jessie with the familiarity of a father. For the first time in ages, Shane wondered if perhaps keeping his distance — from Jessie, from their hometown, and from his dad — had been a mistake.

But then Jessie was back, a bag in her hand and a smile on her face, and he couldn't think of anything other than how much he wanted to kiss her. Oh, and how he wouldn't.

She held up the bag. "I brought you a sandwich and some chips."

Beaming Alvin took it from her. "Thank you. As you know —"

"There's no need," Jessie finished, and Alvin gestured for her to follow him and Shane back to the kitchen.

"But," she said as he set the sandwich and chips on a plate, "As *you* know —"

"You like to."

"Right."

Shane could tell the two of them spent lots of time together, and his heart added a layer of guilt on top of the jealousy.

"Anyway," Jessie said. "I'll leave you two to it. I don't want to interrupt your bonding time. I'll check in with you later."

She headed for the door and Alvin called, "Come for dinner! I made soup."

That stopped Jessie in her tracks. "You made soup?" she said, turning around.

"I did." Alvin looked so proud of himself, Shane had to wonder when he'd cooked last.

"That's great," Jessie said. "And you'd better believe I'll be here to eat it. What can I bring? Bread? Salad? Wine?"

Alvin raised a hand to dismiss her, but she said, "I insist."

"Fine," he said. "Bring all three."

And she was gone.

After the door closed, Shane and his dad stood in the kitchen alone again, staring at each other.

"What are you thinking?" Shane asked after a long, awkward silence.

"I'm just thinking that I see something between the two of you youngsters that wasn't there before."

Shane turned away and busied himself fiddling with the flame under the soup. "Is that what you're thinking?"

"I notice you didn't deny it."

Sighing, Shane turned back toward his father. "I didn't."

"Is there something you want to tell me about?"

"I came into town last night," Shane blurted, and wasn't surprised at the look of hurt that crossed Alvin's face. "I know," he rushed to add. "I didn't tell you. I'd mentioned to my friend Mikey that I was coming into town for the weekend, and he invited me to hang out." He shrugged. "I haven't seen him since before sophomore year of college, and we always had a blast together. I'm sorry I didn't tell you. I should have, but I didn't want to you to feel bad. And a good thing, too, because we stayed up way too late and I would have kept you up."

"Fair enough," Alvin said. "Let's get back on topic. But let's do it sitting on the couch."

Once they were seated, Alvin took a healthy bite of his sandwich and Shane said, "Anyway. We ordered takeout from Rita's and when we were leaving, I noticed Jessie and her friends sitting in the corner booth." Remembering that moment, he had to catch his breath. "She jumped out of that booth, flew across the room, and tackled me in a hug. I could swear she felt something, Dad. But for the rest of the night, I told myself it was just my imagination."

"Huh," Alvin said. He steepled his fingers and rested his chin on them. "I'm not so sure it is, son."

Stomach aflutter with butterflies, Shane said, "Why do you say that?"

"I've known you since you were six years old, skinny as a rail, and knee-high to a grasshopper. I've lived with you since you were seven. And I've known Jessie almost as long. Not as well, since I didn't raise her, but we've spent a lot more time together over these past months. And I saw the way she was looking at you just now. Like a woman looks at a man."

"Gross, Dad. It's weird to hear you talk like that." Shane was sweating, despite the fact that he'd noticed his dad had the thermostat set at sixty-eight degrees.

Alvin chuckled. "Just human nature, that's all." In the quiet that followed, Shane heard the old clock ticking and a loose shingle knocking in the wind.

"I never told you about Isabelle, did I?" Alvin finally said.

"You didn't," Shane said, his curiosity piqued.

Alvin's eyes had taken on a faraway look, and a small smile tugged at the corners of his mouth. "She was my first love. My only love."

"What happened to her?" Shane's first thought was that she must have died in some horrible way, but Alvin continued to smile.

"Nothing horrific," he said. "The sad fact is that I didn't fight for her. We were so in love. Then we had a falling out. I always assumed I'd have another chance. When she fell in love with someone else a while later, I simply gave up my dream of having her fall back in love with me and resigned myself to living alone. Well, until you came along."

"Why didn't you tell her how you felt?" Shane asked.

"Well, much like you and Jessie, Isabelle and I were the greatest of friends, even after we broke things off. We didn't grow up together, technically, but we worked together for years and shared all the related experiences. The two of us were joined at the hip. We went to the staff parties together, worked on projects together, attended our colleagues' weddings together, and even bought baby shower gifts together when those same colleagues had children."

"But you were just friends," Shane said.

"Right," Alvin said. "Whenever people would ask us if we were together, Isabelle would laugh and dismiss them, proclaiming we were good buddies."

At that point, bitterness tinged Alvin's voice, and Shane felt somewhat relieved to hear his dad had experienced feelings similar to his own.

"Sounds familiar," Shane said.

"Until now, perhaps."

"Dad, I love you, but I think you're misreading things between Jessie and me," Shane said. "Nothing's changed, as much as I wish they had."

Shane's phone dinged, notifying him of a text message. Jessie's name came up on the screen, and Shane's body reacted involuntarily, his heart racing and his hands shaking. He was twenty-seven years old, for goodness' sake. Why did the mere sight of her name on his phone screen still make him feel like a teenager?

You might want to check and make sure your dad turned off all the burners on the stove.

That wasn't what he'd been expecting, and he realized that his romance with Jessie (or the lack thereof) wasn't his priority. He needed to focus on his dad. Consciously shifting his thoughts, Shane said, "I'm going to grab a drink. Want one?"

"Sure," Alvin said. "I'll take a sparkling water."

Shane wrinkled his nose. "You drink that stuff?"

His dad shrugged. "Jessie keeps me stocked. Says it's better for me than the sweet iced tea I was drinking before this."

Unsure of whether to find the situation funny or to be irritated that she'd stopped his dad from drinking his favorite beverage, Shane headed for the kitchen. He checked the stove first and was pleased to find that with the exception of the burner under the simmering soup, all the burners were off. When he opened the fridge, his jaw dropped. Jessie had stocked it with sparkling waters in several flavors, and she'd also organized the whole space.

Condiments were with condiments. Jarred pickles were with jarred jalapeños. The milk and cream and whipped cream shared a shelf on the door. Leftover containers were neatly stacked and labeled. Labeled! With contents and a date.

"What is this witchcraft?" Shane hollered before grabbing two sparkling waters and returning to the living room.

"Ah," Alvin said as he took the can Shane offered him. "You've encountered the modern marvel that is our refrigerator. Blame Jessie. Or, you can blame me. Damn fool that I am, I ate some leftover spaghetti not realizing quite how old it was, and it made me sick. Jessie came in that day to find me on my hands and knees in the bathroom. After that, she insisted on labeling everything."

Another stab of guilt. Shane should have been here to care for his father and label leftovers. Jessie shouldn't have had to do it. But thank goodness she had.

"I'm sorry I wasn't here," Shane said.

"Oh, son, don't be sorry," Alvin said. "I'm not your responsibility. I'm so proud of you, running your business like you are. That's exactly what you should be doing. I'd hate for you to think you had to take care of me."

Shane appreciated the sentiment, but guilt plagued him anyway. "Thanks, Dad. I'll start visiting more often."

"I wouldn't mind seeing you more," Alvin said, "and I don't think Jessie would, either."

"Oh, Dad."

Shane remembered clearly the day he'd come home with his dad — Mr. Alvin, as he called him back then. After spending almost a year getting to know each other through various outings (fishing, mini golf, watching movies), they'd shared a few home visits, designed to give Shane time to decide whether he wanted Alvin to adopt him. But that time — that was when Shane officially moved in. Walking through the front door, Shane felt something inside his chest unlock. He could remember feeling a release of pressure he didn't even know was there. Mr. Alvin pointed at the stairs. "Remember that room I showed you? I got started on it, but I think we should go shopping, pick out the decorations you want, maybe even paint the walls if you like."

A nod was all Shane could manage. Mute, he followed Mr. Alvin up the stairs and to the door of the bedroom. He put his hand on the doorknob and held his breath. His first bedroom. He knew he would remember the moment forever. He pushed open the door and took in the space. A twin bed sat under the window, a nightstand next to it. A desk and bookcase sat along the adjacent wall, and across from those, a dresser stood. Shane swallowed the lump in his throat. He remembered wondering whether the moment was real.

"Well, are you going to say something?" Mr. Alvin said, giving him a playful nudge.

Shane looked up at him, and even then, at seven years old, he could see the hope and anticipation in his new dad's eyes. He felt a rush of affection for him, this man who was offering him a home and a family.

He felt himself smiling the biggest smile he ever had. "I love it. Thank you so much."

Mr. Alvin's eyes shone. He wrapped his arm around Shane's shoulders and squeezed him. "You're so welcome. Now, I know you like football, but I didn't want to decorate without you. Do you want to go shopping now? Or would you rather get settled in first, and go shopping later, this afternoon or maybe tomorrow?"

Before Shane could answer, Alvin said, "I'm getting ahead of myself. Come in, come in. Put your stuff down. Unpack. You can put your clothes in the dresser, hang stuff in the closet. Whatever you want."

Rigid with uncertainty, Shane moved forward into the room, his legs wooden. He dragged his suitcase — which Mr. Alvin had bought him a couple of days before — into the middle of the room, laid it down, and unzipped it. He never had his own dresser, or a closet where he could put his clothes. He didn't know quite where to start. Mr. Alvin seemed to sense that and sat down on the floor right next to Shane's suitcase.

"Now, some folks like to put their T-shirts in their dresser. But me? I like to hang mine up. Keeps them from getting wrinkled. I stocked some hangers in the closet for you."

Another wave of panic hit Shane. He knew what hangers were, but he didn't actually know how to put a T-shirt on one.

Again, his new dad to sense his hesitation. "I'll demonstrate."

Within a few minutes, they'd worked together to hang up all of Shane's shirts, and to fold and put away his pants, socks, and underwear.

"Tell you what," Mr. Alvin said when they were done. "Why don't we plan a longer shopping day for tomorrow? Looks like you're going to need some clothes along with stuff to decorate your bedroom. For now, let's go downstairs and play some cards. Maybe put on the football game."

Yet again, gratitude rendered Shane speechless. He simply nodded and followed Mr. Alvin back down to the living room.

No sooner had they found football on TV and set up a game of speed than someone knocked on the door. Shane's heart raced in response. Was someone coming to take him away already? Kids in his various foster homes told horror stories of being taken from one home to the next, even when they thought they were going to stay.

Mr. Alvin glanced at him and then put a hand on his arm. "Don't worry, kiddo. I have a feeling I know who that is. And I happen to know cookies are her specialty." He winked at Shane and answered the door.

Shane stayed put, but from his spot on the couch he heard what he'd consider a bossy voice. "Hello, Mr. Alvin. I heard your new son moved in today. I brought cookies. Can I meet him?"

And that's how he met Jessie Monroe. She walked right in, plate in one hand and the other hand extended for a businesslike shake.

"You must be Shane," she said as he took her hand. She pumped his three times. "I'm Jessie."

It was fascination at first sight. Jessie seemed to have everything Shane didn't: confidence, poise, and knowledge.

"Mr. Alvin told me you're going to be in third grade at the elementary school. So am I. You'll probably get Mrs. Byrd. I'm already in her class. Maddy Dublin and Jordan Lee are, too. They're nice. I hear Mrs. Byrd is a stickler for homework. But also, if your behavior is good, she gives you donuts on Fridays."

Shane's head spun with all the new information Jessie fed him, and at the same time, he found himself mesmerized by her big brown eyes and dimples. The following Monday, she showed up again, this time in her first-day-of-school outfit, her hair in a perfect ponytail and her shoes shiny and brand new.

For the first time in his life, Shane, too, had brand-new shoes and clothes, which felt stiff and uncomfortable on his body. He relaxed a little when Jessie didn't seem to notice his discomfort. Jessie and Shane walked to school together, her mom and his dad behind them. Sure enough, he had Mrs. Byrd, too, which meant he was attached to Jessie's hip from that moment forward.

4

———————

Why was she *nervous*? Jessie had eaten dinner with Alvin and Shane countless times. As a gangly kid, an awkward tween, a less-awkward teen, and a young woman. She had nothing to be nervous about, she told herself as she stood in front of her full-length mirror, turning this way and that to view her outfit from as many angles as possible. Still. She didn't want to look like she was trying too hard, and she also didn't want to look like she wasn't trying at all.

After agonizing over her clothing choices for far too long, she finally took a selfie in each of the final contenders and sent the pictures to Taylor and Rose with a message: *Not sure what to wear to dinner at Alvin's. Help me pick.*

Their answers came back right away. Rose wrote, *In all this time, you've never been unsure of what to wear to Alvin's ... could a certain muscular young man be to blame?* She added the smiling devil emoji. Jessie groaned. Taylor's reply came through next: *Hmm. I mean, are you even going to be in clothes for that long, anyway?* She, too, added the smiling devil emoji. Jessie typed, *Guys. I'm serious.* They both wrote back, *The jeans and blue sweater.* Taylor added, *Wear those sparkly dangly earrings I love. The blue and black ones.*

Even with their approval of her outfit, Jessie found herself smoothing her sweater, running her fingertips through her hair, and brushing nonexistent dust from her jeans as she walked over to Alvin's.

When Shane answered the door and gave her a once-over so thorough it ignited a fire in her belly, she decided all the angst had been worth it. Although they'd just seen each other at lunchtime, he opened his arms for a hug, and she didn't waste any time wrapping her arms around his waist and laying her head on his chest. Although the embrace was short and sweet, she had enough time to notice (again) how athletic and powerful his body felt.

"Gosh, it's good to see you," he said as they stepped apart. He held onto her hands, and that contact sent delightful energy zipping around her body.

"It's good to see you, too," she said. "Since you make a point of coming to town when I'm gone at conferences or visiting my parents."

Although she'd cracked the joke only to dispel some of the tension she felt, she saw in his expression that it landed harder than she'd meant for it to.

"That's not true," he said. "Weekends are busy at Jump Zone."

"I was just kidding," she said. "It's been a while since I've seen you in person, that's all."

"True," he said. He dropped her hands. "Come on in. Dad's just finishing things up."

She followed him to the kitchen, where Alvin was slicing French bread on the big wooden cutting board. Piano music played from a bluetooth speaker on the counter. Jessie assumed Shane had brought that — Alvin usually listened to talk shows on the AM/FM radio he'd had since she and Shane were kids.

"There's my girl," Alvin said, grinning up at her. "Perfect timing. We're just about ready. Want to get out some bowls and plates?"

"I could have done that, Dad," Shane said, and Jessie thought she detected a hint of resentment in his voice.

"You get the bowls," Jessie rushed to say, "and I'll get the plates."

Shane tossed her a look so familiar, her heart squeezed in response. It was the same one he'd given her thousands of times as they grew up and he felt exasperated with his dad. Like the time Alvin had caught them red-handed on their way to toilet paper Richard Carter's house and stopped them. Or the time he'd walked right into algebra class with the lunch Shane had forgotten at home. And, just like she had thousands of times in the past, Jessie giggled at Shane.

When they sat down at the table a few minutes later, Alvin beamed at both of them. "It's so good to have you both at my table again," he said. "Some of my best memories have to do with the two of you growing up."

"It's good to be here," Shane said.

"How are the wedding plans coming, Jessie?" Alvin asked.

Shane's head whipped toward Jessie, and his gaze landed on her left hand.

"Not mine," she said, giggling. "Taylor's."

"Oh," Shane said, his relief obvious.

"I would have told you if I was engaged," she said.

"Right."

She beamed at Alvin. "I love that you've been keeping up with my life and my friends' lives. Thanks for asking. The wedding plans are coming along great. We're pretty much done with everything, and we're kind of taking a break until all the festivities next weekend."

"Wonderful," Alvin said. "You know who you should take with you to the wedding, don't you?" He inclined his head toward Shane. "That guy."

A shock passed through Jessie's system. If Alvin had made that comment eight or nine years ago, she wouldn't have thought twice. But now that she'd experienced downright salacious thoughts about Shane, Alvin's suggestion put her on the spot.

Shane shook his head and held up his hands. "No, no. That's not necessary. The wedding is only a week away. I'm sure she already has a date, Dad." He turned toward Jessie. "Right?"

His flustered reaction totally changed her mindset. She wondered whether he was flustered because he didn't want to encroach on her existing plans or because maybe, just maybe, he found her attractive, too. Maybe she *should* invite him to the wedding.

"Actually," she said, "I don't. I know it might be tough to get off work two weekends in a row, but I'd love for you to come to the wedding with me."

Shane's eyes actually widened, the surprise so obvious, Jessie had to laugh.

"You don't have a date?" he said.

Giddy with her sudden enjoyment of the moment, Jessie said, "Nope," and took a bite of her French bread.

"Okay," Shane said, nodding. "I'll go with you. But you'll have to help me decide on what to wear. I haven't been to a wedding since I was a kid."

Jessie glanced at Alvin, whose eyes twinkled with mischief and triumph. His intentions were obvious, but more importantly, what did Shane think of them? He looked like a deer in headlights.

"No problem," Jessie said. "The rehearsal dinner is Friday night. Do you want to come to that, too? You're going to have to find a second outfit."

Shane shrugged. "Sure. I'll just have to check with Roman, make sure I can get away."

"Okay," Jessie said, her nerves creeping in again. "Sounds good."

Were the rehearsal dinner and wedding going to feel like dates with Shane? Several years before, they wouldn't have — the two of them would have been best friends, spending a couple of evenings together. But now?

"You know," Alvin said then, "I met Isabelle at a wedding."

"I thought you worked together at WGL."

"We did," Alvin said. "But the first time I met her was right before she started. A co-worker who'd hooked her up with the job brought her to the wedding." His eyes misted over, and Jessie felt her own throat go tight. "She was a vision in that dress."

"Who's Isabelle?" Jessie stage whispered to Shane.

"Dad's one and only love, who I just found out about today."

"What was her last name?"

"Sorensen," Alvin said. "That was her maiden name. She

married Jack Budgie. Can you believe it? Budgie. Like a parakeet." Shaking his head, he soaked up some soup with his French bread.

"What happened to her?" Jessie asked.

"She was the one who got away," Alvin said. "I never had the courage to tell her how I felt, and she ended up marrying someone else."

Jessie glanced at Shane, who stared studiously into his bowl.

"Not to put a damper on the mood," Alvin said. "But I'm tired after such a busy day and all this visiting. I think I'll go to bed early, if you two don't mind doing the cleanup."

Shane threw Jessie that exasperated look again, and she smiled. "We don't mind," she said. "Do we, Shane?"

"Not at all."

"Sleep well, Alvin."

He pushed back from the table. "You know, I think I will."

After he'd gone, Shane shook his head. "He's getting wily in his old age, isn't he?"

"A bit," Jessie said. "But he's as charming as ever. Should we clean up? And then I'll get out of your hair."

The two of them gathered the bowls and plates and carried them to the kitchen. "Should we clean up like old times?" Jessie asked. "I load the dishwasher while you bring over the big dishes? And you hand wash the big dishes while I wipe down the counters?"

"Sure," Shane said. They fell into an easy rhythm, having shared these chores countless times as kids.

"You know," Shane said at one point, when she'd finished loading the dishwasher and he was hand washing, his back to her, "You don't have to bring me to Taylor's wedding and the rehearsal dinner."

"I know," Jessie said, leaning against the counter and crossing her arms. She wondered if Shane was saying that because he didn't want to go, or because he was embarrassed Alvin had suggested she take him. "I think it would be fun. Do you want to go?"

His back still to her, his massive shoulders flexing as he scrubbed, Shane said, "Yeah. I think it would be fun, too. And I'd love to celebrate Taylor, even though it's been a while since I saw her."

"Then come."

"Okay," he said, finally squeezing out the dishrag and turning to face her. "I will."

"Okay."

"But I think you should know, I'm kind of getting the feeling that my dad has this dream of seeing us together."

Jessie's heart raced, but she acted nonchalant when she said, "Oh, I doubt it." Still, she'd seen that twinkle in Alvin's eyes. She picked up the dishrag and started wiping down the counters. "I think he knows how much I've missed seeing you. I complain every time you come into town while I'm gone."

There. That should make things less awkward.

She heard Shane turn the water on and then off again, and she finished wiping down the counter and stepped over to the sink to rinse the dishrag. Once she'd hung it over the sink's edge to dry, she turned around to find Shane leaning against the kitchen island, arms crossed.

"What do you say we have a drink?" he asked.

"I say that sounds like a great idea. But I think all your dad's got on hand is a six-year-old bottle of scotch."

"We're in luck," Shane said. "I happen to have some vodka left over from last night."

When he returned with the bottle, she gasped. "That's from last night? It's nearly empty."

Laughing, he said, "I know. I totally overdid it. I woke up sick, but Mikey saved the day. Magical hangover cure. So, the good news is that I think one drink is about all I can handle tonight. There's plenty for each of us to have one."

They settled on the couch a few minutes later, and, distraction-free for the first time, Jessie tried not to stare at the man-god before her. His long-sleeved shirt hugged his biceps and pecs, and his shoulder muscles bulged. Growing up, he'd always been just a bit overweight; she often called him her teddy bear. But not anymore. The man looked like someone had carved him from stone. Even his face had taken on a stronger appearance. His eyes, though — they were the same warm brown she'd always loved.

"Penny for your thoughts?" he said.

Jessie jumped, then took a quick sip of her drink. "Oh, I was just thinking about all my bridesmaid duties for the wedding."

"What all do you have to do?"

As she started describing her duties (organizing the bachelorette party for Thursday, confirming the dinner reservation for Friday night, spending the day with Taylor Saturday as they prepared for the ceremony, making a short speech at the reception, and checking in with the wedding planner to make sure everything stayed on track), she finally relaxed.

"Sounds like you're going to be busy," he said. "I hope Taylor appreciates everything you're doing."

"Oh, she does," Jessie said. "She's thanked Rose and me about a hundred times. Tell me about Jump Zone. I didn't realize it had gotten so busy. You must be proud of yourself."

Shane smiled. "I am. But not only because of the business's success. I love making people happy. I love seeing their excitement before the jump, or, when they panic in the plane, after they make the choice to go for it, and feel so proud of themselves."

"That sounds awesome."

"It is," he said.

"Do you still jump?"

"Oh, yeah," he said. "Almost every day."

"Do you still get an adrenaline rush?"

"Oh, yeah," he said again. He sipped his drink. "Every single time. It's great."

The vodka had made it to her bloodstream, and Jessie felt herself relaxing even more.

"Is that how you got so buff?" she blurted out. She slapped a hand over her mouth, and instantly regretted doing that — in the old days, asking Shane that question would have been completely natural. She felt embarrassed only because she suddenly thought he was hot. *Maybe I should set down my drink.* She took another sip.

Shane seemed unfazed. "Nah. Being out on my own, done with

college, I have extra time on my hands. One of my friends up there invited me to the gym, and after a two-week free trial, I was hooked. Weightlifting is cool because you can really keep track of your progress. I started getting stronger and stronger. Being ripped is just a nice side effect."

He was grinning, and she couldn't help but grin back. "Well, you're certainly ripped."

Like some kind of wanton Jezebel, she let her gaze trail over his torso. When she made eye contact again, his expression had shifted. He was no longer smiling at her like a best friend. No, he was looking at her like he saw her differently, too. Like he wouldn't be opposed to tearing off her clothes then and there. Like he hadn't eaten for three days and she was a giant, juicy cheeseburger (he'd always loved cheeseburgers, craved them).

She had to get out of there. But she hadn't talked to him about Alvin yet.

After clearing her throat, she said, "I think we need to talk about your dad."

Shane sighed, his posture deflating. "We do. You said he wasn't getting around as well, and you're right. But it's not like I can tell him he can't live on his own, can I?"

"I don't know." Jessie rolled her glass between her hands. "I don't mind checking up on him, obviously, but I'm worried about him."

"When I first met my dad," Shane said, looking down into his drink, "I thought he was invincible. He was so tall and so strong, and his hands were so big. For one of our first outings together, he took me to the park to play basketball. He could dribble forever. He made every shot and blocked most of mine." He smiled. "He let me get a few in. And he could lift anything. Remember when that branch fell off the tree out front and he just picked it up and hauled it into the yard so he could cut it up?"

"I do," Jessie said, chuckling.

"It's hard to see him getting old."

"It is," Jessie said. "But I think he can still be independent. Just with a little more support."

Shane nodded, and he looked so sad, she wanted to crawl into his lap and kiss him until he felt better. "Well, I'd better get going." She drained her drink and set the glass on the coffee table, then stood up.

Shane raised an eyebrow at her and flashed his familiar grin. "Good thing you live next door, and you can walk."

"I'm not drunk." Her tone was defensive.

"Maybe not drunk, but definitely tipsy. Your cheeks are flushed and your eyes have that look they get."

"What look is that?"

"Oh, I don't know, just a little glazed over. Don't worry, you're still beautiful. I'll walk you to the door."

He stood up. She reached for her glass, but he waved her off. "I'll get it."

"Aren't you the gentleman?" she said.

"Always," he said. As proof, he offered his arm, and she took it, wrapping her hand around his bicep instead of settling it in the crook of his elbow. She gave his muscle a squeeze, and he laughed as he walked her to the door.

"It was really nice to spend time with you," Jessie said, feeling reluctant to leave.

"I agree," Shane said. He opened the door, obviously eager for her to go.

She stepped out into the cold fall night and inhaled as deeply as she could. She turned around to see Shane staring at her, an interesting expression on his face. She could swear he was puzzling through something, but she was afraid to ask.

"Goodnight, Jessie," he said.

"Goodnight."

He shut the door while she was still thinking about whether she should hug him again.

"That's probably for the best," she whispered.

This is crazy, she thought as she made the short trip back to her house, her feet crunching on the fallen leaves. Almost immediately after realizing she was completely, utterly attracted to her childhood best friend, she'd invited him to a *wedding*. Only the most romantic event in the world.

She couldn't even blame the alcohol.

She'd invited him when she was stone-cold sober, and she'd done so because she imagined the two of them swaying to slow songs on the dance floor, their bodies pressed up against each other.

After letting herself into her house and collapsing on the couch from pure mental exhaustion, Jessie texted her friends: *I just invited Shane to the wedding.*

They both responded with emojis: Taylor with the surprised, big-eyed guy, and Rose with a pair of clapping hands.

Then Taylor texted, *This is getting very interesting,* and Rose added, *Indeed. I'm on the edge of my seat.*

5

<hr>

As soon as Jessie left, Shane heard Alvin's bedroom door open and then close, and his footsteps approaching.

"She left already?" he said, his eyes bright and alert and looking nothing like those of a tired man who'd gone to bed.

"Yeah," Shane said, trying to hide his disappointment. He could have asked Jessie to stay longer. He could have hugged her good-night. He could have kissed her. "What were you doing, listening from your bedroom?"

Alvin grinned. "Not quite. I heard the front door open and close. I went to bed so the two of you could have some alone time. Talk. You know." He clapped Shane on the shoulder. "And you didn't seize the opportunity, my boy."

"Oh, my God." Shane ran a hand through his hair. "Who knew you'd turn into a matchmaker in your old age?"

"Got any of that vodka left?"

Shaking his head, Shane said, "Just enough for one more drink. You can have it."

He went into the kitchen to pour the drink, and Alvin followed him. "You've got to tell her, son."

"Tell her what?"

Shane handed Alvin the glass and as they walked into the living room Alvin said, "That you've loved her since you guys were kids."

Sitting down and dropping his head into his palm, Shane said, "I can't tell her that, Dad."

"Why the hell not?" The emotion in Alvin's voice surprised Shane.

"It's embarrassing. She's never thought of me like that."

"But maybe she does now."

"She doesn't."

Alvin lowered himself into the couch, and Shane swore he could hear his bones creaking. "You didn't see the way she looked at you?"

"Just like she's always looked at me," Shane said, exasperation coloring his voice.

"That's where you're wrong."

"Look, Dad, can we talk about something else?"

"If we must. Can you believe this weather?"

"Stop it." A smile tugged at the corners of Shane's mouth, and he found himself thanking his lucky stars for his dad. "Do you remember the first day we met?"

"How could I not?" Alvin asked. "That was a life-changing day for me. I remember knowing immediately that I wanted to adopt you. There was just something about you. Your eyes were so wise for a little kid's. I said to myself, 'That kid's an old soul.' I loved you on sight. Meanwhile, you wouldn't stop giving me the evil side-eye. There we were, in my favorite place — that old ice cream shop over on Gurley Street, and you wouldn't even eat."

Shane chuckled and drained the rest of his drink from his glass. "Right. I was terrified beyond words. I wanted a family so badly, and I was afraid that if I made one wrong move, said one wrong thing, you'd decide not to adopt me. What if I took too big of a bite? What if I chewed too loudly? What if, heaven forbid, I spilled my ice cream? Those were all things I'd been in major trouble for with my birth parents. I knew there were tons of other kids out there waiting for a family. You could take your pick."

"But I warmed you right up, didn't I?"

"Yeah," Shane said, remembering. "You wanted to talk about the weather. At first, I thought it was the dumbest thing. And then I realized you were just trying to get me to settle down and talk to you."

"You actually smiled when I did that fake weather report."

"You've always known how to make me feel better," Shane said. Jessie had said he should spend more time with his dad. Maybe she was right. Not just so he could help Alvin, but so Alvin could help him.

"What are you thinking?" Alvin wanted to know.

"I'm thinking I should spend more time at home. Make more regular visits. I've been so busy. I didn't realize how much I've missed you. But being here, chatting on the couch, it reminded me."

"Good," Alvin said, taking a healthy slug of his drink. "I'd really like that."

"Maybe after Taylor's wedding, I'll stick around for a bit. I think I could take a couple weeks off from Jump Zone. That gives me a week to get organized."

"Good idea," Alvin said. "And didn't Jessie say Taylor's wedding is at the start of their winter break?" His eyes laughed at Shane over the rim of his glass.

"She did," Shane said. "Taylor and Judd planned it that way so they could take a honeymoon without using any of their vacation days."

"Perfect. Jessie will be off work, too. So, the two of you can spend some time together."

Even as Shane said, "Dad. The whole point is for me to spend time with *you*," his heart leapt a little inside his chest. Jessie and his dad apparently loved hanging out together, so Shane being around too would be a win-win-win.

"That's great, son. Really great."

That Monday when Shane returned to work, he said to Roman, "Hey, so, I got invited to a wedding in Prescott next weekend. You cool with me taking a couple weeks off afterwards, so I can spend some time with my dad? Obviously, I'll schedule people to cover my shifts."

The two of them were double-checking the parachutes they'd

use throughout the day, hanging them up behind the bench where the jumpers would get ready.

"Sure," Roman said, pausing his chute check to grin at Shane.

Shane turned around from where he was hanging up his chute, caught Roman's smile, and said, "What?"

Roman shrugged. "Oh, nothing. Who invited you to a wedding?"

How does he know?

"An old friend."

"Which one?"

Shane growled, caught. "Remember that girl I told you about? Jessie?"

"Sure do." Done checking his chute, Roman turned and hung it on the hook.

Shaking his head, Shane said, "She invited me."

"And now you want to stay in town for two weeks. Sounds suspicious to me."

"I'm going to spend time with my dad," Shane said.

"Right."

"Whatever, man."

"Whatever."

Another busy day left the two of them without much time to talk, but in the early evening when they were packing parachutes again, Roman said, "So, are you going to tell this Jessie you still have the hots for her?"

"Absolutely not."

"I didn't get a chance to ask. Did you see her this weekend?"

Fast and furious, a blush zipped up Shane's neck and into his cheeks. "I did."

"And?" Roman had gotten on the computer, but smiled when he glanced up and saw Shane'd red-stained face.

Shane didn't know why he said it, but when Roman looked back at the screen, he blurted out, "My dad thinks she might have feelings for me."

"Ah," Roman said, turning away from the computer screen to pin Shane with his stare. "And what do you think?"

"I don't know ... I mean, there were a handful of moments, you know? Where we looked at each other and ... maybe there was something there?"

"You said she hasn't seen you since you got ripped."

"I did. She hasn't."

"I mean, not that *I'm* attracted to you, bro, but you're looking pretty great these days."

Shane shrugged. Was that enough? "She did compliment my musculature."

"I'm sure she did."

"But, I mean, we've been best friends for ages. It could have been a friendly compliment. Like, noticing I've gotten in shape."

"Could have been," Roman said. "But, she *also* invited you to a wedding. In my experience, a lady doesn't invite a man to a wedding unless she's feeling a bit romantic about said man."

"In your experience, huh?"

"I've been to my fair share of weddings." Roman shrugged, wiggled his eyebrows. "And to the romantic shenanigans that follow. Inevitably."

A vision of romantic shenanigans with Jessie — her smooth skin bare, her hands on his chest, his mouth on her neck — hit Shane with an intensity that made his jeans feel tighter.

"I see your wheels turning." Finished with his end-of-day tasks, Roman turned off the computer. "Go to the wedding. Do the shenanigans. Stay two weeks. Take care of your dad. Fall in love."

"That simple, huh?" Shane packed the last parachute and hung it up.

"Who's to say it isn't? We've got things covered here."

"Thanks, man."

The rest of the week was a whirlwind as Shane adjusted schedules, jumped with clients, took photos, and planned for Taylor and Judd's wedding.

Early Thursday morning, before he'd even left for work, Jessie texted him: *You ready for this weekend? I'm texting you now to make sure you're not going to bail on me.*

He wrote back, *Not bailing. Although, you might wish I did if I choose the wrong outfits. What should I wear?*

Then he panicked. Was talking about what to wear akin to sexting?

Haha, she texted. *You'll be fine. Tomorrow night is casual — all the ladies are going to be beat after Taylor's bachelorette party tonight. Jeans and a sweater are fine. Do you have a suit for the wedding? I probably should have brought this up sooner.*

He didn't. He wrote back, *Shit. I'm panicking. I don't.*

Her next text came through, sending his heart rate sky high. *No worries. Let's go shopping. I have to work on Friday because it's finals week, but the wedding's not until four on Saturday. I have to be there at two, but I can totally go shopping before that.*

Shopping for suits, with Jessie? Shane didn't know whether the sick feeling meant he was experiencing a deep dread or an anticipation.

Great, he typed, nerves (or excitement?) making his stomach all fluttery. *Thank you.*

Because Shane had to work Friday, too, he drove into town just before he and Jessie had to leave for the rehearsal dinner. His dad met him at the front door and whistled.

"Looking pretty dapper, there, Shane. If you can't muster up the cojones to tell Jessie how you feel about her, I'm sure you can snag another young lady."

Shane made sure Alvin saw him rolling his eyes before he wrapped him in a hug "Thanks, I think."

"I know you've got to leave right away," Alvin said as he stepped back, "so don't feel like you have to hang out with your old man. Jessie's a stickler for punctuality. I'd suggest you drop your bag and go. I'll put it in your room for you."

Shane nodded and handed his bag to Alvin. "Thanks. I don't want to be late on our first date."

"You're calling it a date, eh?" Alvin winked.

"I shouldn't have said that," Shane said. He gave his dad a light punch on the arm.

"Freudian slip," Alvin said. "Seen it a million times."

"It's not a date. I just didn't know what else to call it."

"That's because it's a date," Alvin said. "It's a social engagement and that fits the definition of date. I know because it's been a cross-word clue."

"Fine. Whatever."

"Fine. Whatever," Alvin mimicked as Shane turned around to go back through the door. Shane scowled at him and he said, "Just have a good time, all right?"

"I will," Shane called. He walked down the walkway and made a right to go to Jessie's.

When she opened the door, he literally gasped. Even though her outfit was simple — jeans and a sweater, just as she'd suggested he wear — she looked more beautiful than he'd ever seen her. She'd swept her hair into an updo, and although she wore minimal makeup, her face practically shone.

"Everything okay?" she said.

"Great," he rushed to say. "Everything is great. You look really nice."

"Thanks," she said. "You don't look so bad, yourself."

Reading into that half-compliment wouldn't do any good. So, he offered his arm just like he had the previous weekend, and again, she wrapped her hand around his bicep. This time, she didn't give it a playful squeeze. He could swear she caressed it. He dwelled on that, and the goosebumps it produced, only for as long as it took them to walk over to the passenger side of his truck — he'd offered to drive — and she had to let go to get in.

"Thanks for driving," she said once they were on the road. "Especially after you made the trip down to Prescott today."

"No problem," he said. "I figured you must be exhausted from wedding festivities and finals week."

She slumped in her seat. "Totally. That was really thoughtful of you. Fortunately, I've carried out most of my responsibilities now that the bachelorette party's over. Tonight should be pretty relaxing. We'll run through the ceremony first — you get to relax and enjoy that part — and then we get to eat. And then I can go home and fall into bed."

Why was he imagining falling into bed *with* her? By then, Shane found a parking spot near the hotel where Taylor and Judd would get married and have their reception, and the conversation switched gears as Jessie described the plans for the next day.

The ballroom where the ceremony would take place was already set up, chairs in rows and a giant, flower-laden wooden arch front and center.

"Tomorrow, we'll have flowers at the end of each row, and petals on the runner," Jessie said.

"That'll be nice," Shane said, relieved when several other people came through a door at the other end of the room.

The more distractions, the better — he couldn't stop picturing Jessie in bed, her hair a halo on the pillow as she waited for him. Within a few minutes, the whole bridal party had shown up, and Shane took a seat in the audience while they practiced the ceremony. The mood was festive, with lots of laughter and teasing.

When the officiant announced, "You may now kiss the bride," Judd dipped Taylor low and kissed her long and hard, while the members of the bridal party cheered and laughed before the bride and groom walked back down the aisle. As Jessie and her partner came past Shane, she winked at him, and that single gesture lit him up.

Judd could see why Roman had said weddings led to romantic shenanigans ... this was his first wedding event — not even the real thing — and he was already in the mood for those shenanigans.

Jessie skipped up to him then, beaming. "Ready for dinner?"

He stood up. "So ready."

She grabbed both of his hands and squeezed them. "I'm so glad you're here. Dinner's just down the street, at Rita's, so we can walk."

She kept hold of one of his hands as they fell into step. Pretending that contact didn't send pleasant shivers racing all over his body, Shane said, "I love Rita's, but I'm surprised they're not having the dinner somewhere ..."

"Fancier?"

"Yeah. I mean, it seems like most people want upscale dining for wedding stuff."

Jessie laughed. "You know Rita. She swears Taylor and Judd found true love because they met at her diner."

"They did?"

"Yeah. They ran into each other while coming in the door, and he bought her coffee. Then he pulled her over for almost hitting him, head-on, and the rest is history. So, Rita's giving them a huge discount on the food."

"That's sweet," Shane said, remembering then that he'd seen Jessie at Rita's the last time he'd come back — and that she'd given him that huge hug. Was that foreshadowing?

Rita winked at him when they walked in, still hand in hand, and he winked back. If Rita thought her diner could propagate true love, who was he to argue?

Once everyone was settled and Rita and her husband Sal had brought out the food — platters and platters of it — Judd's parents announced that some people wanted to give toasts.

Rita yelped and hollered, "Let me bring the champagne! I nearly forgot!"

Realizing she could use an extra set of hands, Shane jumped up to help her. While they stood at the counter, pulling corks, she whispered, "You're Jessie's date, huh?"

Smiling, he said, "Yep."

"You know true love starts at Rita's. This is where the magic happens."

"So I've heard," he said, a fizzy, happy feeling bubbling up inside him.

They poured champagne, loaded flutes onto trays, and carried the trays to the table. Once everyone had a glass, Shane grabbed one for himself and settled into his spot next to Jessie.

Just as he did, she grabbed his wrist and said, "It's me. I want to make a toast," and got to her feet.

The guests quieted and looked up at her. She cleared her throat. Shane had never known her to be the nervous type. She was always the outspoken one. He reached up and squeezed her hand.

She squeezed back, released his hand, and started talking. "Rose, our resident wordsmith, is making a toast tomorrow night, so I asked if I could make one tonight," she said. A few people chuckled and Rose smiled up at her friend. "I just wanted to say that I'm so glad

Taylor met Judd. When we first saw him at a staff meeting at the high school ... well, when we first saw him, Taylor freaked because he'd given her a ticket a few days before." More laughter. "But also, she thought he was hot." Jessie looked at Taylor with a semi-apologetic expression, and Taylor laughed. "I mean, Rosie and I didn't think he was half-bad, but you could see there was something between them. And they took a chance on each other. Things weren't always easy, but because they're so in love, they persevered. And here we are." She held up a hand, and her little audience cheered. "Taylor and Judd are proof that life sometimes puts love in your path ... and that when it does, you've got to seize it. It might take grit and work and determination, but if you find that kind of deep, true love, you've got to hang onto it and just go for the ride." Jessie's voice sounded thick with emotion. "I'm so happy for both of you, and I can't wait to share in your special day tomorrow and in the rest of your life together. You're in for a beautiful adventure."

Shane felt his own throat tightening and tears prickling in his eyes. Not because Taylor and Judd were in love, but because he was in love with Jessie. He wanted a beautiful adventure with her. He just had to convince her they belonged together.

6

———————

Jessie woke up before her alarm went off Saturday morning. She couldn't remember the last time she had so looked forward to a day, she thought as she lay in bed, cozy under the covers. Winter break had begun, Taylor's wedding was finally happening, and she got to go suit shopping with Shane.

She hadn't anticipated the latter for long — they'd only just planned it on Thursday — but the idea of spending the morning with him, watching him dress up, and participating in selecting the suit that best showed off his powerful masculine form, really warmed her blood. She took her time stretching before getting out of bed. It really would be nice if she brought Shane coffee, she thought. So after her shower, she threw her hair into a bun and went to Rita's.

When she ordered two coffees, Rita raised an eyebrow at her. "I admit, I was disappointed to see you coming in alone this morning. But now I see you're ordering for two. Is someone waiting for you at home, perchance?"

Jessie smiled at her. "Nobody's waiting at home. But, I'm taking Shane suit shopping this morning and figured it wouldn't hurt for me to bring him a coffee."

"I do make the best coffees," Rita said, pulling two paper cups off her stack, "and I'm sure he'll appreciate the gesture. You know what he'd appreciate even more?"

"I can only imagine what you're about to say."

Rita turned around to face the espresso machine. "He'd appreciate even more if neither one of you spent the night alone after this wedding."

Jessie rolled her eyes. "You're such a romantic."

Rita finished making the coffees and pushed them across the counter. "Don't I know it. These are on the house. I'll see you tonight."

When Jessie arrived at Alvin's house, Shane opened the door right away, almost as if he were waiting for her to knock.

"Good morning," he told her, something unusual and fun in his voice.

"Good morning," she replied, wondering if her smile looked as goofy as it felt.

"You look chipper this morning," he said, making her laugh.

"So, my smile does look as goofy as it feels."

"It looks beautiful," Shane said, and if Jessie wasn't mistaken, he gave her a look that qualified as smoldering.

"It's coffee. Rita's." She paused. "Wait. That's not what makes me beautiful, it's what makes me chipper."

Shane shook his head. "You *are* chipper. Maybe I should have had another cup."

"You're in luck. I brought you some. Shall we?"

"Yes. Let the torture commence."

"Hey!" She punched him on the arm and he pretended to flinch. He rolled his eyes, then hollered goodbye to his dad, who hollered back at him from somewhere deep inside the house.

"I've been wondering when I'd get to—"

"Don't even ask to drive it again."

"I wasn't!" He held up his hands in mock surrender. "I was going to say I've been wondering when I'd get to go for a spin in the Jeep. I've learned my lesson. Every time I ask about driving, it's a hard no."

"Is that true?" She knew it was; the Jeep was her baby, and she never let anyone else get behind the wheel.

"I'm afraid to say."

"Anyway," Jessie said. "It's always fun, but even more so when it's warmer. Spring and fall are the best. Let's go again in a few months. I mean, if you want to."

Why did everything feel so awkward all of a sudden? Once they were in the vehicle, Shane lifted his coffee from the cupholder and held it out. "Cheers to a day of torture and fun."

"Hey," Jessie said again, laughing. "It's going to be all fun. Don't tell me you think shopping is torture."

"Sort of. I mean, I prefer jeans and a t-shirt. But since I know wearing a suit will make you happy, I'll do my best to enjoy the process."

"That's the spirit."

Jessie had been inside the suit store only a handful of times with her dad. It was set up almost like a bridal shop, with mirrors lined up outside the fitting rooms and racks of suits along the walls and crowded into the giant store's center.

"What are there, like a million suits in here?" Shane wanted to know. "Where do we start?"

"Well, I guess we start with style. I think you'll look nice in the slightly more fitted suits."

"You're the boss," Shane said. "Lead the way."

Right away, Jessie noticed and appreciated that Shane was easy to shop for. He was game to try on just about anything, and she had seven suits slung over her arm within a few minutes.

"This is a good start," she said to Shane. "Should we hit the fitting room?"

"Sure."

They went in together and Jessie relished in the intimate feel of the two of them in that tiny space, working side by side to hang up the suits.

"All right, get to it," she said when they were done, giving his shoulder a squeeze. "I'll be waiting for you on that really comfy couch out there."

The fitting room door didn't come all the way to the floor, which gave Jessie a chance to watch as Shane took off his shoes and pants.

She'd never been so turned on by the sight of a man's stockinged feet before, but she couldn't stop imagining what he looked like in his underwear. What kind of underwear did he wear? Silk boxers would be nice. The feel of those hard muscles, wrapped in silk, under her hands ... She shivered.

The sound of the lock sliding open broke her out of her trance. The fitting room door swung inward. Shane stepped out, and Jessie's breath caught.

"Wow," she whispered.

His shoulders looked broad and his waist trim. He'd left the jacket open, and the shirt laid over his pecs, making them look irresistible. Was it a coincidence that her hands would fit there just perfectly?

When she finally looked at his face, he wrinkled his nose. "Not good?"

So good. *So so good.* Jessie cleared her throat. "It's good," she managed. "In fact, I can't imagine any of the others could beat it, but we should see. Just in case."

He beamed. "Really? You like it? My dad always called these things penguin suits and complained about them being uncomfortable. I think his distaste for them transferred over to me. Osmosis or something. But it's been a long time since my dad wore a suit, and this is more comfortable than I expected."

Jessie smiled. Her voice sounded strangled when she said, "Comfort and style. You may have found a winner."

Shane pulled the jacket off his shoulders and let it fall to his wrists. He took it off and hung it over his arm. A growling noise came out of Jessie's throat. How was it even fair for the man to look that good in dress pants and a shirt? She couldn't quite see the definition of his abs, but her mind couldn't stop envisioning a chiseled torso.

She lifted her chin toward the fitting room. "Go on. Try the next one."

As soon as he was safely in the fitting room, a slab of wood between them, her imagination dreamed up all the ways she could take a suit off Shane, and delight in his gorgeous physique.

"What is wrong with you?" she whispered, dropping her forehead into her hand. "He supposed to be your best friend, not a piece of meat."

The lock slid open and Shane came out, this time grinning broadly. Jessie smirked. "You look so proud of yourself. Like that time in fifth grade when you played that prank on your dad."

"Yes!" Shane said. "The cookies that looked like poop."

Remembering, Jessie shook her head. "You were so very self-satisfied about that one."

"I was. And you know what? To be perfectly honest, I'm proud of myself now, too. I've never felt comfortable in anything remotely fancy. Much less my own skin. It feels good to feel good — and look good — in clothes as nice as these."

He shrugged, his easy smile bringing Jessie back to her center. There it was. That connection they'd always had. They were still best friends. She just happened to think he was hot, as well. Those two ideas coexisted in her mind like eggs being scrambled. Somebody was in there with a whisk mixing everything up.

"You do look great," Jessie said. "Like, seriously great. I can't believe I'm going to say this, but I think I like the second suit even better than the first one. And the first one was ..." Jessie brought her fingers together and kissed them, imitating a chef's kiss.

"Do I even need to try on another one?"

Jessie shook her head. "Either of those is fabulous. Like I said, I think the second one is even better, but it's up to you. All the ladies are going to be jealous when we walk in together."

Shane suddenly looked sheepish, and Jessie laughed out loud. "Come on. You want all the ladies to be jealous, don't you?"

"I —" Shane froze, then lifted a hand with his pointer finger extended. "Never mind. I almost said something I'd certainly regret. I'll get the second suit."

Several hours later, Shane knocked on Jessie's door. As she went to answer it, her high heels clicking on the hardwood floor, she experienced gratitude that she'd already seen him in his suit. Because if he'd caught her off guard looking that good, she might very well swoon. She took a deep breath, consciously pushed any impure thoughts from her mind, and pulled open the door. She nearly swooned, anyway. Even with the preview earlier that day, Shane's appearance stunned her.

Apparently, her appearance stunned him, too, because his eyes raked shamelessly over her body and then met hers. "That dress should come with a warning."

Jessie held up her hands. "I didn't choose it! Taylor did."

Shane whistled. "Still." He cleared his throat. "You look very ... ah ... nice."

Jessie felt a self-satisfied smirk on her lips. "Thank you. I may not measure up to you ..."

"Oh, you do."

They stood there, staring at each other. Jessie could practically feel the heat waves between them. And, as much as she loved Taylor, for a moment she considered skipping the wedding so she could spend the evening having her way with Shane. *Oh, the fun we could have with that tie.*

Fortunately, their ride-share driver pulled up to the curb then.

"I guess we should go," Shane said.

Jessie smirked. "I guess we should."

The drive downtown took only a few minutes. *Thank goodness for that*, Jessie thought. If she had any longer to envision herself and Shane, limbs tangled in the backseat of this stranger's car, she'd self-combust for sure.

At the hotel, Shane helped Jessie out of the car, and his hand felt electric in hers. "I've got to go into the bride's room with the ladies," she told him as they walked in. "You can find a seat in the ceremony room, and I'll see you after."

The urge to kiss him goodbye was strong. She practically ran away from him to get to her friends.

"Are you okay?" Rose asked when she blew into the room where the three women would wait for the ceremony to start. "You look ... well, I don't know how you look. But it's something else."

"I'm fine," Jessie said. "Just fine."

Taylor emerged from the bathroom, looking like a ballerina

goddess in her wedding dress. Tears sprang to Jessie's eyes, and Taylor laughed. "Don't ruin your makeup. It's just a dress."

"I know it is, but the reality of the day just hit me. You're getting married! You've found the love of your life and that's just such a beautiful thing. I'm so darn happy for you."

Taylor opened her arms, and Jessie and Rose embraced her.

"Now," Taylor said, stepping back so she could look at Jessie, "why do you look like you do?"

"Like what?" Jessie said. "Like, as Shane said, my dress should come with a warning?"

"He said that?" Rose demanded, and Jessie giggled. "He did. I don't even know what to make of it."

"Oh, I do," Taylor said. "I know exactly what you should make of it. A night of hot, glorious sex. And the reason you look like you do right now."

"Yes," Rose said, nodding, her lips pursed and eyebrows raised in an expression of wisdom. "That's exactly what you should make of it."

"But he's my *best friend*," Jessie said. "We can't have *sex*."

"I mean," Taylor said, "I'm pretty sure the two of you have all the right anatomy."

The three of them dissolved into giggles, which made Taylor's eyes water. "Okay, okay," she said, swiping her fingers under her lower lashes. "We're going to ruin my makeup. Let's be serious."

"Yes," Rose said, adjusting her hair pins while looking in the mirror. "Let's. I seriously think you should just go for it. Make sensual, mind-blowing love to Shane West tonight. Isn't that what weddings are all about? I mean, besides two people getting married."

"You guys!" Jessie said. "I'm scandalized!"

"Why?" Taylor walked over to the table in the corner, picked up a couple of nuts, and popped them into her mouth. "You've had sex before, right? It doesn't have to be scandalous. It can just be fun."

"Right," Jessie said, drawing the word out. "But what if we have sex and it ruins our friendship?"

Taylor took a swig of water from a wine glass. "Would it? You guys have been friends for, like, *ever*. I don't think a little nookie could ruin years of memories and experiences."

Although Jessie thought Taylor might be right, the conversation made her uncomfortable, like little ants were crawling up her arms. "I hear you. But let's focus on you now. This is your day."

"Even so," Taylor said. "When I manage to tear my eyes away from my new husband this evening, they'll be on you and Shane."

During the ceremony, Jessie found herself watching Shane from her spot behind Taylor. And she found him watching her. His gaze was sharp, interested. She was positive hers was, too.

When the officiant announced that Taylor and Judd could kiss, not just as part of a rehearsal, but to seal their new vows, Jessie kept her eyes on them. But when it came time to walk up the aisle a minute later, she locked gazes with Shane the whole way. Maybe Taylor was right. Maybe they *could* have sex. Doing so would alleviate all the sexual tension she'd built up over the past week since he'd come to town the first time.

She didn't have to decide right this very minute. She'd play it by ear.

For a little while after the ceremony, she was so busy, she was able to stop thinking about Shane and muscles and suits and silk boxers and sex. She and the rest of the bridal party posed for photos, sat at the head table to eat, and toasted the married couple. Finally, the DJ made the traditional announcement, introducing the members of the bridal party as they walked onto the dance floor, and then Jessie was free of her duties and able to hang out with her date.

He was sitting at one of the giant round tables situated around the dance floor, and he stood up when he saw Jessie approaching. A slow love song played on the speakers, and the chandeliers twinkled as Jessie's heart propelled her toward him. "Having fun?" she asked.

"Absolutely," he said. "Mostly because I get to enjoy watching you in that dress."

Up until that moment, she could chalk up every compliment he paid her to friendliness. But not this time. Heat simmered in his eyes. He took her hands and said, "I can't stop looking at you."

Her body responded, pulsing and throbbing with need in a way she'd never experienced.

"Do you want to dance?" Although she'd love nothing more than to strip him down right in the middle of the reception, that might take the attention away from the bride and groom. Dancing seemed like the next best thing.

"I would love to," he said.

Still holding hands, they made their way to the dance floor, and he swung her around to face him. He held onto her waist so they remained a few inches apart, and he rested his forehead on hers. They swayed, and she felt an almost impossible urge to draw him closer so they were touching from chest to hips.

"This is nice," he said.

"It is," she said, doing her best to keep her voice even despite the feelings zinging through her consciousness and her body.

In all the time they'd known each other, they'd never broached a more-than-friends relationship. What would kissing him feel like? Would it lead to more, or would it reveal that they were right to remain friends all this time?

"Penny for your thoughts," Shane said, his voice a husky whisper.

When she sighed, Jessie inhaled the rich, spicy, woodsy scent of his cologne. Should she tell him the truth about what she was thinking? When had she ever held back? That, at least, didn't have to change. "Things feel different," she said, and almost immediately wished she could take it back.

They swayed for a few beats and Jessie held her breath while she awaited his response.

Finally, he said, "They do."

Her heart beat just a bit faster when she said, "I think I might like to kiss you. Just to try it. Have you ever thought about it?"

She felt Shane's body still, just for a split second. If she hadn't been so tuned into him, she might not have noticed. "Once or twice."

"Should we try it?"

Before he could answer, the romantic slow song ended and a

hard rock song, with heavy, fast bass and loud, shrill electric guitar blared through the speakers. Jessie jumped, and Shane laughed.

"Well, that put a little damper on the mood, didn't it?"

Jessie wasn't sure whether to feel relieved or disappointed. Shane grabbed her hand and pulled her toward the edge of the dance floor. They made their way through gyrating bodies and banging heads. A waiter passed by with a tray of champagne flutes, and Shane grabbed two.

"Here," he said, yelling so she could hear him over the music, and promptly tipped his back.

Jessie followed suit, and almost immediately after the bubbles burst in her mouth, she felt a delightful buzz, a softening of the nervous edges.

"Thanks," she yelled back.

She took his champagne flute and set both empty glasses on a nearby table, and then gestured to the back of the room, where she hoped the music wouldn't be as loud. He followed her into a corner, where the lighting was dim and, sure enough, they could speak at a normal volume.

"Who picked this song?" Shane demanded, and Jessie smiled. "Probably Judd. I don't know."

Now that they'd talked about kissing, Jessie couldn't stop thinking about getting her lips on his. But had the crazy music ruined the moment for good?

"Let's go outside," Shane said. "Isn't there a patio?"

Maybe the music hadn't ruined the moment.

Double doors at one end of the reception room led to a patio, where space heaters radiated warmth. They stepped outside, and when the doors closed, silence wrapped around them.

Shane grinned at Jessie, and anticipation flared in her torso. "Now," he said. "Where were we?"

She smiled back and took a step closer to him so they were almost touching.

"I want to hear you say it again," he said.

Shyness gripped her, and obviously sensing that, he laughed, which eased a bit of her tension. She said, "I'd like to try kissing you."

His eyes lit up with triumph or satisfaction or both. He put his hands on her waist and pulled her in, and then his lips were on hers.

$$7$$

Shane had imagined kissing Jessie too many times to count. And there they were, the cold air biting at their noses and ears, the heater hissing above them, and he was finally getting his chance.

As soon as he brought his lips to hers, his body jumped to attention. *Yes*, he thought, this was exactly what he'd waited for. The pleasure was almost too great to bear as years' worth of desire came rushing to the surface. She tasted like champagne and the cake's strawberry filling and part of him worried she'd come to her senses and stop him before they really got going.

But that didn't seem to be the case. After a few gentle kisses, a hunger seemed to possess her and she wrapped her hands around his upper arms and kissed him deeply, teasing his lips apart, licking his lower lip, and then brushing her tongue over his. Every action, every movement, sent a fresh wave of bliss through his veins and he wished he could be in this moment forever.

His own moan caught him off guard. Releasing her waist, he wrapped his arms around her and her hands slid into his hair. He'd hardened instantaneously, and he pressed against her belly. She didn't seem to mind. In fact, she pushed her hips forward and her breasts against his chest, and her kissing became even more intense.

Would it be completely unthinkable to strip that otherworldly dress off her body right this very minute, on this very patio?

Jessie's hands made their way from the back of his head to the front of his body, and roamed over his pecs and abs.

"Mmhmm. Exactly as I suspected," she murmured against his mouth. "*So* nice."

She was driving him wild. Her hands traveled downwards, leaving trails of chills in their wake, and she hooked her fingertips into his waistband. God, how he wanted her to touch him.

"Touch me, Shane," she whispered, making all the fantasies of his youth come true.

Keeping one arm wrapped around her, he used his free hand to explore the body he'd lusted after for years. As he'd always imagined, that hand fit perfectly in the curve of her waist. When he brought it to her breast, she groaned and leaned into him. He thanked the make-out gods when he realized he could edge down the neckline and put his mouth there. Holding onto the back of his head, Jessie pulled him closer, gasping when he found her nipple and took it gently between his teeth.

He was so hard, he thought he might explode and then she unzipped his pants. He sprang free, and she made another "Mmm" sound, taking him in her hand and pleasuring him with long, slow strokes.

Just when he thought he couldn't stand another stroke without getting inside her, the patio doors clicked and started to swing open. Jessie gasped and let go of him, and he slid up the top of her dress to cover her before zipping up his pants.

They both whirled around, and another couple stood there, frozen, wearing shocked expressions.

To her credit, Jessie laughed out loud. "Hey, guys," she said. "It's all yours."

She grabbed Shane's hand and pulled him back inside. Shane did his best to tuck his full-force erection into his waistband, and Jessie gave him a wicked smile.

"I'll get back to that," she said. It sounded to Shane like a promise—one he knew he'd be thinking about for the rest of the night.

Another slow song played, and without speaking, the two of them returned to the dance floor.

"Oh, my God," Jessie said. "That was the last thing I expected."

Delighted, Shane felt himself smiling. "Me, too."

"I thought I was going to be like, 'Okay, that was nice,' and we'd move on with our lives. But I can't wait to do that again, Shane."

It was music to his ears. Still, he kept his feelings close to his heart. If she knew he'd thought of her like that for all these years, she might turn tail and run. "I can't, either."

"You know," she said, her breath warm in his ear, "maybe we should just get a room here tonight."

Shivers ran over his skin at that thought ... the two of them in a hotel room, him ripping off that dress and having his way with Jessie in whatever she wore underneath.

But what would it be like in the morning, when they woke up, wedding festivities over? Was Jessie's sudden interest in him a result of the wedding excitement? That's why, as Roman had said, post-wedding romantic shenanigans were a thing ...

"This is not the reaction I was hoping for," Jessie said, and Shane could see a mixture of worry and humor in her smile.

Deciding full honesty was the best course, Shane said, "I panicked! I mean, first, I imagined everything we could do together in a hotel room overnight. And *then* I freaked out, thinking about whether your feelings might change when we woke up together tomorrow morning."

Jessie looked thoughtful for a moment. "I see."

"And?"

"I honestly don't know," she said. Then, a gleam in her eye, she said, "Maybe we should get a room and talk things over, first. And then decide if we want a simple, casual sleepover, or a sleep-together sleepover."

"Sounds reasonable," Shane said, relief rushing through his veins. "But do you think you might like to try kissing a little more while we still have music and mood lighting?"

She nodded, and this time when he kissed her, she melted against him, quelling some of the nerves that had cropped up.

"Should we go make sure there's even a room available?" she asked as the song wound down a minute later.

He nodded and she said, "Don't look so terrified, Shane. It's just a sleepover. We might even have a pillow fight."

The hotel did have a room, and Jessie slid her credit card across the counter without a care in the world. Then she turned to him and said, "I'm starving. Want to eat?" as if he wasn't vibrating with desire and yearning for her and food wasn't the last thing on his mind.

"Sure," he said, because he wasn't quite ready to face the idea that she might change her mind when they got up to the hotel room.

He shouldn't have been surprised when they sat down at the hotel restaurant and Jessie ordered a burger and a beer — it had been their go-to dinner before he moved away.

"There's just something incongruous about you, in that dress, eating a burger," he said, smiling as she took a giant bite.

"I know," she said after swallowing. "But I've been eating mostly salads for the past three months in preparation for this dress."

He laughed. "Well, I've never passed up a burger, for a wedding or anything else."

"You know," she said, "all this wedding stuff has got me thinking."

"Uh oh," he said, thinking again of Roman and his romantic shenanigans comment. What if Jessie was about to say she'd realized her more-than-friends feelings for him were related to Taylor and Judd's wedding, and that they'd go back to the status quo after that?

"It's nothing bad," she said, flapping a hand. "It's just—your dad never got married. But he has mentioned this Isabelle lady several times. What do you think about trying to find her?"

"Now? After all this time?" Shane said, mostly just relieved they weren't talking about *their* relationship.

"Well, yeah," Jessie said. "Your dad's not getting any younger."

"But Isabelle got *married*," Shane said. "Chances are, she's still married. Do you really think that if I came to her now and said my dad was in love with her, she'd welcome me with open arms? Who knows if she even remembers him?"

"True," Jessie said. "You make some good points. What if I do a little groundwork, find out if she's alive, if she stayed married, if her husband is still around, that kind of stuff?"

Shane chuckled. "I'm not totally against the idea, but why are you so into it?"

"I don't know," Jessie said, her eyes going dreamy. "Like I said, maybe it's all this wedding stuff. Focusing on true love and all that."

Shane tried to hide his sigh. Roman was right: the wedding stuff was getting in her head.

"If your dad has a chance at that," Jessie went on, "I don't want him to miss out on it."

"I see what you're saying. I'm just afraid of getting dad's hopes up and leaving him disappointed."

Jessie looked thoughtful. She took another bite of her burger and chewed slowly. "What if we didn't tell him?"

"I don't know," Shane said. "Can we sleep on it?"

Jessie winked at him. "I mean, that might take an extra night. Because I don't think we're going to be doing much sleeping tonight."

Once again, a fire ignited in Shane's belly. She wanted to keep him up all night. He couldn't wait. They polished off their food and went back to the reception. Walking in with Jessie on his arm, Shane felt like the luckiest guy alive. She told him the ladies would be jealous of her, but he was certain the men were jealous of him. Getting caught on the patio had defused some of the sexual tension simmering between them, and eating giant burgers together wasn't the most sensual activity, although the way Jessie ate hers, like she was ravenous, turned him on. But what—about Jessie—didn't turn him on?

Getting back on the dance floor ratcheted the tension right back up. Newly energized, Jessie moved against Shane like she was some kind of sex goddess or mystical witch. Every one of his senses was attuned to her. Her skin felt so soft under his palms, and she smelled like the most heavenly combination of flowers and citrus. Every time their lips met (and they met countless times out there on the dance floor), he luxuriated in her taste. Her laugh was like music, but the quieter noises, her moans and sighs and gasps, drew him to her like a magnet. His sixth sense, too, drew him to her. He felt this thing between them on a spiritual level.

Although he could dance with her forever, he was looking forward to the hotel room and was glad when the DJ announced it was time to say goodbye to the bride and groom. Jessie and Rose distributed containers of birdseed and the bridal party and guests rushed out the front door and stood in two lines. Taylor and Judd ran between the two lines while everyone cheered, whistled, and showered them with birdseed. They got into a limo and after everyone waved goodbye, with more cheering and whistling, the crowd started to scatter. The whole process seemed interminable.

"Does this mean we get to go up to our room now?" Shane asked, hoping he didn't sound too eager.

"It does." She raised an eyebrow at him.

The two of them quietly slipped away from the remaining crowd. In the elevator, Jessie backed him up to one wall and leaned against his body, running kisses along his jawline until her lips to his. *How is this possible?* Joy and arousal tangled together. He cupped her butt and then ran his hands over her waist and up to her breasts. The elevator dinged and its robotic voice announced, "Seventh floor."

Pressing her hands against the wall behind him, Jessie peeled her body away from his. They held hands as they walked to their room, and remained silent while Shane unlocked the door.

Once they got inside, Jessie gasped. "Look at this view!"

It *was* quite a view: the room overlooked the courthouse plaza, downtown Prescott's crown jewel. The whole thing shone with Christmas lights twinkling from the trees, adorning the light posts, and illuminating the majestic courthouse. Jessie had run up to the window, and Shane let the door close and locked it. He came up behind her and put his hands on her shoulders. He kissed the back of her neck and her shoulder, tucking his pointer finger under the tiny strap on the right and pulling it down. He did the same with the strap on the left before trailing kisses down her spine.

Goosebumps rose on her skin. She turned around to face him, and in the glow of the Christmas lights outside, she looked luminous, ethereal. Wrapping her arms around his shoulders, she kissed him on the lips, tender, gentle. He felt himself relaxing into the contact, following her pace as she increased the intensity. Starting with his collar, she unbuttoned his shirt, moving slowly and carefully until she had to untuck it to finish. She paused her kissing to unfasten the buttons at his wrists, and then let his shirt fall to the floor.

"Take a step back," she commanded. "I want to look at you."

He did and had to tell himself to stand confidently in his new body. He was no longer the awkward, out-of-shape teenager he'd once been.

"Pretty," she said, her smile revealing her satisfaction at seeing him without his shirt on. "Lose the pants."

For just a beat, a fraction of a second, Shane blanched. She wanted him to undress? In front of her? He took a deep breath, hoping she couldn't sense his anxiety, unfastened his pants, and let them drop to his ankles. His erection throbbed. Before he knew what was happening, Jessie ran up to him and grabbed his ass with both hands. "Ah, just what I was hoping for. Silk boxers. And you look as amazing in them as I imagined."

She worked him with her hand, over the boxers, and he nearly came undone. "Stop," he growled, "or I'm going to finish before we even get started."

With a wicked laugh, she pulled his boxers down and motioned for him to step out of those and his pants. He motioned for her to turn around and when she did, he unzipped her dress. Because he'd already pulled off the straps, the heavy fabric fell to the floor. He groaned when he saw what she wore underneath: a tiny g-string she shouldn't have even bothered with ... but he was glad she had. Kneeling behind her, he ran his hands over her ass, then used one finger to pull aside her G string so he could access her center. She arched against him, and he decided he couldn't wait any longer. He pulled off the underwear, cast them aside, and led her to the bed.

"You're so beautiful," he said to her.

"*You're* so beautiful," she said back. They were at it again, kissing with an intensity Shane had never experienced. He poured every ounce of longing, every bit of love he'd felt for her over the years into his kissing. If this was his one chance, he was going to make the absolute most of it.

Jessie lay on the bed and pulled Shane down next to her. "I want you inside me," she whispered. He had no choice but to oblige.

"Your wish is my command," he said, making her smile as he lifted himself above her and plunged into her. He looked into her eyes as he started to move. She held his gaze. He wanted to tell her, then and there, that he loved her, always had. He wanted to tell her he'd dreamed of this moment for ages. But he wasn't ready. So instead, he poured that love into her with every stroke, every movement, until they both went over the edge.

Afterward, Jessie flopped onto her back and put her hands on her forehead. "Well," she said. "Who would've thought?"

I would. "That was really nice."

Jessie's laugh was a cross between a sob and a gasp. "Nice? I'd call it incredible. Earth shattering. Axis tilting."

That gave Shane a confidence boost, and he rolled toward her and rested his hand on her bare stomach. "Good."

"I'm so tired. I know I said we wouldn't be getting much sleep tonight, but I'm going to need a nap, at least. It's been such a busy week."

"I'll wake you up in a couple of hours," Shane said, lifting his head to wink at her. He pulled the sheet and duvet over Jessie's body, kissed her on the cheek, and said, "Get some sleep."

She smiled and caressed the side of his face. "Okay. But wake me up!"

She drifted off, her breathing becoming even. A few minutes later he heard tiny, quiet snores. Which were adorable. Shane considered getting up and closing the drapes to give Jessie more darkness. But she was already sleeping soundly, and he loved the way she looked in the glow of the Christmas lights. As tempting as it was to touch her, to run his fingertips up and down her arm or his hand along her hip, he let her sleep — for now.

Shane always told himself he had Jessie's every detail memorized, but as they lay there, he noticed features he never had before. A dark, pinprick-sized freckle sat just under the outside corner of her left eye, and she had the faintest line between her eyebrows from the way she squinted when she concentrated.

Maybe because the room was dark and quiet, or maybe because Shane had always faced insecurities, doubt about his relationship with Jessie started to creep in. He imagined it as a villainous, smoky substance, entering his body through his skin. Yes, she called their lovemaking axis tilting. And it was for him, too. But he couldn't shake the feeling that this whole thing, whatever it was, was a novelty to Jessie. Kind of like test driving the latest model of a car after an upgrade gave it some new bells and whistles.

Shane loved Jessie, not like a best friend, but with a deep, tender affection that could last a lifetime. He rolled onto his back and closed his eyes. Images from their night together paraded through his mind. Jessie smiling at him from her spot behind Taylor during the wedding. Jessie winking at him as she walked back up the aisle. The wicked gleam in her eye when they got on the elevator and it was empty. The pure, unbridled pleasure when she came while he was inside of her.

God, he had it bad. Reverting to "just friends" might actually kill him. He opened his eyes again and stared at the ceiling. What if he could resolve to enjoy this time with Jessie while it lasted? What if he could love her with everything he had, for now? What if he could let her go, when the time came?

He gave the ceiling a nod, as if it had participated in the conversation with him. That's what he would do. Seize the day. And every night he could get.

8

―――――――

Jessie woke up the next morning to find Shane sound asleep beside her. "So much for being up all night," she murmured.

At the sound of her voice, he stirred and pulled the covers up under his chin.

She still couldn't believe she'd never seen the potential for Shane to transform into the stud he'd become. Even more, she couldn't believe they'd had that earth-shattering sex the night before. She knew she should think about that, and about what it all meant, and about what might happen after winter break when he went home. But she couldn't bring herself to.

Emotions had never been her strong suit, and although she and Shane hadn't discussed it, she could pinpoint the event that led to the shift in their friendship, the precise moment they'd gone from talking several times each day to talking a couple of times each week, and then even less.

Spring semester, senior year of high school. Jessie and Shane were seventeen. One evening, she dressed to the nines, curled her hair, and waited outside for Ian O'Brien to pick her up. Back then, her family had a swing in the front yard, hanging from the big oak tree. While she waited, she sat in the swing, using her feet to push herself. The late-afternoon sunlight was bright, so she kept her eyes closed. She did *not* want to be squinting when Ian showed up.

The sound of footsteps on the sidewalk announced someone's arrival. She simultaneously opened her eyes (which made her squint), and smiled, thinking Ian was the one approaching ... and felt her smile fade when she realized it was Shane. His own smiled faded when hers did, and when Ian pulled up in his car at that very moment, Shane's shoulders literally slumped before he did an about-face and walked away.

Shane's obvious disappointment unlocked uncomfortable feelings for Jessie. Guilt, for sure, and also uncertainty. Did their relationship mean the same thing to her that it did to him?

The clock on the nightstand next to the glorious, luxurious king-sized bed read 10:00. Gasping, Jessie sat up and looked around the room, cursing herself for not thinking to plan for clothes to change into. Or a toothbrush. She called down to the front desk and in a whisper, requested a late checkout and two toothbrushes.

Just as she shut the door after someone brought the toothbrushes, Shane said, "We definitely slept through the night." He sat up, exposing his chiseled statue of a torso. "I slept like the dead."

"Me too," Jessie said, walking over to sit on the edge of the bed. "And now I'm famished. Should we order room service? I usually check in with your dad for breakfast, but we missed that boat."

Shane groaned and dropped his head into his hands. "How humiliating. I'm going to have to do the walk of shame at the age of twenty-seven."

"I hadn't thought of that," Jessie said. "I'll just have the ride-share drop me off at my house."

Shane shook his head, a rueful smile on his lips. "Well, I guess the damage is done." He inhaled, like he was about to speak, but then closed his mouth. After a beat, he said, "Should we order breakfast? And then I'll hop in the shower."

Once he got in the shower, Jessie took off her makeshift sheet dress and put on her bridesmaid dress. Out of habit, she turned on the TV and flipped to what looked like a Christmas movie. While the characters did their thing, Jessie let her mind wander. The energy between Shane and her felt different this morning. He seemed subdued, pensive. She wondered if he was disappointed she hadn't kept him up all night. But she really had been tired. And, apparently, so had he. She vaguely remembered waking up in the middle of the night, just enough to see him sleeping.

Based on how she felt last night, she wondered why she hadn't jumped at the chance to hop in the shower with him. Before she could even consider going in the bathroom, she heard him turn off the water. And then he was back, wearing those silk boxers and his dress shirt.

A knock sounded at the door, announcing the room service.

"I'll get it," Shane said. He spoke to the hotel employee for just a minute before wheeling the cart into the room. "Your feast, my lady."

They laid the food out on the small table and ate in companionable silence. Once they polished it off Jessie said, "What do you say, after we go home and put on real clothes, we talk to your dad about finding Isabelle?"

"I don't know," Shane said again, and Jessie gave him a playful poke on the shoulder. "You just don't want your dad to have someone to focus on besides you!"

Smiling, Shane said, "That's not it. I'm just thinking, like you said last night, maybe we should do a little groundwork before we bring it up. Make sure she's still alive, not happily married for forty years, and not on her deathbed or anything."

"Oh, right," Jessie said. "I'd forgotten about the groundwork. But that seems reasonable."

An hour later, the ride-share driver dropped them off at Jessie's. They stood there on the sidewalk, and for the first time since they'd shared that kiss on the dance floor, Jessie felt like she didn't know what to say or do, or how to act.

"I had fun last night," she said, quashing the urge to sway back and forth like a little kid.

"Me, too," Shane said. He shaded his eyes from the sun and looked at her, hard. "I hope things aren't awkward now."

"They won't be," Jessie said, infusing her voice with the gusto she knew he expected. "I promise."

He opened his arms for a hug. The embrace felt *normal*, free of all that charged sexual energy from the night before. Jessie didn't know exactly what to make of that, and when he said, "See you in a bit," and headed for Alvin's, she experienced a strange feeling she couldn't quite identify.

After showering and getting dressed, she fired off a text to Rose and Taylor. *Good afternoon! How are we all doing today?*

Rose responded right away: *I'm doing just fine. I didn't get to sleep in, but hey, I don't want to sleep away all of my winter break anyway. Sleeping in is overrated. More importantly, how are YOU today? Did my eyes deceive me, or did you and Shane get a room last night? I saw the two of you heading for the elevator.*

Even though she was alone in her house, sitting on the couch, Jessie blushed fiercely. She hadn't planned on *not* telling Rose and Taylor she'd slept with Shane, but she hadn't exactly planned on telling them, either. At least, not yet.

Taylor joined the conversation with a big-eyed emoji. *Did the two of you get a room?*

By the way, the weather in Cabo San Lucas is divine. She sent a picture of Judd and her on beach chairs, both of them wearing sunglasses, Taylor wearing a giant sun hat.

That looks lovely, Jessie typed. She left it at that. After a couple of minutes passed without any further conversation, Rose sent another message: *Jessie? Are you going to dish or not? I know you didn't miss our questions.*

Jessie sighed. She couldn't put her finger on why she was reluctant to tell her best girlfriends what happened between her and Shane. All she knew was that it made her uncomfortable. She didn't want to dwell on her discomfort, though, so she went ahead and wrote back. *Yes, we did get a hotel room. Yes, we had sex. And then room service. Great omelets.* The following pause in the conversation was so long, Jessie sent a cricket emoji. Then, at the same time, both of her friends sent back a mind-blown emoji.

Haha, Jessie typed. *My mind is blown, too. I don't even know what to make of it.*

How was it? Taylor wanted to know.

Yeah, Rose wrote. *Tell us everything.*

Great. It was great. I never would have imagined Shane would be such a good lover. Actually, she should have known he would be attentive in bed. He'd always been thoughtful, taking care of others' needs before his own. As a child, he filled her water glass first, dished up her meals first, gave her first choice of whatever snacks they had after school. *This whole thing is just so strange*, Jessie typed, hitting send before she realized her comments could open up a deeper conversation about her feelings for Shane. As quickly as she hit send, she composed another message. *But it's fun, so I'll go with that. He's here for two weeks, and then things will go back to normal.*

Sure enough, Rose responded: *This is going to require a longer, in-person conversation as soon as Taylor gets back.*

Jessie groaned. *Oh, I'm sure no one wants to talk about that. I'm going to want to hear all about the honeymoon.*

Rose and Taylor both responded with eye-rolling emojis, and Jessie giggled. *I've got to go, ladies. Heading to Alvin's for dinner.*

With a bottle of wine and her casserole, she headed next door.

Alvin seemed especially jovial when he greeted her. "Jessie! So wonderful to see you. Come on in! Shane's in the kitchen!"

Shane gave Jessie a funny look, half smile and half grimace, as she came in. In response, she offered what she hoped was a reassuring smile.

"Shane's just whipping us up a salad," Alvin said. "Did you know our boy is good in the kitchen?" Jessie's mind played a trick on her, replacing "good in the kitchen" with "good in bed," and she blanched. Shane must have read the fear, and then the relief, on her expression, because he stared hard into the salad bowl, tossing lettuce leaves and cherry tomatoes with deep concentration.

"Who knew?" Jessie said. "Can I put my casserole in the oven?" She pressed the preheat button and Shane made a strangled sound. "Hey," she whispered. "I didn't say anything about you putting your casserole in my oven."

"I'll be right back," Alvin said. "I just remembered I haven't gotten the mail yet today."

He left the kitchen and the front door opened and closed half a minute later.

"It's Sunday," Shane said. "There's no mail. I think he's trying to give us alone time."

Again, Jessie wondered why they didn't throw themselves at each other for at least a passionate kiss ... during the wedding, she would have sworn that's all she'd want to do the next time she got him alone. "I think I'm going to need some wine for tonight. You?" She was already opening the bottle.

"Please," Shane said. "You should have seen his face this morning when I walked in the door."

"I can only imagine."

"He looked so pleased with himself, like he had something to do with our romantic shenanigans."

Mid-pour, Jessie looked at him and arched an eyebrow. "Is that what we're calling it?"

"It's apropos, isn't it?"

Jessie handed Shane his glass, which she'd poured heavy, and they touched their glasses together before taking a sip. Jessie went ahead and took another healthy gulp. If Alvin was excited about their romantic shenanigans, he was very likely to put them on the spot at dinner. Before Jessie had time to think about how she might respond if he did, the front door opened and closed again.

"I'm back," Alvin said. "No mail today."

"It's Sunday," Shane and Jessie called back.

"Dinner's ready," Shane said, and Alvin came swaggering into the kitchen. "Smells pretty good in here, you two. You make quite the team in the kitchen."

Jessie glanced at Shane, who rolled his eyes. She snickered. The oven timer beeped. While Shane grabbed a trivet out of a drawer, Jessie took the casserole out of the oven. When she set it on the trivet Alvin winked at her as if to say, *See? I told you; you make a good team.* Sure enough, things got worse at the dinner table.

Rubbing his hands together to display his eagerness, Alvin said, "So, tell me about the wedding."

Hoping not to add any fuel to his fire, Jessie said, "The wedding was nice. Lovely. Taylor and Judd looked so happy. Everything went to plan, the food was great, and the music was even better."

"Great!" Alvin said. "And the dancing?"

Jessie looked at Shane across the table. If she wasn't mistaken, a little of that fire was in his eyes as he stared back at her. Alvin looked at Shane, and then at Jessie, and then back at Shane.

Jessie said, "It was wonderful."

"Huh," Alvin said. "Happy to hear it. Did they play any slow songs?"

Shane snorted. "Yep."

"And how was the hotel? You know, I've always wanted to stay there."

"Let's talk about the weather," Jessie said. "A bit chilly, right?"

Alvin made himself scarce again after dinner, leaving Jessie and Shane to clean up. "Have you done any more thinking about Isabelle?" Jessie asked as she transferred the leftover casserole into a container.

Something Jessie couldn't quite identify tinged Shane's laugh. "I haven't. Why don't you do some initial research and find out if she's even alive? And then we can revisit this topic."

His attitude stung. Why wouldn't he want his dad to reunite with the woman he'd loved?

"Fine," she said. "I will."

She used a dry erase marker to label the leftover container, and when she turned around after putting it in the fridge, Shane had stopped rinsing dishes and stood facing her. "I'm sorry," he said. "I've expressed my concerns about this project, and I also realize that maybe the potential benefits outweigh the potential drawbacks. I just don't want him to get hurt."

Jessie nodded. "I understand. I'll tread carefully, I promise. I don't want him to get hurt, either. Let me just look her up, okay?"

"Okay."

She went home a little while later, leaving behind a disappointed Alvin. A notebook at her side, Jessie sat on the couch and used her phone to search the Internet for Isabelle Sorensen Budgie.

"That really is quite a name," she said into the silence. Not liking the way her voice reverberated in the empty room, she switched on the TV. The search results populated. "Bingo."

Isabelle Sorensen Budgie was alive and well, and apparently a busy and well-known member of the community in Buffalo, a small town in Wyoming. From the looks of it, she'd participated in ribbon cuttings, park cleanups, and chili cook-offs.

Jessie scrolled down. After seeing so many examples of Isabelle's community involvement, she shouldn't have been surprised to see a link to a magazine article about her. *Isabelle Sorensen Budgie Talks Life After Divorce*. Intrigued, Jessie clicked on the link. A picture of Isabelle, her piercing green eyes looking right at the camera, took up most of the space on the webpage. Jessie scrolled to the beginning of the article. *Isabelle Sorensen Budgie knows a thing or two about making her own way.*

"I think I like this woman," Jessie said.

Divorcing after six years of marriage, Isabelle has spent most of her adult life doing as she pleased. And fortunately for the community of Buffalo, making an impact pleases Isabelle. "When Jack and I first divorced," Isabelle remembered, "I thought it was the end of the world as I knew it. I felt like my life had burned down. But then one day it hit me. Well, if my life had burned down, I would simply become a phoenix."

The article went on to describe how Isabelle had raised a son and a daughter, co-parenting amicably with Jack despite the divorce. Meanwhile, she'd started her own company and built it into an empire. She retired quite wealthy, and used her time and money to further causes about which she was passionate.

"I realized that if I poured my energy into the things I cared about, I was a much happier person. Instead of dwelling on the past, I created my own future, and hopefully, helped build a better future for Buffalo."

The article stated that Isabelle never remarried, and Jessie pumped her fist. If Isabelle and Alvin had been such good friends, surely she'd be open to seeing him. But a phone call or email wouldn't do. Isabelle was older and might think someone was scamming her. Hands shaking with excitement, Jessie pulled out her phone and texted Shane. *Are you up for a road trip?*

He texted back right away: *Sure, I guess. What do you have in mind?*

Jessie wrote, *I found her.*

Shane wrote back, *Isabelle?*

Giggling madly by that point, Jessie responded, *Who else?*

Shane wrote, *I think this requires a real conversation. Can I come over?*

Jessie sighed. She wanted Shane to agree, right away, to be as excited about the idea as she was. But, apparently, it might take some convincing.

Sure, she wrote. *But what are you going to tell your dad?*

Shane responded, *He'll be in bed in an hour. Why don't I come over then?*

Sure.

While she waited, Jessie poured herself a glass of wine and returned to the couch to continue researching. When Shane knocked on the door an hour later, she couldn't believe all that time had passed.

As soon as he sat down next to her on the couch, she thrust her notebook at him. "Look at this. Not only is Isabelle alive and well, but she's also single. I think we should go visit her, tell her about your dad, see if she wants to come for a visit."

Shane looked at her sideways. "Don't you think you're being a little presumptuous?"

Feeling defensive, Jessie said, "I mean, not really. It's just information gathering. What would it hurt to go talk to her? Maybe we feel her out before we invite her to Arizona. I'm just spitballing, you know?"

Shane's sculpted chest rose and fell with his deep breath. "I guess you're right. Part of me thinks a phone call or email would suffice, but part of me wonders if she would think we were somehow trying to trick her."

Triumphant, Jessie said, "My thoughts exactly."

"You really thought this through," Shane said.

"Now that it's winter break, I guess I have too much time on my hands."

Shane set Jessie's notebook on the coffee table and turned toward her. He tucked her hair behind her ear, and the simple gesture sent a thrill over her skin. He leaned closer and whispered, "I can think of some other things to do with all this spare time."

Jessie felt a moment's hesitation. The transition between friend and lover didn't feel totally smooth. But, as Shane's fingers brushed the back of her neck and he kissed the spot just below her ear, her inner voice yelled, *Are you crazy?* Her body, the memory of Taylor's wedding night fresh in its memory, begged her to let go and give into temptation. Yes, she wanted to plan a road trip to Wyoming. But also, she could do that tomorrow. She set down her wine, took Shane's glass from him and set it down, too, and then got to her knees and pushed Shane into a lying position on the couch. His satisfied smile sent a shot of heat through her body. His hands were under her shirt, unhooking her bra, cupping her bare breasts. She straddled him, and could feel his arousal between her legs as she brought her mouth to his.

She ground against him and he moaned, the sound bringing her closer to the edge. He pulled her shirt over her head and flung her bra to the side, raising up to take her nipple in his mouth. She returned the favor, sliding her hands up his stomach, over his chest, removing his shirt. Skin on skin, they continued to kiss, and Shane ran his fingertips up and down Jessie's back. He pulled her pants down over her hips and one hand moved to her center, stroking, teasing, exploring. She writhed against him, desperate for the contact. Needing a break before she lost herself completely, she pulled down his pants, sliding down while she did so, and then took him into her mouth. He groaned, and after she took him deep a few times, he put a hand on the back of her head and thrust so she had to take him deeper. His grunts of pleasure nearly brought her to release.

"Get up here," he commanded, reaching for her rib cage and pulling her up so they were face to face. "I need to be inside you."

Unable to speak, Jessie nodded, and he grabbed her hips and thrust himself inside of her. She cried out, and he grinned. "Feel that? You did that to me."

Still gripping her hips, he moved against her, matching her rhythm.

"Come for me," he said, and she did, just like that, unwinding and falling apart in a crescendo of sensations. He wrapped his arms around her waist, pulling himself closer while he released, crying out as he pounded into her.

He flopped down flat on the couch, and she flopped down on top of him. They lay there, panting.

Thanks," she said to him.

"Anytime," he said. After a few seconds, Jessie sat up. She felt Shane twitching inside her and said, "Ready to go again?" He laughed, running his hands from her knees to her hips. "Maybe in an hour or so."

"Then I guess we have plenty of time to plan our road trip."

Maybe he looked a little exasperated, but all he said was, "Okay."

"Okay, like, you want to? Or, okay, like, you don't really want to, but you can't tell me no?"

"The latter. But," he said, holding up a finger to stop her protest, "I'll do it as long as you take credit, whether it goes well or badly."

Jessie peeled her body off his and pulled on her underwear and T-shirt. "Fair enough. Here." She tossed him his T-shirt, too, and he put it on before finding his underwear. Jessie had to go on tiptoe to kiss him on the cheek. "Thank you. You won't regret it. And you know what? Those silk boxers are a really nice touch."

Jessie grabbed her laptop and sat on the couch. She patted the cushion next to her and Shane sat down, too.

After unlocking her screen, she clicked on the Internet tab she'd already mapped the route from Prescott to Buffalo. "See? It's sixteen hours to the town where Isabelle lives. I figure, we can do the driving in two days to minimize how long we leave your dad alone."

"Wait," Shane said. "It sounds like you may have already done some planning."

Jessie shrugged. "Not actual planning. Just information gathering. I was waiting for you to plan."

"Were you?"

She gave him a dark look and he laughed. "Just kidding. Kind of."

9

———————

Shane didn't know how Jessie always convinced him to do deeds he considered questionable. But three days after she found Isabelle Sorensen Budgie in Buffalo, Wyoming, there they were, buckled into his truck in the driveway, stocked up with road trips snacks, the town plugged into her navigation app.

He started the truck and Jessie squealed. Maybe that's how she got him to do things with her — by being unbearably adorable.

"Ready?" She looked at him across the console, her smile so bright, he couldn't help but return it. She squeezed his shoulder before grabbing the bag of tortilla chips out of the snack bin and tearing it open. "Want a chip?"

"Not just yet. I'm still getting over what I just did."

"What did you do?"

"I lied to my dad! I've never straight-up lied like that."

"Not even that time we sneaked to the store and bought tons of candy, but told him all we bought were a couple of sodas?" She smirked at him.

"That's different," he said. "I just told him we're going on a road trip related to your work. Which is a complete and total lie."

Jessie's smile faded, and after she looked thoughtful for a

moment, she said, "Well, it's part of my *social* work. It's like volunteer work. Kind of."

"That's a stretch."

"It's a white lie, Shane. And if everything works out it's for his benefit."

"True," he said. Then, after a pause: "You know, this reminds me of the time you convinced me to sneak into that swimming pool down the street."

Jessie gasped, aghast. "This is nothing like that! That was against the rules! That was a foolish teenaged caper!"

Shane put the truck in reverse and backed onto the street. He put it in drive and said, "Yes, in that sense, you're right. This is nothing like that. But in the sense that you officially convinced me to go on this road trip when I am not sure it's a good idea? This is exactly like that."

Jessie made a dismissive gesture, popped a chip in her mouth, and proceeded to talk with her mouth full. "You had fun. Admit it."

He did have fun. A tiny glimmer of it peeked through the terror related to getting arrested and thrown in jail. He remembered that much. "That's beside the point."

"Dare I say, you wouldn't have had half the fun you did in high school if it weren't for me."

Shane considered. She was probably right. But he wasn't going to admit that to her. "The point I'm trying to make, Jessie Monroe, is that you have a habit of convincing me to go along with your schemes, and I have a habit of giving in to you."

"I hadn't thought of it like that."

"I always figured, if we got caught, that's how I would explain myself. So my dad wouldn't be mad at me."

"Hey!" She threw a chip at him and crossed her arms.

He plucked the chip off his lap and ate it. "I thought it was a good idea at the time."

"Fortunately, he never caught you."

They'd made it out of town. Highway 89 stretched north out of Prescott, long and straight, surrounded by grasslands and scrub brush.

"Anyway, it wasn't Dad I was worried about so much as someone else catching us," Shane said.

"Well, like I said, we never got caught. And I still say, even if we did, it would've been worth it."

Shane wasn't sure. His mind flashed back to their little jaunt to the pool. It belonged to their neighbors, the Alvarez family. On one of those hot summer nights, when escaping this heat seemed impossible, Jessie and Shane sat on his front porch swing, lethargic. Sweat beaded on their skin, their arms stuck together where they touched, and cicadas screamed.

"I wish we had a pool," Shane said.

Jessie flopped back in the swing and threw a hand over her eyes. "Me, too. It's sweltering."

Looking back on that moment now, Shane wondered why they hadn't just gone inside to the air conditioning. He supposed they thought they were exercising their independence, staying outside until well past bedtime. He also felt a bit scandalized at the way his teenage self had admired Jessie's body while she sat there with her eyes covered. He knew, too, that his admiration was totally normal. But God, he had it bad for her. Because it was so hot and muggy, she wore only a tiny tank top and the shortest possible shorts. He could see the curve of her breasts above her neckline, and the perfect, smooth slice of skin between the bottom of her tank top and her denim shorts. If he moved his head just a little, he'd probably be able to see her underwear. As tempting as it was, he didn't do that. Sitting there on that swing, he started to feel aroused. And then, immediately, guilty. Even as he continued to ogle her body, she sat up straight and said, "I've got it! We can use the Alvarezes' pool!"

"Are you crazy?" he said, only to receive a single raised eyebrow in response. "Maybe I am," she said. "But imagine how good it'll feel."

It took five more minutes of pleading, cajoling, and bargaining to convince him. Then, because they didn't want to wake her parents or his dad by going inside to get their bathing suits, they agreed to swim in their underwear. She couldn't have known how attracted he was to her. Could she? If she had, she probably never would have stripped down to her bra and panties in front of him.

Shane's adult self laughed out loud, and Jessie said, "What?"

"Nothing," Shane said, adjusting himself in the driver seat and thanking the heavens she couldn't read his mind. "It's just funny that we went swimming in our underwear."

Holding up a chip as if it were a prop in her speech she said, "We went swimming in our underwear, we cooled off, felt refreshed, and had a great time. We didn't get caught and nothing went wrong." She popped the chip into her mouth.

"But it was *close*! Remember?" He risked a quick glance at her. "The Alvaraez dad came home while we were in the pool! We were terrified! Did you block that out of your memory?"

She laughed. "No. But he didn't catch us."

"No," Shane said, "but do you remember his headlights sweeping over the backyard as he turned into the driveway? For a minute there, it felt like we were in a horror movie and the killer had discovered where we were."

"But we got out and went home. He never even saw us. Want a sour string?"

"But he could have!" Shane was almost yelling now, and Jessie looked amused.

"But he didn't. Here, eat a sour string."

Shane shrugged and shoved the candy into his mouth. "I guess you're right."

"Ergo," Jessie said, "everything will go fine on this trip. And, just like back then, I bet you'll be glad you went along with my plan."

"I don't know how glad I was back then, after I nearly had a heart attack." *And had to spend the entire night bathing in sexual tension after spending an hour with you in your underwear.*

"That was a good night," Jessie said, leaning back and putting her feet on the dashboard.

"It was," Shane said, speaking on reflex. Their dip in the pool *had* felt refreshing, but the fact that Jessie swam with him in her underwear and didn't think twice about it was like a slap in the face. Not that he blamed her back then. Although they had a great relationship and told each other (almost) everything, that night made it obvious that she thought of him as a brother, if she thought about their relationship at all.

"Penny for your thoughts?" she said. She reached across the console and squeezed his hand.

"Oh, just thinking about all the crazy shenanigans you've gotten me into."

Maybe one day he could tell her he'd been in love with her for years. But not right now, with this thing between them still so fresh his heart ached with joy and hope and fear.

They'd reached the exit for the interstate and Jessie asked him to stop at the gas station. He waited for her in the car. Instead of wondering what took her so long, Shane should have known she was buying out all the Reese's peanut butter cups in the store. She'd always loved those things.

A bag stuffed with candy over her arm, she climbed back into the truck, grinning. "You're going to help me eat these, right?"

Shane waved his hands in protest. "No, no, no. That's another shenanigan you got me into. The time you convinced me to help you eat an entire extra large bag of popcorn at the movies, with extra butter flavoring. And then you insisted that I help you polish off the refill. My digestion didn't recover for four days. Plus, you think I dropped my pudgy-boy physique by eating *candy*? I didn't. I'll eat one or two, but that's it."

"Hey," she said, frowning. "Don't call your physique a pudgy-boy physique! That's my best friend you're talking about."

Shane shook his head and started the truck. "It was. I'm okay with that now, because I worked so hard to change it. But," he said, pulling onto the onramp, "I'm not falling back into old habits, no matter how much you try, you temptress."

She laughed at that, and the moment passed. The road took them further north, into pine country, and Shane could see patches of snow in the shady areas.

"You know what I think we should do?" she said.

"What?"

"I think we should play some music from our high school days. That'll be nostalgic, right?" She was already connecting her phone to his stereo system.

"I guess," he said, and she paused what she was doing to look at him.

"You guess?"

How could he tell her that most of the songs she was likely to choose would remind him of the angst he'd experienced back then … angst over his unrequited feelings for her?

"Sorry," he said. "It will be fun. I was just distracted."

Satisfied, she went back to her task. Sure enough, the first song she chose reminded him of the homecoming dance their junior year. It was a love ballad, so popular at that time, the radio played it several times per day. It came on during the dance, and Shane took it as a sign that he should ask Jessie to dance.

Why he'd considered it a sign, he didn't know … maybe he was looking for any reason to believe he could finally tell her how he felt.

He didn't have to spend much time looking for her. His subconscious kept track of her, and he always knew where she was. At the moment, she stood near the snack table with a couple of friends. Slowly, cautiously, he approached her. His stomach roiled with nerves. He shouldn't have paused; it cost him his opportunity. Just before he took another step forward, a trio of boys walked up to Jessie and her friends. Shane couldn't hear their conversation over the loud dance music, but he assumed the boys asked the girls to dance, because they were off, paired up and on the dance floor. He slunk back into the shadows. Bringing himself back to the present moment, Shane felt a little sad for that uncertain, tentative, insecure version of himself.

So," Shane said after they heard a few more songs. "I assume you have a plan for when we get there?"

"Not really," Jessie said. "What do you think we should do?"

"Oh, no," Shane said. "This whole thing is your idea. I'm just along for the ride. You come up with the plan and then tell me."

"You're no fun." Jessie crossed her arms.

Shane laughed. "Pouting isn't going to change my answer.

Imagine we're driving into town. What's the first thing were going to do?"

Uncrossing her arms and sitting up straighter, Jessie said, "Well, I guess we go eat."

"Of course. After that."

Jessie pressed a button on the stereo to skip a heavy metal song. "I guess we find Isabelle."

"Okay," Shane said. "And how do we do that? Just start knocking on doors?"

When Jessie didn't answer right away, Shane looked over at her. She was grimacing, her shoulders slightly raised — an indicator of guilt if he'd ever seen it. "What did you do?"

"I'm glad you asked." Twisting in her seat, she reached into the back and grabbed her backpack. After looking through it for a couple of minutes, she pulled out a folder. "I just happen to have her address."

Shane used one hand to rub his forehead.

"What?" Jessie said. "I'm not bringing us all the way to Wyoming for a wild goose chase. We have to get back to your dad."

"How did you get her address?"

"Property records. Just like anyone else." She shrugged.

Shane admired Jessie's dedication to the cause — true love. He'd never thought of her as much of a romantic. In fact, she seemed to shy away from talking about her feelings. But there she was, traveling hundreds of miles from home just to give true love a chance.

"Aren't you the detective?" he said. Although he wasn't looking directly at her, he could tell she was beaming at him from the passenger seat.

"I am," she said. "So we'll start at her house."

"Okay," Shane said.

They'd been in the car for ten hours when they found a motel — a long, low building that looked like it had sat there for a few decades, maybe half a century. Still, when Shane parked in front of the office sign, he saw that the property looked clean and well kept.

"Not as fancy as the hotel the other night," Jessie said, "but it'll do."

Images of the night they'd spent together flooded Shane's mind, and Jessie swatted him on the shoulder. "Are you blushing?"

"Let's go." Before she could force him to admit he was, in fact, blushing, Shane stalked over to the office door and opened it for her. Although she didn't speak as she walked past him, her smile revealed her amusement.

10

———————

That wistful nostalgia still creating a heavy feeling in his stomach, Shane was relieved the springs were squeaky, and sank into bed with relief when Jessie said, "I'm beat. Sleep well."

He might have liked a kiss on the cheek at least, but the absence of one didn't stop him from falling into a deep sleep.

The next morning, they set out before the sun came up.

"I love watching the sunrise," Jessie said.

They stopped for coffee (and Jessie bought more Reese's peanut butter cups) and did exactly that as they continued their trek northward. The winter sky blazed bright orange and purple, then gave way to an equally bright blue as the sun lifted off the horizon.

"I'm gonna need lunch," Jessie said when at noon, they saw the *Welcome to Buffalo* sign.

"I figured."

The town's historic main street featured several shops and a diner, and Jessie exclaimed, "How cute!" when they walked inside and saw the Western décor.

"I'm not sure I'd call a stuffed deer on the wall *cute*," Shane said, "but to each her own."

"I wasn't talking about the deer head," she told him darkly. "I was talking about all the cute pictures. They show the town back in its heyday."

Properly chastised, Shane gestured to a booth.

"I can't believe how nervous I am," she told him as they scooted into it. "I don't know if I can eat."

"You can always eat."

"Very funny."

A server brought the menus, and Shane quickly decided on chicken barley stew and a ham sandwich. Jessie stared at her menu, unmoving, until the server came over to take their orders.

"You go first," Jessie said.

As soon as Shane was done, Jessie said, "I'll have what he's having." Once the server was gone, she said, "What if this doesn't work out? What if we can't find her? Or worse, what if we find her and she doesn't want anything to do with us? Or, even *worse*, what if we find her and she comes to visit and she and your dad don't even get along anymore?"

Shane felt the buzz of his own anxiety as she spoke. He plucked a sweetener from the little dish on the table and pinched it between his thumb and forefinger. "And you didn't think about any of this before you convinced me to drive a thousand miles to Timbuktu, Wyoming?"

Flopping against the wall on one side of the booth, Jessie said, "I don't know. I guess I was feeling pretty optimistic."

"Well, that optimism is the only thing that's going to give this little scheme of yours any possibility of working out. So try to hang onto it."

"Little scheme," Jessie muttered.

The server was back with their food, and Jessie ate with her usual voracity. Back in the truck, she said, "I thought about asking the server if she knew Isabelle."

"Why didn't you?" Shane asked.

"I don't know." Jessie looked at the ceiling. "I guess because I was worried she would think we were up to no good. From what I can tell, Isabelle is practically a celebrity around here. But what if I missed an opportunity?"

He turned to face her. "Jessie Monroe. I have never known you to second-guess yourself or shy away from a challenge. Do I need to give you a pep talk?"

"Maybe," Jessie said, her voice tiny in the quiet cab. Her forlorn expression made Shane's heart ache. She turned to face him, too, and leaned her back against the passenger door.

"Here's my pep talk, then. Let's just take each moment as it comes. Your heart is in the right place. You wanted to do this for my dad, so he could have another chance with Isabelle. That is noble. And sweet. And if it doesn't work out like you hope, then at least you tried. Because there is nothing worse than wondering, what if? What if you had taken action on that thing? I think that's the feeling my dad is living with now. So, like I said, let's take this one moment at a time. We're here, we just had a good lunch —"

"Did we?" Jessie said. "I barely tasted it."

He reached over and grabbed her shin. "It was delicious." She put her hand over his and he said, "Now, we're going to start carrying out your mission. We're going to go to Isabelle's house and knock on the door. If she doesn't answer, we'll try something else. But let's not get discouraged before we've even started."

"That was a great pep talk," Jessie said.

The talk seemed to energize her. She sat up and leaned across the console to kiss him on the cheek. "I'll put her address in my phone. Ready?"

"Ready," Shane said. He started the truck and she gave him his first instructions. He pulled away from the curb, and they were on their way.

Isabelle lived just outside of downtown Buffalo. Victorian houses painted in soft pastels lined the side streets and, Jessie exclaimed about a million times, were "so cute!" Isabelle lived in one such house.

Jessie said, "Aww," when they pulled up. Then she said, "Oh my gosh, I'm so nervous. Look." She held out her hands, which trembled.

"Do some deep breathing," Shane said, thinking he didn't know if he could keep up with the emotional roller coaster she was on.

She inhaled through her nose, held her breath, and exhaled through her mouth several times. Then she nodded. "I feel much better. Thank you."

"You're welcome," he said. "Now let's go. The longer we wait, the more nervous you'll get." He turned off the car, hopped down from the driver seat, and walked around to open Jessie's door. Her hand felt cold and clammy in his. She didn't let go as they went up the walkway. How many times had he wished she'd lean on him for comfort? And there they were ... on a joint mission, her hand in his, their fingers intertwined. When they reached the front door, she took another deep breath and straightened her shirt.

"You look great," Shane said out of the side of his mouth. She giggled, and a nice rush of satisfaction made Shane smile.

"Ready?" Jessie said.

"Ready as I'll ever be," Shane said.

Jessie squeezed his hand and then knocked.

Nothing. No footsteps, no voice letting them know someone was on the way, no dog barking. Just silence.

"Well, this is anticlimactic," Shane said, again, out the side of his mouth. Again, Jessie giggled. "Should I ring the bell?"

Shane shrugged. "Sure."

Again, nothing. Jessie groaned, and Shane released her hand and wrapped his arm around her shoulders. "It would have been too easy if she just answered the door and invited us in for tea," he told her. "Come on, we'll try something else." Her shoulders slumped and he said, "Chin up," as they walked back down the walkway.

When they reached the sidewalk, a man called, "Good afternoon" and raised a hand in greeting.

"Hello," Jessie called. "Do you live around here?"

Shane panicked. People in small towns could be wary of outsiders. But, Jessie had always been charming. Hadn't she charmed him into coming to Wyoming?

"Sure do," the man said. He hooked a thumb at the sidewalk behind him. "Just a couple of houses down."

"Do you know Isabelle, by any chance?"

"Sure do," the man said again. "We've been neighbors for years."

"I'm Jessie." She extended a hand and the man took it.

"Vince. Nice to meet you."

"This is Shane." Vince shook Shane's hand next, his expression open and friendly.

"Shane's dad, Alvin, is an old friend of Isabelle's," Jessie said. "Shane and I were in town, so we thought we might look her up, see if she might be interested in reconnecting."

We were in town. Shane did an internal eye-roll.

"Oh, I see," Vince said. He turned to Shane. "Your dad, you say? He live around here?"

"No, we actually live in Arizona," Shane said. "They knew each other a long time ago."

"Well isn't that nice? I'll tell you what. Isabelle is a very busy lady. Sometimes she's gone from dawn until dusk. I don't know exactly where she is, you understand, but as you know, she lives here, so I'm sure she'll be back at some point. Anyway, it was nice meeting you two. Good luck."

He tipped his hat and went on his way.

"Should we just do an old-fashioned stakeout?" Jessie said. "Sit in your truck and eat snacks and wait for her to come back?"

"It's always snacks with you," Shane said.

She punched his shoulder and feigned an injury.

"A stakeout might be the simplest thing to do," Shane said, "but also, we could explore this cute little town. Who knows? We might run into her while we're out. Chances are she'll be home in the early evening, right? I mean, older folks like to be home before dark, don't they?"

"Your dad sure does," Jessie said.

He watched her consider his suggestion, and loved that her thoughtful expression was the same as it always had been: lips pressed together, eyes slightly squinted and looking up and to the left.

"You're right," she said, finally. "Let's explore the beautiful town of Buffalo. We planned on staying overnight, anyway, so we can catch Isabelle this evening or tomorrow morning."

They headed back into town and checked out some of the shops on the main drag. Shane had almost forgotten how much fun they had when they were together. He'd spent so long avoiding her (and the feelings she stirred up in him), he nearly let go of what he enjoyed about their friendship.

In an antique shop, Jessie disappeared for a few minutes, and then leapt out in front of Shane wearing a wooden mask with an unidentifiable face. Shane practically jumped out of his skin, and the two of them fell into fits of giggles before Jessie dragged him out of there.

Still breathless with laughter, they went into an art gallery, where Jessie insisted on taking photos as they reenacted scenes from the paintings. Again, they left in stitches, this time after she pretended to have been gored by a bison.

They gorged themselves on fudge at the candy shop, where they overheard a family talking about sledding on the library lawn. From the candy shop they went straight to the hardware store to buy sleds and took turns dragging each other across the snowy field as fast as they could.

By late afternoon, Shane's face hurt from smiling and his sides ached from laughing. He tried not to show his disappointment when they got back into the truck, shivering, and Jessie said, "Should we go back to Isabelle's house?"

"Sure," he said, wishing he could extend this trip to five weeks instead of five days.

Just like before, Shane parked in front of Isabelle's house, went around the front of the truck to open Jessie's door for her, and held her hand as they walked up to the door.

Just like before, Jessie knocked.

This time, they heard footsteps approaching, and a voice calling, "I'm coming! Just a minute!"

Jessie looked up at Shane like he'd just given her the exact Christmas present she wanted. He wondered how he could recreate that expression over and over, until the end of time, but before he could ponder that, the door swung open.

And there she was: Isabelle Sorensen Budgie, all five feet, four inches of her. She beamed at them as if they were friends, and Shane could see right away why his dad had fallen for her years ago. Her eyes were the most startling shade of green, light like the ocean.

"You must be Shane and Jessie," she said. "Vince told me you stopped by earlier. I'm guessing, from your rosy cheeks and the sleds in the back of your truck, that you've been playing outside."

"We have," Jessie said. "We went sledding at the library."

"That sounds marvelous," Isabelle said. "But you must be cold. Why don't you come in, have some tea?"

Jessie looked up at Shane and grinned. "We'd love to."

"Come on. Kitchen's in the back."

Shane noticed lots of framed pictures hung on the walls and sat in on top of furniture. This woman had obviously lived a very full life, surrounded by people she cared about.

Quite suddenly, *Shane* was nervous.

Isabelle meant so much to so many people ... would she even be willing to consider seeing his dad?

"Have a seat," she told them, gesturing at the kitchen table. "I'll just put on the kettle."

After she filled the pot and turned on the stove, she came to sit with them. Her eyes locked on his. "So, Vince said you mentioned your dad and I were friends?"

Heart thumping in his ribcage, Shane nodded and gulped. "Alvin West."

Isabelle's entire face lit up, her smile as big as could be. "Alvin West. Well, I'll be."

Jessie's hand gripped Shane's thigh under the table. He covered it with his.

"He mentioned the two of you worked together."

"Yes, for years at WGL. Al and I used to call it Wiggle." She laughed, the sound almost childlike. "The higher-ups would have hated that. They were quite stuffy, you know. Anyway, how is Alvin? I've thought about him often over the years. We went our separate ways before social media was even a thing. And to be honest, I'm not on social media, anyway."

Jessie gave Shane an "I-told-you-so" look, and he gave her an "I-know-you-did-and-you-were-right" look.

Feeling as if his description of his dad was some kind of test he *had* to pass, Shane cleared his throat. "He's good. He's living in Arizona. Retired, obviously. He volunteers at the humane society every week, plays poker with his friends, and is an avid Phoenix Suns fan."

"Alvin always did love his basketball," Isabelle said.

The tea kettle whistled. Isabelle got up slowly and turned off the stove. Her back to them, she said, "And what about family? Did he have any other children?"

She'd arranged the kettle, cups and saucers, and a selection of teas on a tray, and turned around to carry it to the table.

Shane shook his head. "Nope. It was just Dad and me. He adopted me when I was seven. He never married but didn't want that to stop him from having a family."

Beaming again, Isabelle set a teacup at each of their places. "What a wonderful man. He's a great father, isn't he? I always knew he would be."

Jessie sat stock still, her mouth clamped closed, but Shane could practically hear her thinking, *Can you believe this?*

"He *is* a great father," Shane said. "The best. I really lucked out."

"I'd say he lucked out, too. You seem like a very nice young man." She pushed the little basket of teabags toward Jessie, who chose one and handed the basket to Shane. He chose his and handed the basket to Isabelle.

She said, "And what about you, Jessie? Where do you fit into all this?"

Jessie tore open the wrapper on her teabag. "Well," she said, dunking the bag into the water just after Isabelle poured it. "I, too, am an only child. So you can imagine my delight when Alvin, the next-door neighbor I adored as a child — and still do — told me he was adopting someone my age. We grew up together, from the time Shane moved in until Shane moved out a couple of years ago."

"You still live nearby?" Isabelle asked.

Jessie nodded. "My parents wanted to downsize, so they moved into a senior community. I bought the house from them, so I still live next door to Alvin."

"And now?" Isabelle fixed Jessie with a hard stare and then shifted her sights to Shane.

"What do you mean?" Jessie asked, all innocence.

Again, Isabelle's laughter filled the room. "Oh honey, you know what I mean. What's going on between the two of you now? And, at the risk of sounding direct, why are you really here? Vince told me the two of you were in town, but why?"

At that point, the nerves seemed to hit Jessie again. Shane heard her gulp and she picked up her teacup and blew across the tea's surface before answering.

"The truth is, we came here just to find you." Shane noticed she skipped over the answer to Isabelle's question about the two of them. "As you know, Alvin is getting older. I wanted Shane to come back to town so he could decide how much help Alvin really needs. And that's when Alvin started talking about you. We decided —"

"*You* decided," Shane interjected.

Jessie's cheeks flushed. "*I* decided I wanted to contact you to see if you'd be interested in reconnecting. I did a quick Google search and saw that you divorced and never remarried. And," she rushed to add, "that you have lots of other accomplishments under your belt. Anyway, I sweet-talked Shane into coming with me."

"I see," Isabelle said. She drizzled some honey into her cup, watching the honey come off the dipper stick. Without looking up, she said, "What did he say about me?"

The air in the kitchen went very still all of a sudden. Jessie glanced at Shane, giving him the chance to answer. He inclined his head. "Go ahead."

"He said the two of you were the best of friends," Jessie said. She glanced at Shane and he squeezed her hand, which was still on his thigh. "At the time, he wished for more. He was glad you found happiness, but to be honest, he sounded pretty wistful when he talked about you."

Finally, Isabelle looked up from her tea and honey. "Is that right?"

Emboldened by her hopeful expression, Shane jumped in. "That's right."

"To tell you the truth," Isabelle said, "I didn't find the happiness I thought I would with my husband, Jack. He's a good enough person, but we never quite had that spark, you know." She sipped her tea, winced, and blew on it before saying, "We agreed we'd be better off as friends, so we divorced. It was all quite friendly and the opposite of passionate, just like our marriage."

Shane thought he detected a hint of sadness as she spoke. "Jessie said you had a couple of children, though, right?"

Smiling again, Isabelle said, "Yes. Theodore, who goes by Theo, and Violet. They turned out pretty great, if I do say so myself. But, we digress, don't we? You didn't come all the way to Buffalo just for tea and my wonderful company. You said you're here because you want to see if I'd be interested in reconnecting. What are you thinking?"

"It sounds almost silly now that we're sitting here in front of you," Jessie said. "But we were hoping you might be interested in coming for a visit. Prescott is such a nice small town and a lot of people vacation there. But also, Alvin's there. There are plenty of hotels, but you're welcome to stay with me, if you like. Over the past year or so, I've come to love Alvin like a second dad. The way he talked about you, I — I just didn't want him to miss out on the chance to tell you how he really felt about you." She shrugged, almost as if she thought she should provide more of an explanation, but didn't quite know what to say.

Her hand was still on Shane's leg, and his hand was still on hers. He interlaced their fingers. She gave him a grateful smile.

"What do *you* think, Shane?" Isabelle asked.

"To be honest," he said, grimacing, "When Jessie first approached me with this idea, I thought she was a bit crazy. I thought, what if we told Dad about this and then you didn't want to see him? What if your memories of him weren't as fond? What if you told us to take a hike? What if we hurt him?"

Isabelle nodded, the movement slow as she considered his words. "I see," she said again.

"I'm sure you need some time to think about it," Jessie said, which Shane thought was totally out of character. Under normal circumstances, Jessie would be pushing for an immediate answer.

"I'd like some time to think about it, yes. I would love to see Alvin, I really would. I mostly just need to figure out how to offload my responsibilities so I can get away for a week or so."

She laughed again, and Shane couldn't resist joining in with her. She said she wanted to see his dad ... that was a step in the right direction.

11

———

Isabelle insisted they stay for dinner and Jessie's heart soared. She couldn't wait to tell Alvin.

"Let's make a nice soup," Isabelle said. "If you two help me, I think we can make one in a jiffy. Jessie, how are you at chopping?"

Forty-five minutes later the three of them sat down at the table, bowls of steaming chicken noodle soup in front of them.

"So," Isabelle said. "Tell me about growing up with Alvin."

The smile that came to Shane's face made Jessie even happier. It served as proof that he'd enjoyed a wonderful childhood with his dad.

"It was the best I could ever ask for," Shane said. "He was always there. For every school function, every soccer practice and game, every fever. We definitely had our share of fun, going to the arcade, seeing movies, playing basketball at the park, you name it. But he also made sure I did my homework and studied for tests and showed up for the stuff I committed to. I, too, turned out pretty great."

Isabelle winked at him. "Tell me about growing up *together*," she said to Jessie.

"We had the best time," she said. "Shane would say I always convinced him to do things he considered questionable, but I like to think of it as bringing a little adventure into his life."

Her eyes twinkling, Isabelle said, "Like what?"

"Like the time she convinced me we should toilet paper Mr. Friedman's house."

"And who is Mr. Friedman?" Isabelle wanted to know.

Jessie was already giggling. "Our English teacher freshman year. Nicest guy, but so serious. He made us take these vocabulary tests every single week. Every. Single. Week."

On each of her last three words, Shane lifted his pointer finger into the air, making her laugh even harder — that was exactly what she'd said and done when she explained why Mr. Friedman deserved to have his house toilet papered.

"We wrote vocabulary words on the toilet paper," Jessie said through her squeals of laughter. "Not every sheet or anything, but enough that he couldn't miss it when he walked outside the next morning."

"And enough that he recognized our handwriting," Shane added.

Isabelle hooted with laughter.

"He called our parents," Jessie said, and Shane added, "We had to do the walk of shame over to his house and clean it all up."

"And write apology letters," Jessie said.

"Sounds reasonable," Isabelle said. "If you were my kids, I would have been furious."

"Were your kids without shenanigans?" Jessie asked.

"Ha! Absolutely not," Isabelle said. "They never toilet papered anyone's house — at least, not to my knowledge — but they did their share of prank phone calls. I think their favorite was to call someone, ask who they were talking to, and then insist that the person had called them. That made people furious. I had to put an end to it. But oh, how they laughed."

"Maybe we should do that now," Jessie said to Shane.

He gave her a dark look, to which she responded with a sweet smile. She was walking on clouds as they finished eating and cleaned up the kitchen. The plan was going perfectly. They'd leave the next morning and head home to Alvin. He'd be so happy to hear Isabelle wanted to reconnect.

The Buffalo Inn, a square three-story building painted bright red, looked a little more promising than the first motel where they'd stayed.

The woman behind the counter resembled the structure—tall, equally wide, and red-faced. She wore her hair in tight curls close to her head. A pearl necklace sat above a white, lace-edged collar, and a powder-blue sweater completed the look. Jessie figured she was probably wearing bobby socks. Rather than speaking in greeting, she raised her eyebrows and looked down her nose at them.

"Uh, can we get a room? Just for one night."

The woman made a show of looking at Shane's left hand and then Jessie's. Then she sniffed and opened a paper ledger on the counter. "The rate is eighty-five."

That lady smokes a few packs a day.

Shane pulled out his wallet.

"Would you like one bed or two?" the lady asked, and Shane could hear the challenge in her voice.

Amused, Jessie squared her shoulders. "One, please."

The lady tilted her head forward and looked at Jessie over the frames of her glasses with what someone might call a withering glare. Instead of withering though, Jessie had to hold in her laughter.

Without speaking, the hotel clerk turned around and took a key off the hook on the wall behind her. She held it out to them, pinching the keyring between her thumb and forefinger as if she wanted to avoid touching either one of them. "You can have room five."

Shane took the key, careful not to touch the woman's hand, and he and Jessie walked back outside.

As soon as the office door closed behind them, laughter burst from Jessie's mouth. "Gosh. I can't remember the last time I felt so judged."

Room five contained the bare essentials and nothing more. A king-size bed took up most of the space, a TV sat on top of a dresser, and through the open bathroom door, Jessie could see a shower and a sink. Obviously anxious to take off his shoes, Shane sat down on the bed. The springs creaked so loudly, Jessie was sure the woman in the office could hear them.

Another bark of laughter erupted from her mouth. "Good thing we're only staying here for one night."

The next morning when she woke up, her watch told her it was 8:30 a.m., but the light coming through the window looked dimmer than that. Slipping out of bed, she went to the window and opened the drapes. She gasped, the sound loud enough to wake Shane, who said, "Everything okay?"

Jessie laughed out loud. "You're not going to believe this. It's snowing. Like, *really* snowing. There must be a foot of it on the ground already."

"Are you kidding?"

"No!" Pulling the drapes open all the way, and then the sheer curtains, Jessie stepped to the side to give him a better view.

He sat up, the sheet falling down around his waist. "Wow," he said. "You weren't kidding."

"You'd better call your dad. I don't think we're driving home today."

Jessie and Shane both jumped when the motel room phone rang, shrill in the otherwise silent room.

When Jessie answered, a nasally voice came through the earpiece. "Good morning, Miss."

Jessie immediately recognized the voice as belonging to the woman from the front desk. To Jessie, it sounded like those words tasted bitter in the woman's mouth.

"Good morning," Jessie said. She infused her voice with extra cheer.

"This is Midge from the front desk."

Jessie winked at Shane. "Hello, Midge from the front desk."

Shane raised his eyebrows.

Midge said, "I just saw that you opened your drapes."

Jessie's mouth dropped open.

"As you can see," Midge said, "we got a bit of a storm overnight. The drifts are pretty high on your side of the building, but if you're willing to brave the snow, you're welcome to come in to the conference room for a hot breakfast. The door is just off the office. We're going to shovel the snow soon, but I don't suppose the roads will be clear today with as hard as it's coming down. We'll have breakfast on until about nine."

"Thank you very much," Jessie said. "We'll be there shortly." Once she hung up, she told Shane, "Breakfast in the conference room."

"There's a conference room?"

Jessie shrugged. "I guess so. Hungry?"

When they opened their motel room door a half-hour later, they found a drift of snow about two feet high.

"When I packed these boots," Jessie told Shane, "I had no idea how handy they'd come in."

"Lucky for you," Shane said. "My jeans are going to be soaked."

Jessie pointed at the parking lot. Snow blanketed the expanse, coming up as high as the top edge of the tires on most of the cars. "You can hang them to dry in the room after we eat. I don't think we're going anywhere anytime soon."

"Oh, boy," Shane said. "First you dragged me all the way to Timbuktu and now we're snowed in. Remind me of this the next time you come up with one of your schemes."

That stung, but then he smiled at her and stepped into the snow. Hand in hand, they made their way along the building, lifting their feet to knee height to walk through the drifts.

"Was the storm in the forecast, by any chance?" Shane asked.

Mid-step, Jessie froze. "Um, I don't know."

"You didn't check?"

Jessie shook her head. "Didn't even occur to me."

Shane sighed, and full-fledged guilt swamped Jessie. She stopped right there on the walkway, the snow up to her knees, and took both of his hands in hers. "I'm sorry," she said. "Truly. It's been so sunny at home, I didn't even think of checking the weather up here. I'm sure you're worried about your dad. I'll call the girls during breakfast and see if they can check up on him until we can get back."

He nodded, the worry still evident in the angle of his eyebrows. "That would be great. Thank you. And Jessie?"

"Yeah?"

"Let's check the forecast, okay? It would be nice to know how long we can expect to be stuck in room five."

She winked at him. "Okay. I'll call the girls and check the forecast while we eat our hot breakfast, courtesy of Midge."

Over oatmeal with all the fixings, hot coffee, and bacon, Jessie called Rose and Taylor to tell them what was happening, and asked if they could look after Alvin for a couple more days.

"Ooh, snowed in!" Taylor said. "That is so romantic! I can't wait to hear all about this when you get back. Take your time. We'll be here to keep an eye on Alvin."

Jessie wished she could tell them about the creaky bedsprings, but she couldn't — not with Shane sitting right there.

"I'm jealous," Rose said. "I'd love to be snowed in with Mac for a couple of days with nothing to do but—"

"Let me guess," Jessie said. "Celeste just walked in."

"She did," Rose said. "She says hello."

"Hi, Celeste," Jessie and Taylor said at the same time.

"Anyway," Jessie said, "thank you both, so much. I checked the forecast, and it looks like it's supposed to snow all day today and clear out tonight. It's really cold, though, so it may be a couple more days before it's safe to drive."

"Have fun," Taylor said, drawing out the second word for emphasis.

"Yeah," Rose said. "Enjoy the alone time."

Thinking of Midge commenting on how she'd noticed her opening the drapes that morning, Jessie rolled her eyes. "We'll do our best."

"So?" Shane said when she disconnected and set down the phone.

"They said they'll work out a schedule to check in on your dad," Jessie said.

"Your ears are turning pink. What else did they say?"

"Basically, that being snowed in sounds totally romantic and they hope we enjoy it."

Smiling, Shane said, "I was so stressed about my dad, I didn't even think about romance."

"Well," Jessie said, gathering her dishes to carry them to the sink. "Now you can."

That idea hanging in the air between them, they made their way back to room five in about half the time it had taken them to get to the conference room. Hoping Midge was watching, Jessie pulled the drapes closed.

"What were we saying about romance?" she said, pulling off her knee-high boots.

Smiling, Shane removed his own hiking boots and wet jeans. "I'm not sure, but I'm open to ideas."

He hung his jeans on the hook on the bathroom door and approached Jessie in his underwear, shirt, sweater, and jacket.

"My first idea is that you're going to have to remove some layers," she said, tugging his jacket off and flinging it onto the bed before pulling on his sweater sleeve. "My second idea is that we're going to have to find somewhere other than the bed to pursue any romantic notions we might have."

"I like your thinking," he said, stripping off his shirt before moving toward her and pulling off her sweater.

One piece at a time, they removed the rest of each other's clothes: her sweater, his underwear, her shirt, his socks, her pants and underwear.

"It's cold in here," Jessie said. She shivered, and Shane said, "I guess we're going to spend most of the day under the covers. But first, I think we should warm up with a hot shower."

"I like your thinking," Jessie said, "but will we have hot water if the power's out?"

"Some," he said. "We'll have to be quick."

Heat already pooling between her legs, she wiggled her eyebrows at him. "Let's go."

Within a few seconds, hot water came out of the shower head, and they squeezed into the motel's tiny shower, giggling, both facing the warm spray.

"This is cozier than I expected," Shane said. "Turn around."

Jessie rotated right into his arms, and brought her mouth to Shane's. His tongue slipped between her lips and teased her tongue, and she reached down to stroke him.

"Feels like you're already ready to go," she murmured.

"I am," he said. "But I've got to get you a little more warmed up."

"I like the sound of that," she said.

Taking the soap from the little shelf, he unwrapped it and lathered up, then moved his slippery hands to her breasts, circling her nipples with his thumbs. She pushed her hips toward him, rubbing against his wet shaft as he continued to massage her breasts, his mouth ravishing hers.

"I think I'm ready, too," she told him, and he wasted no time grabbing her hips and lifting her, then sliding her down onto him.

"Oh, yeah," she said as he sighed in pleasure. "I'm definitely ready."

He wrapped an arm around her waist and used his other hand to brace against the shower wall as he moved inside of her once, twice, and a third time.

Without warning, her body let go, an explosion, a wave of rapture that made her weak in the knees. A second later, his body let go, too, and he shuddered against her as the water went cool.

"Just in the knick of time," Jessie said, reaching behind herself to turn off the faucet.

Shane buried his face in her neck, his pleasure still wracking his body.

"Just in the knick of time," he repeated, his voice husky. "And it's already freezing. Let's dry off and go to bed."

Once they warmed up, they got dressed and then sat on the bed and played cards, read books, and talked for the rest of the day. Midge called again at dinnertime to invite them to eat in the conference room and didn't hide her disdain — she looked over her nose at them when they came in, and they spent the meal giggling.

The power came back on just after they returned to their room, and they spent the evening snuggled under the covers watching Christmas movies.

As they prepared for sleep that night, Shane figured that was just about the best day he'd had in forever. He didn't tell Jessie that, because he worried she might not feel the same way, but he drifted off feeling satisfied and content, visions of a future with Jessie dancing in his mind.

The next morning dawned sunny and bright (and frigid: "it's exactly zero degrees Fahrenheit," Midge told them during conference-room breakfast). Crews had cleared the roads, and according to Midge, officials declared travel safe.

Shane felt reluctant to leave the snowed-in cocoon he and Jessie had enjoyed, but also eager to get back to his dad. He and Jessie stopped at the Buffalo gas station to fuel up and get snacks, and then they hit the road. Walls of snow rose up from either side, stacked so high, Shane could hardly read the road signs.

"So, how do you plan to tell your dad about Isabelle?" Jessie asked after they'd driven for a while.

"I thought you'd want to tell him," Shane said, "but either way, I think we should wait until we get a final confirmation that she's coming."

"You're probably right," Jessie said, and Shane gasped, pretending to be shocked. "Did I hear you correctly?"

She swatted his arm and he grinned at her.

"Anyway," he said, "I'm not sure I'm ready to face his disappointment when we tell him the real reason for our trip. I'm pretty sure he thought we were going for a romantic getaway."

"Weren't we?" Jessie asked, all innocence, and Shane felt a stab of hurt.

He wished they'd taken the trip purely for romantic reasons, but he suspected that for her the romance had been a nice side benefit and nothing more.

They reached their halfway point at dinnertime, and had traveled far enough south that everything was dry — not a flake of snow in sight.

"I say we finish the trip tonight," Shane said over dinner. "That way, we can relieve Taylor and Rose of their duties."

Eight hours later, Shane pulled into Jessie's driveway. Leaving the truck running, he grabbed her bag out of the back and carried it to the front door. She gave him a big hug and thanked him again for coming, then added a quick kiss on the lips and went inside. In his bleary-eyed, middle-of-the-night state, Shane told himself not to be disappointed she hadn't given him more than that quick kiss; they'd been together for several days and that shower sex? It was awesome.

Back at home, the front door's hinges announced his arrival. He wasn't surprised to see the table lamp on in the living room (he'd told his dad they'd get in late), but he was surprised to see Alvin sitting in his recliner working on a crossword puzzle ... although his eyelids did look heavy.

"Hey, son," he said. "It's so good to see you. Welcome home." He got to his feet and opened his arms, and Shane stepped into them, more grateful for his dad than ever.

"Thanks, Dad. It's good to be home."

"How was your trip?" Interest had replaced the exhaustion in Alvin's eyes, and Shane laughed.

"It was good. I'll tell you all about it tomorrow. We should both get to bed, though. It's two a.m."

"Two a.m. That was nothing to me fifty years ago, but I suppose those days are gone."

"Same." Alvin raised an eyebrow. "Well, not fifty years ago. More like seven years ago. Come on, let's go to bed."

Once he'd changed into his pajama pants and brushed his teeth, Shane knocked on Alvin's door.

"Come on in, son," his dad called.

Alvin was just turning back his bedding.

"Thanks again for waiting up for me," Shane said, and Alvin smiled. "You're welcome. I admit, you're kind of a closed book, but I'll get the details out of you tomorrow."

Smiling, Shane nodded. "After a good night's sleep for both of us."

He wouldn't share *all* the details, he thought as he closed Alvin's door. He was going to have to come up with enough info to keep Alvin from asking too many questions.

But first, it wouldn't hurt to fantasize about Jessie, just like he had so many times. They were rarely sexual fantasies, although now that they'd gone there, he was positive sex would show up. Typically, he fantasized about the two of them living together: grocery shopping, cooking, watching and discussing movies, going to their favorite community events like arts and crafts shows and Christmas lighting ceremonies and parades, and returning home together. What he wouldn't give to go to sleep next to her every night and wake up next to her every morning.

12

———————

The next morning, Jessie met Taylor, Rose, and Celeste at Rita's. She'd offered to take them to breakfast as thanks for checking in on Alvin while she and Shane were gone.

Within a millisecond of sitting down, she was under fire.

"So. How was it, sleeping in a hotel with Shane?" Taylor demanded.

Celeste's eyes went round. "You guys had two beds, right? A boy and girl can't sleep in the same bed."

"We had two beds," Jessie assured her.

"And how was your slumber party?" Taylor pressed.

Jessie rolled her eyes and looked at her menu as if she didn't have it memorized and know exactly what she was going to order. "Fine."

"Fine?" Rose said. "That's not the rave review I was expecting."

"I heard slumber parties are lots of fun," Celeste said, "but Mommy says I'm too young to have them."

"Maybe in a few years?" Jessie hoped the change in direction would stick.

Celeste shrugged. "Yeah. That's what Mommy says."

"It will be here before you know it," Taylor said. "In fact, maybe we can have a practice slumber party before you have one with friends your age. I'd love to have a sleepover with you."

"Perfect." Celeste nodded and colored in one of the hamburgers on the kids' menu.

To Jessie's relief, Rita chose that moment to come over and take their order.

"The usual?" She snapped her gum.

"Yep," Celeste said. "The usual, all around."

Jessie cursed silently, wishing the ordering process had taken a bit longer. But Rita — her buffer — was already gone.

"Dish," Taylor said, and Rose said, "You can't hold out on us forever."

"The sleepover was great. Despite the cold weather, the hotel room was hot. Like, *so* hot."

"But you couldn't open the windows, could you?" Celeste said. "Because it was snowing."

"Right," Jessie said.

"How are you feeling about Shane at this juncture?" Rose wanted to know.

Again, Jessie stalled. She tucked her tongue into the space between her bottom teeth and her cheek as she slid Celeste's kids' menu closer and took a turn at tic tac toe.

"This is interesting," Rose said to Taylor.

"Certainly is," Taylor said back.

"Real interesting," Celeste said, and Jessie poked her in the ribs, making her giggle.

"The truth is," Jessie said, "I don't know how I feel about him at this juncture."

Rita came back to refill their coffees, and when she left again Rose said, "You can take as long as you want putting cream and sugar in your coffee, and we're still going to be here, waiting for you to answer."

Jessie's chest rose and fell. "I don't know. I mean, I haven't thought about it."

Taylor and Rose shared a glance and an unspoken conversation.

"What are you guys thinking?" Jessie asked.

Celeste pinned her gaze on Rose, then Taylor, and then Jessie. "They're thinking you never want to talk about your feelings."

Rose sat up straighter, and her hand inched toward Celeste's, as if she wanted to stop her from speaking. Jessie guessed that would have been too obvious, because Rose's hand then moved to the back of her neck as she looked at Taylor.

Celeste went on, "Every time you get a boyfriend and things get serious, you bail. I'm not exactly sure what that means."

Jessie's face was on fire. She could literally feel flames on her skin when she looked from Rose to Taylor as Celeste had just done. "You guys spent some time together while I was gone, huh?"

If her ego hadn't been stinging from Celeste's comments, Jessie would have laughed at the twin shrugs her friends did then.

"I mean, we did have dinner," Taylor said. "Before we checked in on Alvin one of the days."

"We brought him food from Rita's," Celeste said.

Jessie remembered one evening when the group had come to Rita's and Celeste had dished on Rose and Mac going on a couple of dates. Rita had called her "a font of information." At the time, Jessie thought that was funny. But here they were, Celeste's information sharing related to *her*, and the situation felt completely different.

"That was really nice of you," Jessie said, giving Celeste's arm a squeeze.

"Thanks," Celeste said. Her attention returned to the maze on her menu, and Jessie looked at her friends again.

"Dish," she said. "What were you saying?"

Taylor lifted a hand, palm up, and tilted her head toward Rose. "I'll give you the floor."

Smiling, Rose rolled her eyes. "Thanks a lot." She cleared her throat. "Um, so, it's basically what Celeste said. Whenever it comes time to talk about your feelings, you shut down. And when it comes to men wanting to talk about your feelings, you turn tail and run. I mean, think about it. How many times have things gotten semi-serious between you and some wonderful guy, only for you to end things?"

Her first instinct was to deny, deny, deny. She even opened her mouth to do just that.

But Taylor held up a hand. "Wait. Before you answer, just think about it. We'll wait."

Both friends stared at her, which made it hard to follow Taylor's suggestion and think about what Rose said. So, she looked at her hands, which rested on the table. Was it true? Did she turn tail and run when things got too emotional? And if it was true, why did she do it?

After a few minutes, Rose said in her gentlest mom voice, "I can see some realization dawning on your face."

Jessie nodded. "You might be right. I guess I need to do some soul searching."

"The thing is," Taylor said, her voice just as gentle, "this is different. This is Shane."

"I know," Jessie said. "We've been best friends for as long as I can remember."

Rose and Taylor exchanged another look and Jessie's stomach fluttered.

"What, you guys?"

"I made Rose go first on the last one, so I'll take this one," Taylor said. "I almost can't believe I am about to spell this out, but you've proven before that you can be kind of oblivious."

Jessie gasped, ready to defend herself, and Taylor held up a hand. Again, Rita's timing was impeccable. She arrived then with a tray and handed out their food, buying Jessie a little time. But not enough.

As soon as she left, Taylor said, "Shane's been in love with you for years, Jess."

"No. That's impossible. That's one of the crazier things I've heard you say." She looked at Rose, assuming she'd take her side, but Rose simply shrugged. "He's not in love with me. We're friends and that's all."

"Explain the slumber parties," Taylor said, her intense eye contact in direct contrast to her casual tone of voice.

Even more heat flooded Jessie's face. She couldn't think of a time she'd ever blushed this hard. "That's just ..." unable to find the words, she took her time buttering her waffle.

"I mean, did it occur to you to wonder why he was so eager to have slumber parties?" Rose said.

"Because slumber parties are *fun!*" Celeste said, helpful as ever. "Will someone cut my pancakes?"

Jessie grabbed Celeste's plate and fork and started slicing, her movements a little more aggressive than necessary.

"I mean," she said, "not really. When we saw him here that first night, it was like a switch flipped."

"For you," Taylor said.

"Right," Jessie said, wondering for the first time whether a switch had flipped for Shane, too, or whether he'd always been attracted to her. "I never even paused to wonder whether he had that same experience or …"

"Or whether he's had the hots for you for, like, ever." Rose said.

"Let's eat," Taylor said.

Jessie looked from one friend to the other and realized the girls were sitting at their spots with their forks and knives in hand, staring at her as if they were trying to help her come to the same realization they had. Mute, she nodded and poured syrup on her waffle. As was tradition, she cut off a piece of waffle and popped it into Celeste's waiting mouth before taking any bites, herself.

Her appetite had decreased. Her stomach felt heavy and full, but she went about eating, anyway, methodically cutting her waffle and eggs and inserting bites into her mouth. Every bite felt like dry cement, but she polished off her food, anyway. Eating less than usual would tip off her friends to the turbulent emotions swirling through her body.

As she chewed and swallowed, she thought about whether they were right. Was it possible that Shane had been in love with her for *years*?

"No," she said, her voice carrying too loudly across the restaurant. She felt her head shaking, of its own accord. Her three companions looked at her like she'd lost her mind. "It's impossible."

"Is it?" Rose said. "Think about what happened before he moved away."

"His friend wanted to open a skydiving business," Jessie said, realization dawning, her ears burning. "And also, I'd just started dating that guy ... what was his name?"

"Godzilla," Celeste said.

Laughter came bubbling out of Jessie's throat. "You guys *did* talk about me while I was gone, didn't you?"

Her friends exchanged another glance.

"That's right," Jessie said. "It was Godrick. You guys did not like him."

"You were completely obsessed with him," Taylor said.

"It was kind of creepy," Celeste said, and Rose shushed her.

"Wow. Your discussions know no bounds," Jessie said, smiling to play off the memory of Godrick breaking things off with her after a couple of dates. "You just don't meet my standards for conversation," he'd said. "I want to go *deep*, Jess." That comment hurt more than the actual breakup, especially because he was right. She'd go deep when it came to sex, but not when it came to conversation.

"It's not that they don't love you," Celeste said, finally looking up from her plate. "It's just that they want you to let your walls down."

"Wow." Jessie was flummoxed by all of this information. "I have walls?"

Another exchanged glance.

"Okay," Jessie said, her shoulders tensing. "Fill me in, here. Explain why you think I have walls."

Both of her friends looked down at the tabletop. Taylor drummed her fingers. Rose spoke first. "I don't know, Jess. It's almost like you refuse to get close to anyone. I mean, even Shane. You told yourself you were close to him, but you didn't even realize he was in love with you. Even now ... I mean, we haven't spent that much time around the two of you, but we saw you at the wedding. He looks at you in exactly the same way he did when we were in high school."

"And how is that?"

"Like," Rose said, drawing out the word.

Taylor cut in, "Like a lovesick puppy dog. He has it bad for you, Jess."

"He doesn't take his eyes off you," Rose said.

"It's like you hung the moon," Taylor said.

"It's like he wants to take off that bridesmaid dress," Celeste said.

That caught all three women off-guard, and Jessie relished in the hoots of laughter and watery eyes of her two friends. For her part, Celeste looked around the table, blinking as if she didn't know what was so funny.

Rita was back with the bill and Jessie grabbed it, excused herself, and followed Rita back to the register to pay.

"How are things going with you and Shane?" Rita asked while cashing her out.

Jessie flung her head back and looked at the ceiling. "Why is everyone talking about Shane?"

Rita shrugged. "Oh, I don't know." She tore the receipt off the machine and set it on the counter for Jessie to sign. Jessie snatched a pen out of the container and scribbled down a tip and a signature. Rita said, "Maybe because everyone has always seen the way he looks at you, and finally we see you looking at him the same way. Well, almost."

"What is that supposed to mean?" she shoved the signed receipt across the counter. Rita took it and tucked it into the spare compartment in the register drawer.

"Oh, only that since he came back this time, you've had hearts in your eyes whenever you're together."

Jessie's gaze remained firmly on the countertop.

"Wait," Rita said. Tucking a finger under Jessie's chin, she lifted gently, bringing their gazes to even. "Don't tell me you never noticed how Shane West looked at you. The whole town of Prescott, Arizona has seen it since the two of you were teenagers."

"The whole town of Prescott, Arizona has gone crazy," Jessie shot back.

She crammed her copy of the receipt into her pocket and hurried back to the table. Although she didn't know why — she was under scrutiny there, too.

Instead of sitting down again, she stood with her thighs against the table and said, "Well, I'm off. I'm beat. Thank you again, so much, for keeping an eye on Alvin while we were gone. Breakfast isn't nearly enough to repay you, especially since we ended up staying an extra day, but I'll make it up to you, I promise."

After a quick ninety-degree turn, Jessie marched out of the restaurant, the girls calling her name from the table. She didn't turn around. Hearing more of their observations would only give her more to think about, and she had plenty already.

As she pushed open the door and the cold air stung her cheeks, she made a plan: she'd go to the grocery store, stock up on drinks and snacks, and hole up in her house alone. All. Day. That would give her time to think without interference.

When she returned home, she carried her chips, candy, and sparkling water inside and organized everything on the kitchen table. Although thinking was absolutely the last thing she wanted to do, she forced herself to sit still and consider what her friends said.

Does Shane really love me?

The idea was almost preposterous. She tore open a bag of chips and took one out, popping it in her mouth. They'd grown up together ... and done everything together while they did: learned to drive, learned to cook, built snowmen, watched movies and TV shows, made forts, did homework.

He was more like a sibling than anything else.

Only, if she were being honest with herself, maybe she'd noticed once or twice that he changed the subject or shut down when she talked about her crushes or upcoming dates. She'd figured he didn't want to talk about those things because he wasn't interested in anyone at the time.

She got up and paced to the refrigerator, removed a seltzer water, and popped it open. Then she paced to the end of the living room.

Had he avoided talking about crushes and dates because he had a crush on her, and he wanted to date her?

It was almost unbelievable.

She stopped pacing and took a drink of the seltzer. She suspended her disbelief, just for a moment. So, Shane had feelings for her — beyond brother-sister, best-friend feelings. Why had he never *said* anything?

This called for candy. Returning to the table, she tore open the

Reese's peanut butter cups package and devoured a cup without even bothering to eat the edges first.

She knew the answer to her own question. He'd never said anything because even if she had erected walls after Ranger Tillman invited her to the homecoming dance as a joke (a cruel, barbarous joke), she'd always seemed totally boy crazy.

From his point of view, she had no interest in him and never would. Until he walked into Rita's the other night looking like a steak on display.

To her surprise, their chemistry was pretty much off the hook. Out of this world. Incredible.

The obvious next item to examine was how *she* felt about *him*. She stopped walking. She loved him. But did she *love* him, love him? Or was she just enjoying their incredible chemistry, no strings attached?

She shoved another handful of chips into her mouth, kept pacing. What if she proposed an experiment? She chewed faster as the idea took hold and picked up the chip bag on her next pass by the table. She could propose that they get together for a certain amount of time just to see what things would be like between them. At the end of that time frame, they could decide whether to stay together or go back to being friends — no hard feelings. She stuffed her hand into the bag for another chip. The idea was either genius or destined to fail.

13

———————

Roman pulled open the door of the airplane and Shane could taste the tang of adrenaline in the back of his throat as the wind rushed in.

"Ready?" his friend yelled.

Shane gave him a double thumbs up, which Roman returned before Shane jumped. The wind roared in his ears as gravity pulled him down, fast, so fast it was hard to breathe. Shane screamed, a loud, uncontrolled scream that drained at least some of the tension from his body. His senses were on high alert. He felt the sting of the cold, 10,000-foot air on his skin, smelled the fabric of his jumpsuit, zeroed in on the formation of the buildings below him. Thought was impossible. He pulled the cord and felt the parachute open, slowing his downward fall abruptly. Now he could think. But he didn't want to. So, he hyper focused on his next step: landing. He took his time, steering himself east and west, making slow, lazy half-circles in the sky. And then the ground came up to meet him. The impact was hard, just painful enough to ensure his brain didn't work for at least the next thirty seconds. Smiling, refreshed, he turned around and scanned the sky for Roman. There he was, just a few meters away, his grin stretched as wide as Shane knew his own was.

"Yeah," Roman shouted once he'd made the landing, his enthusiasm level matching Shane's. "Great jump!"

They threw their arms around each other and whacked each other on the back — a good old-fashioned man hug. After they'd both pulled off their goggles and hoods, Roman said, "Feels good to jump without clients once in a while, doesn't it?"

"It sure as hell does," Shane said. "Man, I needed that."

They gathered up their parachutes and stuffed them back into their bags, then headed for the pickup truck they'd parked near the landing zone earlier.

"Man, that hit the spot."

Roman put the truck in drive and headed for the main office. "I admit, I was surprised when you called to say you'd be back for the day. I thought, with your dad and the girl and everything, I might not see you ever again, let alone in the two weeks you planned."

Shane laughed. "Yeah, I thought the same."

"It was the wedding, wasn't it?" Roman nodded, validating his own prediction.

Shane shook his head before he flexed a bicep and pointed at it. "No, it was these guns."

Once Roman parked at the shop, the two of them got out and hauled in their parachutes. While they repacked them, Shane decided he may as well unload everything on Roman. The guy had been his friend for years and had some serious knowledge when it came to the ladies.

"Bro, I was being serious. These guns have got me in a world of trouble."

Roman looked up from his packing job and quirked an eyebrow at Shane. "Yeah?"

"Yeah. I told you I've had a thing for Jessie for as long as I've known her. And when I got back into town, she practically threw herself at me."

Again, Roman paused to look at Shane. "So, what's the problem?"

Shane sighed. Spending all that time with Jessie had stirred up such a mixture of feelings ... feelings that were difficult to put into words. "I should be happy, right? For all intents and purposes, I got exactly what I always wanted."

Another quirked eyebrow from his friend.

"We had fun. The sex is great. She even called it axis-tilting."

"Atta boy," Roman said.

Shane chuckled. "Thanks. But here's the thing."

"Uh-oh. There's a thing?"

Shane kept working the parachute into the bag. "I'm not exactly sure how to put it into words without sounding all ... emotional."

Roman barked out a chuckle.

"I know she likes me, but I have serious doubts she feels as deeply for me as I do for her."

Finished packing his parachute, Roman covered his eyes with the heels of his hands and tilted his head back. "No," he moaned. "And you're worried, because you feel like a stereotypical girl, in love with some stud who doesn't love you back."

The words should have been offensive, but Shane found himself amused. "Yeah. Pretty much sums it up."

"Look, man. You've got to talk to her. If she has no idea how you feel, she might not tell you how *she* feels."

Shane pondered that for a moment. Could he talk to her? Of course he could. But did he want to? Of course not. Opening the relationship up for discussion was akin to laying his heart on the floor. Jessie could either pick it up, cradle it, treat it with tenderness, or she could stomp on it. The visual made him wince.

"I know what you're thinking," Roman said. "You're thinking that if you tell her how you feel and she doesn't feel the same way, things will be over between you. Not just as lovers, but as friends, too."

"Bingo," Shane said, touching his finger to his nose. "Right on."

Roman put both hands on the countertop and leaned forward, his gaze so intense, Shane was worried about what he might say. "What's your other choice? Break things off? Go on like you are, wondering how long it will last?"

Shane shrugged, then severed eye contact, taking a sudden interest in a stain on the counter, which he tried to scrape off with his thumbnail. "Either of those, I guess."

"What if she says she loves you, bro?

What if she doesn't?

His friend's words still fresh in his mind, Shane started the one-hour drive back to Prescott shortly after hanging up his parachute. He would definitely consider Roman's advice — later. At the moment, he had to focus on his other pressing problem: his dad. The two of them needed to have a serious talk about the living situation. Shane couldn't decide whether to be grateful or resentful that the scenery on the commute between his business and his home wasn't a great distraction. Mostly rolling grassy hills, dotted with oak shrubs and granite boulders, with a few houses sprinkled in.

Alvin was healthy as a horse, Shane thought, but maybe he shouldn't be living alone. Shane could probably convince him to come stay near the business in Cottonwood, although moving out of the house where he lived for years might break his heart. Jessie said she was willing to check on him every day, but they couldn't really expect that of her. Maybe Shane could hire someone to come over, tidy up, make sure Alvin had food in the fridge.

The hour felt like it stretched into two, but it was only lunchtime when Shane drove into Prescott. He didn't feel like cooking, so he parked outside of Rita's and went in to order. The place was pretty busy. Rita and Sal had a decent daily lunch rush from what he could gather. Which meant, he noted with relief, Rita wouldn't have as much time to grill him about Jessie. After ordering, he sat at one end the counter to wait. Sal got up from his spot at the other end and hobbled over to the stool next to Shane's.

"It's nice to have you back in town," Sal said, grunting as he sat. "We've all missed you, especially your dad."

And to think, Shane had hoped to avoid Rita talking about Taylor. Hearing that his dad missed him produced a physical pang of guilt.

"I'm sorry to hear that," Shane said. "I'm really enjoying running my business. But I've also realized I need to spend more time at home."

Sal made a dismissive gesture. "You're a good kid. I didn't mean it like that. I just meant, I'm happy to see you and I'm sure your dad is, too."

"Thanks, Sal."

Shane remembered a time when he'd found Sal intimidating, with his bushy eyebrows, perpetual five o'clock shadow, and gruff voice. But sitting there side by side with the guy, Shane thought he might have a soft interior.

Wiggling those bushy eyebrows Sal said, "Rita tells me you and Jessie finally got together. Eh?" He elbowed Shane. "Not bad. I know you've always had a thing for her."

Pressure built inside Shane's torso. He could explode. He suddenly realized his jaw ached from grinding his molars. "Is it that obvious?" he blurted out. He'd meant to say something like, "Yeah, it's great," or, "I'm not really sure, but I'm holding onto it with whatever I've got."

Sal's chuckle was a deep rumble in his chest. "Okay, okay, I get it. This topic is off-limits."

Shane sighed. "I'm sorry. It's just that all of this is so new, and I don't really know what to make of it just yet."

"You young people," Sal said. "Always trying to define these things. Want my advice?" He didn't wait for Shane to answer before he plowed on. "Just talk to her. Ask her what she thinks. You might be surprised."

Shane bit back a groan.

"That's what happened with Rita and me," Sal said.

"You and Rita?" Shane repeated.

"Yeah," Sal said, drawing out the word. "Man, you should have seen that girl in high school. Prettiest girl you ever laid eyes on. And what was I? Some chess club nerd. Well, I finally got Rita to notice me. She was riding her bike home from school one day, wearing my favorite white jeans. You should've seen those things. Anyway, the chain came off her bike. I was driving by then, you know. Well, when I saw Rita there, bent down, trying to fix that chain, I said to myself, 'Sal, this here is an opportunity. Don't mess it up.' You better believe I pulled over to help her, then and there. You see, that Rita, she knows what she's doing. She didn't want to get any bicycle grease on those white jeans." He paused and looked up at the ceiling, then made the sign of the cross. "I wish she still had those things. Anyway. I digress. She knew how to fix the chain but didn't want to ruin her pants. She figured that if she knelt down and fiddled with it long enough, someone would stop by and help her. That someone was me."

"And the rest is history?"

Sal laughed, a hearty, a head-thrown-back laugh that made the corners of Shane's mouth tilt upward. "No. Not at all. But it put me on her radar. It was months before I gathered up the courage to tell her how I felt. And when I finally did, she laughed in my face."

Shane felt the muscles in his own face go slack with shock. "Why are you telling me this story, Sal?"

"Well, don't you see?" He gestured with one hand, encompassing the restaurant and Rita herself. "Even though she didn't realize she had feelings for me then, she came around. She thought on it and realized she was crazy about me. I only wish I had spoken up sooner."

Again, Shane shook his head. Rita reappeared, sliding Shane's to-go bag across the counter. "Here you go," she said. "Sal is telling you our love story, isn't he?"

"So what if I am?" Sal said. "Kid needs to hear it."

Rita laughed, the sound so free, Shane felt his heart lift.

"It's a great story," Shane said. "Thanks for this." He grabbed the bag and headed out.

Alvin didn't answer his knock on the door when he got home, so he let himself in. He found his dad asleep in his recliner, a blanket draped over his bony frame, his head tilted back and his mouth open. For one horrible second, Shane thought maybe he had died in his sleep. But then a small snore came out, rousing Alvin just enough for him to close his mouth.

After carrying the food into the kitchen, Shane returned to the living room and sat on the couch. He wanted to reach out and touch his dad, to let him know he was here, to convey some of the affection he had for him. Unable to sit still, Shane decided to tidy up, let Alvin sleep a bit longer before waking him for lunch. The kitchen was already squared away — Shane figured Jessie had probably stopped by earlier, when he was at 10,000 feet. The bathroom, too. Alvin kept only the bare essentials and habitually wiped down the counter every night. Energy buzzing through his body, Shane found himself wandering down the hallway and into his dad's office, which wasn't nearly as tidy as the everyday spaces. In fact, it looked like Alvin might have taken a recent trip down memory lane. An open file box sat on the floor next to the desk, and pictures, school papers, awards, and newspaper clippings sat spread across the desk's surface. Curious, Shane sat in the desk chair and picked up the newspaper clipping on top. The headline screamed, *Prescott Duo Wins Countywide Science Fair.*

In the black-and-white picture, Jessie and Shane stood next to their project, grinning at the camera. He could see the little clay pots lined up on the table behind them, a poster with labels and charts standing behind that. The weeks he and Jessie spent working on that project together were some of the happiest in his childhood. They had tested different soils to see if any of them produced bigger plants, faster. They worked together every day, checking the plants, watering them, and recording their growth. At the end of each school day, he'd run up to her, eager to go home and work on the science fair project. And every day, she teased him for being a science nerd. Little did she know, his excitement centered around spending time with her. He could care less about the plants. Although, winning the science fair and being featured on the front page of the newspaper were definitely nice perks.

Shane set aside that clipping and picked up a piece of lined paper. A spelling test from seventh grade. His eyes jumped to the score at the top of the page — ninety percent — and he smiled. Before that test, he'd been a horrible speller. The worst. His English teacher told him that if he didn't bring up the spelling grade, she was going to force him to come to spelling tutoring every week over the summer.

When he shared the news with Jessie, she was outraged. "You will not spend your summer in spelling tutoring," she said. "Starting now, we're going to practice every single day." She kept her word.

She quizzed him daily, and he never got less than a ninety on a spelling test after that.

Jessie was tangled up in so many of Shane's memories. Maybe that's why he was afraid to tell her how he felt. If he did, and she didn't reciprocate, he didn't know if he could bear to be around her. He'd be cutting out a major piece of his life, a thread that ran through everything. Leaving the mementos as they were, Shane went back into the living room. He rubbed Alvin's arm. "Dad," he said. "I'm home. I brought lunch."

His dad blinked a few times as he woke up. When his eyes focused on Shane, he offered him a smile that lit up the room.

"I guess you caught me sleeping," he said.

"I did. Pretty soundly, too. I've been here for a while."

"You could have woken me up sooner. I'm retired. I can sleep any time."

The two of them moved to the kitchen for lunch.

"I was thinking," Shane said.

"Did it hurt?"

It was an old joke, and Shane shook his head, smiling.

"As a matter of fact, it did. What do you think about hiring someone to come check in with you every day? They could pick up around the house, maybe run small errands for you, and make sure you have food in the fridge."

Alvin shook his head. "No, son, that's too much of a bother. I don't need anything like that. Are you telling me I'm getting old?"

Shane debated whether to take a humorous approach but decided against it. "All I'm saying is, Jessie has come over a few times and noticed something amiss. The stove turned on without a flame. You falling down in the driveway, unable to get up. Your refrigerator open and warm."

"Hmm."

"I'm not suggesting a babysitter, or anything," Shane said. "It's more for me than it is for you. I'd give me peace of mind knowing someone is scheduled to stop by every day." He shrugged. "I think it would be good. Peace of mind for you, too. It's so nice of Jessie to come by after work, but it means you're on your own all the way until four p.m."

"I've been on my own for years." Alvin had stopped eating and glared at the space in front of him.

"I know. But you haven't done things like leave the stove on until more recently. That could kill you, Dad."

Shane waited, letting that sink in. Alvin took a bite of his sandwich and after chewing and swallowing, swiped a couple of fries through the ketchup on his plate. After what felt like an eternity, he nodded. "I suppose you're right. But how much is a thing like that going to cost?"

"Don't worry about that. Not only have I gotten more good-looking, but I've gotten richer, too. I can afford it."

"Fine," Alvin said.

And that was that. The conversation went so well, Shane figured he was on a roll. Maybe he should go ahead and talk to Jessie, too. After lunch, he decided. He'd clean up and then head next-door. If she was there, it was meant to be. If not, he'd have to work up the courage another time.

Ten minutes later, he headed out. He made a point of squaring his shoulders and lifting his chin so he looked more confident than he felt. On the inside, his nerves were a tangled mass of yarn. He walked down the walkway and turned onto the sidewalk, only to see Jessie coming toward him, a smile on her face.

I love her.

She waved. "Just the guy I was hoping to see."

Shane made a show of looking all around them.

She laughed, and he said, "Me?"

"Yes, you. Can we talk?"

14

———————

What timing. No sooner had Jessie decided to talk to Shane and headed for his house than he came out, presumably headed for hers. When she asked if they could talk, she saw a flickers of surprise and then doubt in his eyes. Overcome by a desire to put him at ease, she grabbed his shoulders and rubbed his arms. "It's nothing bad!"

"Well, that's a relief," he said, the lines between his brows smoothing out. "In that case, we can talk. But let's do it inside because it's cold out here. And at your place, because my dad's home."

Inside the front door, they took off their jackets and hung them on the coat tree. That small act of domesticity felt so significant in that moment, Jessie had the chills.

"Want a drink?" she asked.

"Whatcha got?"

"I have a couple of sodas in the fridge." She looked at her watch. "And since it's officially afternoon, I have a couple of beers, too, I *think* a little vodka if you want something harder."

He cocked his head. "Do I?"

She wondered if he could read the sudden fear in her expression. "A beer should do it."

She got out the bottles and opened them, noticing her hand shook slightly as she handed one to Shane. They tapped the necks of the bottles together and even as they said, "Cheers," Jessie wondered why her chest felt fluttery.

Maybe because, if this doesn't go as planned, you lose your best friend.

Shane settled on a barstool. He leaned forward, putting his elbows on the counter, drawing attention to his massive muscles. Deciding she'd rather sit next to him than across from him — looking into his eyes might be too much — she came around and sat.

"So?" he said. "What you want to talk about?"

Well. He was going to jump right into things.

Jessie nodded. "I want to talk about us."

He froze, almost imperceptibly, the bottle halfway to his lips. He went into motion again immediately, but she didn't miss that pause.

"What about us?"

Jessie realized she was holding her breath and took a gulp of oxygen. "Well, I should start out by saying that you're my best friend." Another almost imperceptible movement: his shoulders slumped, just the tiniest bit, before he straightened them again.

She suppressed a laugh. "I don't want anything to come between us."

Shane nodded but left the air clear for her to continue.

"When you came home this time," she started. She fidgeted with the label on the beer, noticing the way her fingernail polish complemented the logo. She cleared her throat. "It seemed like things changed."

For the first time, Shane's reaction wasn't subdued. His bark of laughter echoed in the quiet house. "Well, that's true."

Despite her nerves, Jessie felt herself smiling. "As surprised as I am, I've also really enjoyed our time together."

She looked at him, gauging his reaction. He raised one eyebrow and she added, "Both in the bedroom and out of it."

He laughed again. "That's good to know."

Suddenly desperate to hear whether he had enjoyed it, too, she elbowed him. "Have *you*?" She hoped he heard the humor and not the fear.

"Can't you tell?" There was an edge to his voice, one she wasn't sure she liked.

She swallowed the sudden thickness in her throat.

"I can tell." After a few beats of silence, she said, "I was thinking."

"Did it hurt?" Shane asked.

Smiling, she said, "I'll tell you, it felt foreign."

"What were you thinking?"

Jessie spun her bottle on the countertop, watching as the condensation made a swirly pattern. She blew out a breath. "I can't believe how hard this is to say."

Shane grabbed her elbow. She dared to make eye contact.

"Jessie. I've never known you to have trouble saying exactly what you're thinking. In fact, sometimes I think life would be easier for you if speaking up was a little more difficult for you."

She offered him a weak half-smile. "You might be right. But this is different."

That statement seemed to ratchet up Shane's nerves. He let go of her elbow and took a big swig of his beer. "Go ahead and lay it on me. We'll both feel better once it's out there."

She nodded. Took another sip of beer. Wished she felt certain. "I'm just going to say it."

"I wish you would."

"I've been thinking."

He grinned. "So you said."

"We've always been the best of friends."

Nodding, Shane said, "Go on."

"And, recently, we've been more than that."

The sound of Shane's swallow was loud in the near silence. His Adam's apple bobbed. She was making him nervous. God, she really needed to put them both out of their misery. The words came tumbling out of her mouth in a rush. "I've really enjoyed it, and I was wondering if you might want to, you know, try out being more than friends. Like, on an experimental basis."

Shane's gaze, which had been stuck firmly on his beer bottle, met Jessie's. She almost laughed at his deer-in-the-headlights-expression.

"Are you serious?" he asked.

She wished she could climb inside his body and feel his emotions. Was he hopeful? Awkward? On the spot?

"I mean, yeah. Our chemistry is pretty good, isn't it?"

"Some might even call it axis-tilting."

"Exactly." She could hear the *whoosh* of blood as her pulse quickened. "I know it's kind of awkward because we've been friends all this time. And I know you probably weren't expecting me to say anything. This is an awful lot like talking about my feelings. You don't even live in town anymore. You're worried about your dad. And also —"

Shane stood, making the barstool scrape as it scooted back. He grabbed Jessie's hands and pulled her to standing while simultaneously using his foot to scoot her barstool back, too. His hands were in her hair, and his mouth was on hers, tender but certain. He ended the kiss but kept his forehead on hers and looked into her eyes. "I would like that. Very much."

Jessie could breathe again. "Good. When should we start?"

"How about now?"

She nodded, and he gave her one more quick kiss before sitting back down.

"I do think we might want to talk about what this looks like, though," he said.

Knees weak, she sank down onto her barstool. "We should. What do you think?"

"It might be fun to go on actual dates."

Jessie nodded. "Dates sound fun."

"And obviously, I'd like us to be exclusive, for now."

"Absolutely. So would I."

"And I know this might be impossible," he said, "but can we agree that if things don't work out, we can still be friends?"

Filling her lungs with air, Jessie mentally crossed her fingers. She sure as hell hoped so. "Of course."

"What would our first date be?" Shane wanted to know.

"I don't know."

They both sat quietly for a while, until Shane said, "Let me surprise you."

Jessie's stomach jolted, like one of those plasma balls that shoot static electricity to someone's finger when they touch it. "Surprise me?"

"Yeah," Shane said. "You love surprises."

Jessie did love surprises, but she wasn't sure how she felt about a surprise in this particular area. She hadn't heard much about his dating life. What if he planned something she hated?

What is wrong with you? Jessie could kick herself. She didn't have to be the one to plan every single thing.

"Sure," she said. "You can surprise me."

"Wait," Shane said. "I feel like that was a 'sure,' like, 'I-don't-actually-like-this-idea-but-I-feel-like-I-have-to-say-yes.'"

One drawback to dating someone you'd known forever, Jessie realized in that moment, was that he'd be able to read your every thought. That could come in handy — or not.

"No it wasn't!" Jessie lied. "You can surprise me. It'll be fun."

He looked at her sideways but said, "That's settled. When should we go?"

"How about this weekend?" Jessie said. "A weekend seems like a good time to go on a date."

"Perfect. Now that that's out of the way, have you heard from Isabelle?"

Jessie shook her head. "Not yet. But it's only been a couple of days. I wouldn't have expected her to call just yet."

"Wouldn't it be fun if she came before Christmas?"

His expression was so dreamy, Jessie laughed. "Have you always been this much of a romantic?"

"You ain't seen nothing yet," he said to her, eyes crinkling at the corners.

God, he was cute.

Standing, he picked up both their beer bottles and threw them away. "Although I'd love nothing more than to stay here and explore what our new official 'dating' title means, I'd better get going. My dad's expecting me back. Game day. I forgot how much I enjoy watching football with him."

"Okay," Jessie said, disappointment like a firehose on her excitement. "Meanwhile, I'm looking forward to this weekend."

She took her time admiring his broad shoulders and trim waist and the way he filled out his jeans as she followed him to the entryway. She nearly salivated. Somehow, the fact that they were dating, and she had implied permission to ogle him made him even more appetizing.

Shane put his hand on the doorknob, then dropped it.

"Wait," he said, turning around. "Since we're dating, does that mean I get to kiss you hello and goodbye?"

"Absolutely," Jessie said, her body vibrating with anticipation as he closed the distance between them and brought his mouth to hers, intertwining his fingers with hers. She sighed into the contact, her body warming up and becoming pliable, and the heat rushing to her core. Lifting one hand, he cupped her breast and ran a thumb over her nipple.

She moaned. "I wish you didn't have to go."

He flashed her a smile and opened the door. "I'll text you tonight to make a plan for our date."

He was gone and only in his absence did she realize she hadn't even asked him why he was heading toward her house when she met him on the sidewalk.

15

"Everything okay?" Alvin asked when Shane walked back into the house.

"Yeah, everything's great." He could still feel Jessie's lips on his, warm and greedy.

"You weren't gone very long." His dad sat in his recliner, his newspaper folded in half so he could work on his crossword puzzle.

Shane sat on the couch and turned on the TV. "I know. I wanted to get back to watch the football game with you."

"That's right. Starts any minute now, doesn't it?"

Picking up the remote, Shane said, "It does. Kickoff is in ten. Maybe we can catch some of the pregame."

He turned on the TV and found the game. His dad scratched his head, puzzling over the crossword. Apparently unable to come up with the answer he needed, he swore and set down the newspaper, quite forcefully, on the table.

"Think the Cardinals can pull off a win today?" Shane asked.

Alvin had always followed Arizona's football team. He knew all the players, stats, and how likely they were to win.

He shrugged. "Hard to say. We just got this new QB. He's untested. So, I guess we'll just have to see how he does."

Shane settled back onto the couch and propped his feet on the coffee table. He enjoyed watching the games, but his interest level was just a fraction of his dad's. While Alvin knew every statistic and up-to-the-minute injury reports, Shane's "following" of the team meant he had a general idea of whether they were having a good season (and he wasn't always right). As the announcers discussed the new quarterback and the team's chances for victory, Shane let his mind shift over to Jessie ... and planning their first official date. They'd already done so much together. Shane wanted this new phase of their relationship to be special. Memorable. If he played his cards right, maybe he could get Jessie to see that they were meant for each other.

Shane watched the TV screen absently. A youth choir sang the national anthem and belted out the last note. The football players put on their helmets, jumped around, and smacked each other on the back, and Shane considered his options. He and Jessie had grown up in their small hometown and while they had gone to many of the local restaurants, coffee shops, and events, new places popped up all the time.

Rita's diner was definitely out. He chuckled at that. No way would he and Jessie have the privacy to explore their feelings for one another. The Cardinals won the coin toss and set up for kickoff. Shane reached for his phone and texted Roman. *I'm taking Jessie on a real date. What should I do?*

Roman sent back a gif of a teenage boy doing a celebratory dance, confetti fluttering in the air. And nothing else.

Come on, man. I need advice.

Roman wrote, *Don't you see what an incredible advantage you have here? You know this girl so well. Better than anyone else, it sounds like. You should be able to come up with something delightful.*

Shane smirked at Roman's use of "delightful." Was he going for *delightful*? He didn't even know.

You've been to Prescott, he typed. *Where would you take a date?*

Roman sent back an eye-rolling emoji and then, *What's your end goal? I mean, if I wanted to show a girl a good time, I might take her out to play pool and get drinks. If I wanted to send best-friend vibes, I would take her to a sporting event.*

Blushing even though they weren't face to face, Shane wrote back, *But if you wanted to show her you were madly in love with her and convince her she felt the same way?*

He must have stumped his friend my because the typing bubble appeared, disappeared, and reappeared.

Finally, Roman's response showed up: *I don't know man. That's a lot of pressure. I'm going to have to think about this.*

Great. Shane had hoped for a quick expert answer. The game was well into the first quarter. No one had scored, but the Cardinals had gotten a first down on the kickoff.

Maybe instead of starting with a place to eat with Jessie, he should start with a thing to do. He used his phone to search for upcoming local events. There were all the usual things — the courthouse lighting, the light parade, the gingerbread village — and there were also some new things he hadn't seen before. The holiday selfie stroll caught his eye. He tapped to bring up the website and explored the different selfie stations. Jessie was always taking pictures. She would absolutely love something like that. And after a drink or two, he'd be relaxed enough to enjoy it as well.

So. Drinks first, then. Dinner after. He'd never planned a three-part date with someone he didn't know, but he felt pretty safe doing so with Jessie. Romance or not, they always had a good time together.

"You're not even watching the game, kid," Alvin said, grabbing his newspaper, rolling it up, and bopping Shane on the foot.

Looking up from his phone, Shane said, "You're right. You know why I went to Jessie's earlier?"

"Nope. I figured it was for some nookie."

Shane leapt up, grabbed the rolled-up newspaper from his dad, and whacked him on the head with it, repeatedly.

Laughing and using his arms to defend against the attack, Alvin said, "What? You're a young man and she's a young woman. Now you know why I commented you weren't gone long."

"Oh my God," Shane said, tossing the paper back onto the table. "My own dad."

"What, son? We're both adults, right? We can talk about this stuff."

Shane sank down onto the couch and put his face in his hands. "No, we can't. I went to her house, Dad, to talk to her about my feelings. Just like you've been saying I should."

Alvin raised his eyebrows.

Shane lifted his head and went on. "And when I was halfway there, who comes down the sidewalk but Jessie. She asked if we could talk, and guess what she wanted to talk about?"

"Nookie?"

"Dad."

"Sorry."

"She wanted to ask if I'd be willing to give things a go ... as a couple."

"That's nice. But did you tell her how you feel?"

It wasn't the reaction Shane expected. He expected his dad to be thrilled. Throw his arms in the air and cheer. Clap him on the back.

"Well, no," Shane said, looking down at his hands, which he'd clasped between his knees.

"Why ever not?"

"I guess I figured, maybe it wasn't necessary since she was asking if I wanted to try dating," Shane said, his confidence deflating.

"Huh," Alvin said.

"What does that mean?" Shane felt his eyebrows pressing together.

"It means, my boy," Alvin said, his eyes intense on Shane's, "that you're going into this dating thing with one foot out the door."

"Huh," Shane said. Then, after a pause: "Self-preservation."

On the TV, the crowd cheered. Both men looked at the screen to see the Cardinals celebrating a touchdown.

"I guess our new QB might be okay after all," Alvin said.

The Cardinals went for the extra point and the kick was good. Alvin pumped a fist.

"Geez, you reacted more strongly to that extra point than you did to my announcement," Shane told him.

Alvin harrumphed. "I just wished you'd talked to her, that's all."

"Well, I didn't," Shane said. "And we're going on a date this weekend, which is why I'm on my phone. I want to plan something that will knock her socks off."

"And the rest of her clothes?"

Shane met Alvin's self-satisfied smirk with a glare, which only made him laugh harder.

"I'm not talking to you about that."

"Fine. What are you planning?"

"I'll let you know when I know," Shane said, cringing a little at the petulance in his voice.

"Great," Alvin said. "You do that."

He stood up, took the remote off the coffee table, and turned up the TV volume. The Cardinals' opponents, the Ravens, had possession of the ball, and Shane watched their run for a few minutes before returning to his research.

Drinks. He already knew he didn't want to go to any of the old haunts. He wanted to give this phase of their relationship a fresh start. Another round of searching revealed a new downtown bar, With a Twist. He was hooked when he found its social media account boasted a new lineup of holiday cocktails.

Next up: dinner.

The Cardinals intercepted the football. Alvin cheered again.

Before he could even begin his next Internet search, Shane remembered he'd always wanted to try the restaurant at the fancy resort that sat on a hill overlooking Prescott. He imagined sitting with Jessie at a table next to a giant window, looking down on the sparkling lights of the city. Talk about romance.

Although he had no idea if the restaurant actually put candles on the tables, he envisioned them flickering, illuminating Jessie's deep, chocolatey eyes and dancing on the curves of her breasts. She might be disappointed the swanky restaurant wasn't the type of place where a person ordered a burger, but she could order a steak. A nice one.

In his mind's eye, she speared a perfectly cooked piece of steak with her fork and put it in her mouth. Her lips closed over it.

Oh, boy.

He'd better stop picturing close-up views of Jessie's mouth, especially when he was sitting just a couple of feet from his dad. He cleared his throat. His dad looked over at him, gave him a thumbs up. Shane glanced at the TV and realized the thumbs up was related to another touchdown for the Cardinals. He returned the gesture and his dad grinned.

When he moved out a few years ago, eager to pour absolutely everything into his new skydiving business, he'd believed he would be so busy, he wouldn't even have time to miss his dad, his hometown, or Jessie. And hadn't that been the point? To distance himself from Jessie so he wouldn't feel the repeated sting of her lack of feelings for him?

Only, in distancing himself from her, he'd distanced himself from his dad.

"You know, I think I'm going to make some nachos," Alvin said then, interrupting Shane's thoughts.

"We just ate lunch," Shane said.

"Bah," Alvin said. "We ate lunch an hour ago. And besides, nachos are tradition. How often do I have my boy here for football games anymore?"

Shane held up his hands in surrender.

"You hang tight," his dad said. "Watch the game. I'll be right back."

Nostalgia made his eyes burn. He didn't know how many more football seasons his dad would be here, how many more plates of nachos they'd eat, how many more touchdowns they'd celebrate.

Instead of watching the game as his dad suggested, he went into the kitchen where his dad stood at the stove cooking meat, took out a baking sheet, and started arranging the tortilla chips.

"Hey," Alvin said. "I thought you were going to watch the game."

"I decided to come give you a hand."

"Worried I might set the house on fire?"

"Or blow something up," Shane said, elbowing his dad. "Just kidding. Nah, I just figured, if I helped assemble while you cooked the meat, we could get these in the oven sooner, so you didn't miss as much."

"That was awful nice of you."

"I'm a nice guy."

"You learned from the best."

The meat was done. Alvin spread it onto the chips, and they added the cheese and beans before Shane put the baking sheet in the oven. They high-fived and went back to the living room. It was halftime by then, and the announcers were discussing the first half of the game. Alvin used the remote to turn down the volume.

"What are you doing?" Shane said. "You always want to hear what the commentators have to say."

"I'd rather hear what you have to say," Alvin said. "About your date." He wiggled his eyebrows.

"Dad, I told you, I'm not going to talk to you about —"

"Not about that!" Alvin said. "Every time I looked over at you during the first quarter, you were on the phone, staring at the screen like your life depended on it." Shane wondered if he'd really looked that intense, or if Alvin might be exaggerating. "If you must know, I thought we would do drinks, then a selfie stroll, then dinner."

His dad's face contorted. "A selfie stroll? What in God's name is that?"

Shane explained, doing his best to make the selfie stroll sound interesting. When he was done, Alvin guffawed. "Kids these days. And all these newfangled things you want to do. Back in my day, if you took a girl out, you went to the diner. Dancing, maybe. The roller rink. And the two of you are going to go for a selfie stroll." He shook his head.

"Thanks, Dad. Not only have you succeeded in tearing down my confidence about what I thought was a fun and unique date idea, but you also managed to make it sound like the world is ending."

"The world is definitely changing, that's for sure," Alvin said. "And don't let my opinion affect your confidence. The selfie stroll sounds like something Jessie will love. She's always showing me pictures on her phone. I think it's a good choice. Weird, but good."

Shane gave his dad a side-eye and said, his tone sarcastic, "Thanks a lot."

Unperturbed, Alvin said, "You're welcome, son. Think the nachos are done?"

They were, and Shane brought them out. Alvin moved to the couch and they both ate right off the baking sheet.

When they were full, Shane put the nachos in a container, which he labeled with the date. He washed the baking sheet, dried it, and put it away. Then, before he went back into the living room, he leaned against the counter and texted Jessie: *Okay, I have a plan for our date.*

She responded right away. *Ooh, the intrigue.*

Let's plan on leaving Saturday at 5, he typed.

Again, Jessie's response came through immediately. *5? What are we, 80?*

It was something one best friend would say to another, but it also took away from the romance, at least a little, for Shane. He shook off the slightly offended feeling and told himself not to be too sensitive. Still, he felt like he had to explain: *I want to get an early start. I have a lot planned. We're doing drinks first, like a happy hour.*

She wrote back, *Ooh, the intrigue. What should I wear?*

Shane smiled at the possible answers. *Wear something festive.*

She sent back a thumbs up. Shane tucked his into his back pocket and returned to the living room. "Fourth quarter already?"

His dad smiled up at him. "Yep. And I think we're going to get a win. I don't know if it's our new QB or those awesome nachos. You think we brought them luck?"

"I'm sure we did, Dad," Shane said. "We'll have to go back to eating nachos and watching football more often."

16

────────

An hour before her date with Shane, Jessie sent out an SOS
to her friends: *I have no idea what to wear tonight.*

Taylor wrote back, *What are you talking about? Shane
has seen you in just about every kind of outfit. Wear something that makes
you feel confident.*

Jessie moved a few more tops along the rod in her closet, then
groaned and threw her head back. Taylor was right. Shane *had* seen
her in pretty much every kind of outfit. But the whole point of this
exercise was for their relationship to feel different than it had before.

"Maybe a change of perspective is in order." She was thinking
about this all wrong. She was thinking about Shane as her friend
and hangout buddy first, and Shane as her date second.

"Let's shake things up, Monroe," she told herself. "Imagine it's
your first date — with someone other than your best friend." With
an encouraging nod she continued scooting hangers down. When
her hand landed on the shoulder of an ice blue cashmere sweater,
she froze, lifted it off the rod, and examined it. "Yes."

She loved that sweater. Typically, she'd never wear it out with
Shane — it was too soft, too feminine. It showed off too much
cleavage and hugged her waist too tight.

But ... she thought back to how Shane had looked at her when he saw her in the bridesmaid dress at Taylor's wedding. Differently. Like she was some kind of seductress, not his best friend. That's how she wanted him to look at her tonight.

Even better, if she paired the sweater with her sparkly snowflake earrings and necklace, it would be festive. She added a pair of faux leather pants that hugged her curves and left almost nothing to the imagination.

With the outfit selection out of the way, Jessie breezed through her getting ready routine. She took the time to blow her hair dry, straighten it, then add in some nice, wavy curls instead of throwing it into a ponytail or messy button. And, even though Shane had seen her bare-faced a million times, she put on makeup she knew high-lighted her best attributes.

All ready, she stood in front of the mirror and decided she was pleased with the finished product. If her goal was to turn on her suitor, she would do it. She gave herself one mist of perfume before double checking her purse and going back to the kitchen to wait. Shane's knock sounded shortly thereafter, about three minutes before he said he'd be there. Just like she would for any other date, she took a deep, calming breath before opening the door.

Shane took her breath away. He wore a thin wool sweater that showed off every ripple and every muscle in his arms, chest, and stomach. His snug jeans, too, accentuated the strength in his legs. After she'd given him a thorough once over, her eyes met his. She never would have imagined thinking Shane's expression was smoldering — especially when it was directed at her — but there they were. And it was.

"You look nice," he said. He put a hand on her upper arm and ran it up to her shoulder. "Soft." The simple, innocent contact felt like pure desire on her skin. "I get to kiss you hello, right?"

Breathless, all Jessie could do was nod.

This kiss was all gentle, simmering heat and Jessie trembled, warring with the desire to unbuckle his belt and have her way with him.

"Hello," he said, his lips still touching hers.

"Hello back."

He stepped back, checked his watch, and jingled his keys in his pocket. "We'd better go."

She groaned in frustration, and he laughed, leading her out to the car.

"Are you going to tell me where we're going yet?"she asked as they pulled into a parking spot a while later.

"Not yet. I want to walk up and get the full effect. Wait here. I'll get your door." While she waited, Jessie realized she was having fun. More fun than she'd ever had on a first date. No one had ever put in the effort to surprise her, and knowing Shane had planned the whole evening with her in mind sent a little pleasant rush of shivers over her skin. He opened her door and offered a hand. Then he helped her into her jacket before putting on his. He offered his arm, and she took it, appreciating the chivalrous gesture.

"The air has quite a bite, doesn't it?"

"It does," she said. "I hope you planned an indoor activity."

"Don't try to dig for info," he said, shooting her an exaggerated dirty look.

"I'm not!" She laughed. "I'm just saying."

She snuggled closer, enjoying not just his body warmth, but also the feel of his rock-hard bicep against her palm. They were both smiling when Shane came to a stop in front of a set of glass doors.

"Ooh," Jessie said, "With a Twist." She paused. "Clever, Shane. Because this—" she pointed at him and then at herself — "is a twist."

"I hadn't thought of that, but you're right. My reason for coming here was more straightforward. It's a new place and they're offering holiday cocktails."

She felt her eyes light up. "That sounds amazing!"

His face lit up, too, in response to her enthusiasm. "I thought so." He opened the door and gestured for her to go in.

The first thing she noticed was that everything sparkled. The floor was polished to a sheen, and a mirrored bar and liquor cabinet reflected shimmering chandeliers. She glanced at Shane. and could literally see his shoulders relax.

"Is it cool?"

"Absolutely," she said, and his shoulders relaxed.

She slid her arms under his jacket and wrapped them around his waist. "I love it."

"Want to sit at the bar? Or at one of those tables along the wall?"

Jessie and Shane, the *friends,* would have sat at the bar and chatted up the bartender. But they were Jessie and Shane, the lovers.

"Let's get a table."

As early as it was, the place wasn't too busy and they had their choice, which ended up being a high-top in the corner. A holiday menu sat in the center. Jessie picked it up and instead of waiting for her to finish reading it, Shane came around to stand behind her, nibbling at her neck and sending tingles down her spine.

"I'm going to get a candy cane cooler," she said. "And then we're going to have to find a dark and secluded place."

He kissed her just below her ear and returned to his seat. "The candy cane cooler looks good. I'm going to try the mistletoe mule. And as much as I like the sound of finding a secluded place, I'll have to take a rain check. We have a reservation in ninety minutes."

Jessie's gaze sharpened. "Ooh, a reservation? Is that a clue?"

"No," he said. "Don't try to guess, either."

Snickering, she set down the menu and looked into his eyes. He really did have nice eyes. "Fine."

"Fine," he said. "Want to save the table and I'll order our drinks?"

"Sure," she said, enjoying that he didn't mind waiting on her. She watched him go, once again admiring the sculpted statue of a man he'd become. As he waited for the bartender to take his order, Jessie pretended she was seeing him as if they'd just met and were on a *real* first date. His movements were easy and confident, and those attributes translated to the smile he flashed at a woman on a barstool. The woman smiled back, and Jessie felt an unexpected flash of jealousy. No need, though, because he turned around then and the grin he sent her across the bar spoke to her heart. Her heart answered, pounding out a greeting.

He returned a few minutes later with their drinks.

"To the grand experiment," she said, lifting hers.

He tilted his head toward her. "Cheers."

They took sips of their drinks and then sat there, looking at each other. For the first time ever in their relationship, Jessie couldn't think of something to talk about. She panicked. Was that because they were on an official date?

"I'm not used to you being this quiet," Shane said.

Taking a sip of her drink, Jessie said, "I'm not used to being this quiet."

"Is it because we're on a date? Not just out as friends?"

The fact that he could practically read her mind brought her a sense of comfort. "I think so. I feel all this pressure to talk about something different. Something date-like."

Shane reached across the table and took her hand. "Don't. It's just the two of us, having a conversation over drinks. Except, for the first time since I've known you, I feel like you dressed up, just for me. You did your hair and makeup, just for me. You're radiant, just for me. So, I'm sitting here feeling pretty damn special."

The warm and gooey feeling Jessie experienced had nothing to do with the candy cane cooler. "You're sweet," she said, suddenly shy. She cleared her throat. "Actually, I'd love to hear more about your business. Since you moved away, I feel like we hardly talk anymore. Your dad says Jump Zone is doing great."

An unidentifiable emotion passed over Shane's features. He cleared his throat. "It is doing great. I'm sure you remember I have a business partner, Roman."

"I remember." She would never admit to Shane that she remembered every detail Alvin told her. Even if Shane was too busy to call or text, she kept tabs on him.

"We work really well together," Shane said. "We met when we were both getting certified to skydive. We became great friends and after a few beers one night, we decided to start a business. What began as kind of a crazy idea turned into what's basically become the focal point of my life."

The focal point of my life. Did his life have room for her?

"I love that," Jessie said. "Do you still enjoy jumping?"

"Oh yeah. I ran over there last week to do a quick jump with Roman. I love taking out clients, being with them while they experience their first jump or subsequent jumps. Seeing them feel the thrill. But sometimes it's nice to go up there, just the two of us, and do everything at our own pace. Jumping, you know, it's the only thing that clears my head."

Why did he need to clear his head? She wanted to ask but wasn't sure she was ready to hear the answer. "That sounds amazing. I'll bet it's a rush."

"It is. More than anything I've ever done. Well, almost anything."

Just like they had when he picked her up that evening, his eyes smoldered. Her body, which had developed a mind of its own, went molten at the memory of their lovemaking in the hotel after Taylor's wedding.

"I'm jealous," she said, desperate to move the conversation forward so she'd stop thinking about sex. "Do you think you could teach me to skydive?"

His face lit up. "I'd love to. That's one thing we haven't done together, isn't it?"

"It is," she said. "Maybe for our third date." Before he could ask, she added, "I'm planning our second."

He smiled. "You're going to have a lot to live up to."

They'd finished their drinks, and Jessie offered to get the second round. Shane wanted a cranberry crisp, and Jessie decided she'd go for a gingerbread mulled cider. The bar had gotten busier, and she squeezed into a space to order. Before she could get the bartender's attention, a man waved her over from a couple spots down.

"This round's on me," he said, and smiling, Jessie said, "No, thanks. I'm actually buying this round for my date and me."

The man scoffed. "Why isn't he over here buying them? Honey, you've got to get yourself a quality man. What can I order for you?"

She moved down the bar and away from the stranger. Instead of waiting around for the bartender to notice her, she waved wildly and ordered their drinks. At the other end of the bar, the stranger watched her. Turning her back to him, she asked the bartender about the most popular holiday drinks, and as soon as theirs were ready, she snatched them up and returned to the table.

"Cheers to strangers in strange places," she said as she handed Shane his drink.

"Cheers," he said. "I take it that guy hit on you?"

"He did. But don't worry. He was creepy."

"Cheers to creepy guys at bars."

They each took another drink.

"How's teaching?" Shane asked then.

"Same as always." She smiled, sipped her drink, which tasted exactly like gingerbread with its warm spices. "I love the kids. Love the school. It's still my dream job, and I also love winter break."

"I still remember you making me play school when we were kids," he said.

She covered her eyes with one hand. "Don't remind me. I was so bossy."

"I loved it," he confided. "I'd never admit it back then, but the way you bossed me around reminded me of the way I heard your mom boss around your dad. And it seemed like they really loved each other."

"Really?"

If she wasn't mistaken, Shane's cheeks were looking a bit rosy. He broke eye contact and stared into his drink as if it contained the secret answers to all of life's biggest questions.

"Yeah," he said. "But I shouldn't have told you. I don't want to make this conversation awkward."

"It's not," Jessie said. "It's kind of cute. And now that I know you like me being bossy, maybe I'll be bossy more often."

Shane shrugged. "Suit yourself. Doesn't mean I'll listen to you."

They grinned at each other.

"Shit," Shane said, checking his watch. "We'd better get going if we're going to make our reservation on time."

Jessie threw back her drink, draining her glass, and took his arm as they walked out of the bar.

"Are we driving?" she asked once they were outside. The frigid air stung her nose.

"We're walking," he said. "Just a couple of blocks."

Jessie glanced around Prescott's quaint downtown and felt a

squeal of excitement rise up inside her body and erupt from her mouth. "This is so much fun," she said. "I mean, the lights on the courthouse and in the trees and on the buildings. It's all so festive. And we're here, together, taking it all in. Did you plan this part of it, too?"

Beaming, Shane said, "I did, actually."

She squeezed his arm. "You're a pretty romantic guy."

"I've actually never heard that from a woman before."

"Are you serious?"

"No," he said. "I've been known to be romantic."

"Why didn't you ever tell me about these romantic schemes? I would have loved to hear about them."

His silence caught her off guard, and her curiosity grew as they walked on and he didn't speak. Finally, he said, "I don't know, really."

The answer wasn't juicy as she'd expected it to be. Something in the air between them had shifted, though. Shane steered her up to a set of doors just then, so she didn't have time to delve into what.

"What's this?" she asked as he pulled open one of the doors.

"Wait and see."

Inside, the atmosphere felt festive. A bench sat on either side of the entry, adorned with Christmas pillows. A brightly lit and ornament-laden tree stood in one corner. Front and center, a woman stood behind a desk, atop which sat a few miniature Christmas trees, glittery and twinkling. The woman herself was decorated, too: she wore reindeer antlers and huge ornament earrings.

"Good evening," she said. "How may I help you?"

Jessie found Shane's bright smile adorable. "We have a reservation at six-thirty."

"Shane West?"

He nodded.

"Right on time," she said. "Follow me. I'll get you going on props."

"Props?" Jessie whispered to Shane as the woman swept open a heavy curtain behind the desk.

He shrugged as if he had no idea what she was talking about and gestured for Jessie to go in ahead of him. In the next room, hat racks, clothing racks, and storage trunks lined three walls, and a table with a lighted mirror stood against the fourth.

"Welcome to the Holiday Selfie Stroll," the woman said. "We're so glad you're here. First stop: props. Choose some props you'd like to wear throughout your stroll. These are just to get you started. As you pass through the various stops, you'll find more props available. My colleague, Janine, will be here in about five minutes to give you instructions and take you to the first stop." Still smiling brightly, she gave them a nod and exited through the curtain.

When Jessie turned to Shane, she could tell he was waiting for her reaction. She gave him one — another loud squeal — before running at him and jumping into his arms.

"This is so much fun," she shouted, before realizing her voice was probably way too loud, as close to his ear as it was. She apologized and extracted herself from his embrace.

"You really think so?" he asked, his eyebrows raised.

"I do," she said. "I love it! This is perfect for me! You know I love taking pictures! And we'll have all these souvenirs. What a great idea!"

Shane mimed wiping his brow.

"You're silly. You know me better than most people. You had to know I'd love it."

He mimed wiping his brow again.

"Let's pick out our props," Jessie said. After a brief pause, she raised her pointer finger. "Wait. I have an idea. You pick mine, and I'll pick yours."

"Sounds like a plan," Shane said.

At the end of the five minutes, Shane had chosen a red feather boa and a sparkly Mardi Gras mask for Jessie, and she'd chosen a top hat and a Christmas bow tie for him.

They both turned when someone knocked on the doorjamb at the end of the room opposite the curtain, and another woman, this one wearing a truly ugly Christmas sweater, waved at them. "I'm Janine. Are you ready to begin your stroll?"

Jessie nodded, as eager as a kid preparing for an Easter egg hunt, and Janine led them through the next door. For the next hour, the two of them planned and posed and kissed and laughed their way through the selfie stroll, taking photos in wintry wonderlands, gift jungles, and sugary scenes. After the final stop, Janine met them to collect their props.

"How was it?" she asked as they loaded her up with the boa, mask, hat, and bow tie, as well as a fan, an old-fashioned telephone earpiece, an umbrella, and a rubber chicken.

"It was great!" Jessie said, and when she looked up at Shane, she saw his satisfaction. Knowing it resulted from her excitement made her want to hug him, so that's what she did. In all the dating she'd done, she'd never known a man as devoted to her happiness.

17

———————

So far, the date was a smashing success. The selfie stroll had removed any residual awkwardness and at the moment, Jessie was skipping along beside him, hugging his arm.

"That was so much fun!" she said for about the seventh time. "I am so glad you thought of doing that."

"I'm glad, too," Shane said. "You should have heard what my dad had to say about it."

She stopped skipping and grabbed his hand, pulling him to a stop. "What? What did he have to say about it?"

Despite her indignation, her eyes twinkled with humor.

"Oh, nothing," Shane said. "Only that us kids have all these newfangled ideas, and we should go to the diner and roller rink."

"Sounds about right," she said.

"Oh, and he said you'd love the idea, as weird as it was. He said you're always showing him pictures."

The sound of her laughter sprinkled him with fairy dust. He swore he could fly.

"I am." She shrugged. "Maybe it's silly, but with my parents gone now, I like sharing my life with a parental figure."

Charmed, Shane leaned forward and kissed her on the nose. "I love that. Now, come on. We're moving on to the part of our date my dad actually thought sounded cool."

Jessie gave an excited wiggle-shiver and started skipping again. "Ooh! I'm so excited! Where are we going?"

"Not telling, yet. We have to drive there."

Jessie squealed when they pulled up at the resort, unleashing another rush of excitement in Shane's body. "Are we eating here? I've always wanted to eat at this restaurant! It's supposed to have the best view in town!"

"We are," Shane said. "And we have a reservation. So let's go."

The hostess led them across the restaurant to a table for two right next to the window. Inside, Shane did a mental fist pump when he saw the candles on the table. And on the other side of the window, the city stretched out, lights twinkling under the dark, velvety sky.

"I'm barely managing not to squeal my little heart out," Jessie said under her breath.

The hostess pulled out her seat and then Shane's. "Enjoy."

After she was gone, Jessie jumped out of her chair and ran around the table to hug Shane around the shoulders. "Thank you so much for this. It's really special." After one more squeeze, she returned to her seat.

"You're welcome," he said. "Thing is, I don't know how you're gonna measure up to this for our second date."

"I'm not even going to try," she said.

He let his mouth drop open in shock, and she waved him off.

"Don't worry. We're going to have a great time. But you're right. Nothing can measure up to tonight."

They sat there smiling at each other for so long, the server came and asked if they were ready to order. They asked for another minute and Shane picked up the leather-bound menu, silently celebrating it's heavy, quality feel.

"What are you going to get?"

Jessie looked at him, shoulders slumping in mock despair. "Oh, how can I choose? Can I get one of everything?"

"I wish," Shane said, stopping himself before adding that they'd have to come here for all the special occasions, so they'd have a chance to taste every item on the menu.

"I have an idea," she said. "Let's choose two things we both want and split them."

"Just two?" Shane said.

They settled on braised beef roast with vegetables and garlic parmesan mashed potatoes, and lamb chops with baby potatoes and greens. While they waited for their main dishes, the server brought rolls and creamy butter, which Jessie dug into right away.

"Aren't you gonna have one of these?" she asked, her mouth full.

He laughed. "You haven't changed a bit, have you?"

"Haven't I?"

"I don't think so. But I'm perfectly happy about that."

"Good."

The food was even better than Shane expected. "I can't believe I haven't been here before."

"I know," Jessie said. "We're definitely coming back."

He couldn't let her see how much that comment affected him, so he simply said, "I agree."

They laughed and talked over the meal, taking bites from both plates as if they'd done it a million times. To Shane, the whole experience felt completely natural. If this one date could determine whether they'd work as a couple, he thought as he watched Jessie devour a bite of his beef roast, eyes closed in ecstasy, it was definitely proving they would.

When Jessie opened her eyes and found him staring at her, her smile was warm and affectionate. "This has been a really special night."

"It has," he agreed.

Shane was tempted to order dessert when the server came by with the dessert tray, but only to prolong the date.

"I'm not ready for this evening to be over," Jessie said, echoing his thoughts. "Tell me we have another reservation after this."

An involuntary smile playing on his lips, Shane said, "We don't, unfortunately." Come to think of it, he should have reserved a room at the resort. But no, Alvin was waiting at home, and he hadn't told him he'd be gone overnight. Plus, if they stayed out overnight, Alvin would have a heyday talking about that. *And*, Shane thought, taking the check from the server, maybe it was better to end the date while they both still wished for more.

On one hand, pouring his absolute everything into this dating experiment seemed like the best idea. That might be just what Jessie needed to realize they belonged together. But on the other hand, if he poured in all he had, and she still wanted to be friends ... that might break him.

They pushed back their chairs, and as they walked out of the restaurant, Shane remembered a certain trip to the Kingdom of Dragons amusement park when he was around ten. He and his dad had the greatest time. They did it all: mini golf, the arcade, the ropes course, the bumper boats, and rock climbing. They took the tickets Shane earned from arcade games and went to the store to buy a prize. Over ice cream, Shane asked how much longer they could stay.

"I think it's time to head home, son," Alvin said.

Shane couldn't believe his ears. "What? Why? We're having the best time!"

"We are," Alvin said, taking a bite of his ice cream. "And sometimes it's best to leave while you're still having the best time. Before you get bored or run out of things to do. You ever heard the phrase, quit while you're ahead?"

He had, but that didn't make him want to stay any less.

His dad woke him up when they got home, and Shane groaned. All that food and sugar, combined with the adrenaline of playing all those fun games, had made him sleepy.

"See?" his dad said. "You're tired. Aren't you glad we're home and you can go to bed?"

"I guess so," Shane mumbled. In his exhausted state, he didn't quite see the lesson. But now, years later, as Jessie snuggled up against him on their way back to the truck, he did.

Leave her wanting more.

Down the winding driveway and back into their neighborhood,

Jessie swiped through the photos they'd taken during the selfie stroll.

Her reactions ranged from, "Aww," to giggles. Inside, he celebrated, imagining himself doing fist bumps and jumping around, arms raised. He'd done good. Back in their neighborhood, he parked along the curb between his dad's house and Jessie's. "Want to come in?" Jessie asked.

Shane did want to go in. But he shook his head. "No, but thank you for asking. My dad's expecting me home and we both know he'll give me the third degree or worse, wiggle his eyebrows knowingly if he sees my truck and realizes I'm at your place."

With a wicked smile, Jessie said, "I'm sure he knows by now that we've slept together. Or will."

"Still. I'll take a rain check." Guilt crept in when he saw disappointment pass over her face expression. But, the concept of leaving her wanting more intrigued him. Yes, maybe it went against everything he wanted to do, but he needed to do things differently now that they were dating.

"Let me walk you to the door." Just like she had as they walked to the truck after dinner, she tucked her arm into his and snuggled up against him. He definitely enjoyed that. But he wouldn't let her seduce him — not right now, anyway. When they reached the door, they turned toward each other. Shane tucked Jessie's hair behind her ear and let his hand rest on her shoulder, fingertips at the back of neck.

"Thank you for tonight," she said. "That was hands down the funnest date I've ever been on."

Satisfaction pumped through Shane's veins. "I thought you'd enjoy it."

He brought his lips to hers, gentle, a whisper of a kiss. She wrapped her arms around his shoulders and took the kiss deeper. Her tongue brushed her lips and then found his, and he swelled inside his jeans. He knew she felt it too because she moved her hands to his hips and pulled him against her, offering up a quiet, sensual moan. He groaned in response, the sound involuntary as she rubbed against him. He cupped her head with both hands and channeled his arousal into the kiss. Jessie's hands were on his belt buckle, working to loosen it. It took every ounce of Shane's self-control not to follow suit, reach behind her and unfasten her bra. But that would lead to the two of them going inside. Or worse, getting indecent in front of her house. His dad seeing his truck was one thing, but him seeing them half undressed and groping each other? That would be even worse. Gently, he placed his hands on hers to still them.

"I like where this is going," he said, "but I think I'm going to have to take a rain check on this, too. As small as this town is, I don't want anyone to catch us out here taking off each other's clothes."

Her pathetic whimper in response only turned him on more. She wanted him. Just as he had always imagined. And that felt almost as good as giving himself to her. Almost.

"I had a really nice time tonight, too," he said. "This was my best first date ever."

"Mine, too," she said. "And I look forward to our second date."

She let herself in through her front door and he heard the lock turn. Filled with pent-up tension, Shane power walked back to his dad's house, focusing on the cold air touching his skin so he wouldn't think about the arousal below his belt. Just before he unlocked his dad's front door, his phone chimed with a text from Jessie: *Call me if you change your mind. I'll leave my ringer on.*

Grinning, he put the key in the lock. When he turned it, he realized the door wasn't, in fact, locked.

Sighing, he went inside. His dad was in the recliner as usual and had the TV turned on low. Something football related was on. Shane suspected it was highlights, but before he could get a good look at the screen, his dad said, "You're home early! I wasn't expecting you just yet."

"Geez," Shane said. "You have the wrong idea about me. You think I'm some kind of party animal or something."

His dad gave a snort of laughter. "It's not that. It's just that now that you've finally gotten Jessie to go out with you, I thought you'd, you know, want to keep her out all night." His bushy eyebrows moved up and down, causing Shane to laugh out loud. "Remember that time we went to that amusement park and spent hours there?

We'd done everything and when you said it was time to go, I wanted to stay even longer?"

"I do," his dad said. "And I told you that we should go home while we were still having a good time."

"That's right," Shane said. "So that's what I'm doing with Jessie."

"I have to say, I'm surprised, son."

"How come?"

"Oh, I don't know. Like I said. You've pined after her all this time. But you know what? I think this is smart of you. I'm impressed with your savvy. How did she like the strange selfie picture-taking journey?"

"Very funny. She liked it. I told her you thought it sounded weird. But like you said, she loves pictures and during the drive home she oohed an ahed over all the ones we got."

"Good. You know, kid, I don't know where you got it, but it sounds like you're a pretty decent romantic."

"Thanks. I think. Well, I'm going to go get ready for bed." Shane paused in the entrance to the hallway and turned toward his dad again. "Did you leave the door unlocked on purpose?"

Alvin's eyes sharpened on his. "I left it unlocked for you. This is Prescott, son. Not Chicago."

Shane smirked. "Thanks. Aren't you up past your bedtime?"

His dad guffawed. "Way past my bedtime. But I wanted to hear all the details about your date."

Shane couldn't believe how warm and fuzzy that made him feel. There he was, twenty-eight years old, and his dad was waiting up to hear all about his date. "Then I didn't give you nearly enough details. Why don't I make some popcorn?"

Popcorn popped, Shane returned to the living room and sat down. Eyes bright, his dad said, "So? Sounds like the take-pictures-of-yourself-escapade went well. How did the rest of it go?"

Shane hadn't really dated as a teen — he wasn't interested in anyone other than Jessie. So he and his dad had never shared these post-date conversations. But, Shane figured, as a teenager he probably wouldn't have appreciated his dad's interest.

He told his dad all about the bar with its sparkling, ice-like surfaces and fancy holiday drinks. He texted Jessie and asked her to send him some of the photos from the selfie stroll, and then described for his dad all the props and scene setups they'd used. A handful of pictures came through, and Shane held his phone up for his dad to see. He flipped through a couple of them, one where they both wore reindeer antlers and held oversized mugs of hot chocolate, and another where they were dressed like snowflakes.

"I can't believe I'm saying this," his dad said, "but that actually looks like a lot of fun. Right up Jessie's alley."

Shane elbowed him. "See? I knew what I was doing."

Holding up his hands in surrender, his dad said, "All right, all right. You knew what you were doing. Tell me about that restaurant at the resort. Was it as swanky as everyone says it is?"

"It was," Shane said. He described the view and the heavy, leather-bound menu and the beautifully laid-out food. "It was like art. I felt weird eating it."

"Sounds like a lovely evening. I heard your truck pull up, and I was surprised when you came in less than five minutes later. I worried maybe the evening didn't go well."

"Oh, it did," Shane said, remembering the way Jessie had moved her hips against his outside her front door. "Very well. But like I said, I'm keeping a few cards up my sleeve. I left her wanting more."

"Atta boy," his dad said. "And now that I have all the details, I guess I'll go to bed. This getting old stuff is for the birds."

Shane had just lay down in bed when he heard a quiet *tick*. Then another. And another. The sounds came from his closed window. He was almost positive someone was throwing rocks at the glass. His mind's eye produced an image of the flower bed just outside. His dad had used small, round, gray pebbles as a ground cover. Without a doubt, Shane knew he heard the sound of those pebbles hitting his window. And there was only one person who would be throwing them. Already grinning, he got out of bed and pulled open his window. The icy air nearly took his breath away. Sure enough, Jessie stood there, the light from a tiny flashlight illuminating her face. In the dark, he could barely make out her sheepskin boots, pajama pants, and parka.

"It's me," she hissed.

"What are you doing?" he whispered back.

"I missed you," she said. "Can I come in?"

Shane pointed toward the front of the house. "You could use the front door."

The shrug she gave him ratcheted up her adorableness factor. "I know. But I didn't want to wake your dad, and anyway, isn't this more romantic?"

"Yeah," Shane said, looking down at the skin on his arms. "If you consider goosebumps and chattering teeth romantic."

Taking a couple of steps toward the window, Jessie said, "Then let me in, will you?"

Shane removed the screen and Jessie put her hands on the windowsill and hoisted herself up. The sound of flesh banging against wood made Shane jump, and Jessie swore, dropping back onto the ground. "Shit. I hit my knee."

"This is a terrible idea," Shane said.

Hands still on the windowsill, elbows lifted, Jessie's smile bordered on maniacal, which made Shane laugh again.

"It might be. But now I'm determined to see it through. Stand back."

Shane took a big step back and Jessie tried again, hoisting herself up and straightening her arms before attempting to swing a leg over the windowsill. She managed to get a knee up before her progress halted. "I think I'm stuck."

A full-on case of the giggles overtaking him, Shane moved forward and put his hands under her armpits, pulling her in through the window in what had to be the least graceful, least romantic entrance he could have imagined. Apparently, the giggles had overtaken her, too, and her shoulders shook as she made almost-silent squeaking noises.

"Wow," Shane said as they both straightened up. "That was quite the entrance."

Jessie held up a hand, pointer finger extended. "But you won't soon forget it."

"That's a fact."

Jessie turned around and closed the window. When she faced him again, Shane said, "So. To what do I owe the pleasure?"

"First of all, I feel like I should tell you that that is not how I planned this to go."

"I wouldn't have thought so," Shane said.

"Well, I was lying there, thinking how much I already missed you. I wanted to see you again."

Shane attempted to tone down the huge smile that gave away his reaction. He was pretty sure he failed. "That's really nice. But you could have warned me. I'm in my underwear."

"I mean, it's not a bad look." She ran a hand over his abs, and he felt a stirring between his legs. "Should we, like, sit and talk or something?"

This time, Shane didn't even attempt to control his reaction. He laughed out loud, a big belly laugh that made Jessie break eye contact. "What was your plan?"

Was it bad that he hoped she'd come over to seduce him, even though he'd said he'd take a rain check on spending the night together?

"I don't know, really. I just wanted to be with you."

That was music to his ears. "Let's sit." Shane gestured at his bed. They did, side by side. Jessie took both of his hands in hers and for a moment, Shane worried she was about to deliver bad news. But then she said, "I had a great time tonight."

"I did, too."

"I'm thinking of printing out some of our photos and making a little album."

"You should," he said.

"I haven't been in your room in forever." She looked around. Her eyes came to rest on the Arizona Cardinals poster he'd hung up when he was in high school. "I remember when you got that."

"It was the same night we had that giant Nintendo tournament," Shane remembered. "My dad had to kick you out of here at midnight because he couldn't sleep with all our yelling."

"And also because you were so worked up because I beat you."

"You cheated," Shane said.

"Did not," she said, pouting like she would have back then. "That was fun."

Jessie nodded, bit her lower lip. "Do you still have that Nintendo?"

"You know I do. I couldn't part with that thing."

"Do you think it still works?"

"I know it does," Shane said.

"Want a rematch?" Her eyes glittered with the competitive spirit he so loved.

A video game tournament rematch wasn't exactly what he would have imagined when the woman he'd loved for years showed up at his window in the middle of the night, but he felt the thrill of adrenaline hitting his veins. "You're on."

Together, they pulled the console out of his cabinet and hooked it up to his TV. They blew out the video game cartridges just like they used to do when they were kids, and found a couple that still worked.

It was after two a.m. when Jessie declared Shane the winner and yawning, stood up.

"I guess we can't have a sleepover," she said. "It would be kind of awkward to go in for breakfast and see your dad there."

"I agree. Any sleepovers are going to have to be at your place."

She kissed him, long and deep, and said, "Fair enough. I'll use the front door this time. And before you offer to walk me home," she said, running her hand down his abs again, "don't worry about it. I'd rather have this final vision of you in sweatpants without a shirt than have you walk me home."

He settled for walking her to his front door. And so what if he literally jumped around in glee after closing it behind her?

18

———

The first image that floated into Jessie's mind when she woke up the next morning was Shane in his pajama pants kissing her goodnight at his front door. Heat flooded her body as she remembered his arousal pressing against her. The night before felt ... spellbinding.

I never would have guessed.

Which was the whole idea behind the dating experiment.

This felt newsworthy. She had to tell Rose and Taylor. Just as she took her phone off the nightstand to text them, her phone lit up with a notification from the messages app. A pleasant electric jolt hit her when she saw Shane's name there.

Thank you for a magical evening.

He'd sent the message the night before, just after she went to bed. Which meant he was still thinking about her. Goosebumps traveled from her scalp to her ankles.

She wrote back, *Thank YOU. Can't wait for our next date. I'm in full planning mode.*

Then she sat up, leaning against the headboard, and texted her friends: *Can I tell you all about our first real, official date?*

Rose responded immediately: *Of course. I've been dying to hear.*

Taylor chimed in a couple of minutes later as Jessie was typing her response to Rose: *Me, too! Dish!*

She recapped the date, from the bar to the selfie stroll to the restaurant, and added, *That was the end of the date, but I climbed through his window afterwards and we had a Nintendo tournament.*

Rose: *That sounds like a lovely evening! I assume you thought it was, too, since you texted us first thing this morning?*

Jessie: *Yes. I'm astonished to say, it was quite dreamy.*

Their responses came through simultaneously: *Dreamy?!*

Jessie: *Yep. I'm still on Cloud Nine.*

Taylor: *Please send pics.*

Jessie did, and her friends gushed over them.

Rose: *OMG, you guys make the cutest couple!*

Taylor: *Yes! Yes, yes, yessss. You ARE so cute together. Why have you never dated before this?*

Jessie sent back a laughing emoji and Rose wrote back, *I'm serious. Why HAVEN'T you?*

She considered. The simplest answer was that she just hadn't thought of him that way ... but when he showed up at Rita's with a smokin' hot body, things changed. But what if she went outside her mental comfort zone and dug a little deeper? She and Shane had grown up doing everything together, like siblings. He was always there: her go-to partner in crime, her confidant, her best friend.

I took him and our relationship for granted.

That realization made her gasp.

His moving away left a void in her life. At first, she'd pick up the phone several times a day to call or text him. His responses were slow to come back, if they came back at all. She'd forgotten about that. She nursed her hurt feelings by attributing his lack of communication to him being distracted as he got his business off the ground. Eventually it became the status quo.

She threw back the covers and headed for the kitchen. Her phone rang as she removed the carafe from the coffeemaker. Although she didn't recognize the number, she answered.

"Ms. Monroe?"

Jessie recognized the voice immediately and her heart swelled. "Isabelle! I mean, Ms. Budgie!"

"Hello, dear," Isabelle said. "How are you?"

"Great!" Jessie said. "Especially now that you called. I hope you're calling to say you've decided to come visit. You know, I was thinking. I could come up and get you, drive you down here."

A magical, tinkling laugh came through the line. "Oh, no, honey, that's not necessary. I can get a flight from Sheridan to Prescott. If you wouldn't mind picking me up there though, that would be wonderful."

Jessie couldn't believe her ears. She put the carafe in the sink and turned on the water to fill it. "Of course! Anything! Would you like to stay at my house? At a hotel? I can make reservations for you. Just say the word. When are you coming?"

More magical laughter. "Oh, my, honey. I think you're more excited than I am. Does Alvin know I'm coming?"

Her hand halfway to the cupboard to get out a coffee filter, Jessie froze. "No. We haven't mentioned it. You know, just in case —"

"Of course. I understand. I haven't picked a date yet, dear. When would a visit be convenient for you?"

Excitement zipped through her body. She pressed the filter into the coffeemaker's basket and got down the coffee. "I'm sure you remember I'm a teacher. I'm on winter break through the first week of January. If you came during break, I could be your chauffeur, tour guide, whatever you need."

"Wonderful. Why don't I come the day after tomorrow?"

Jessie nearly dropped the coffee scoop. "Day after tomorrow? Sure!"

"I understand they call Prescott Arizona's Christmas City. I'd love to see it in all its glory."

"Yes! That would be great. Let me know when you get your flight and I'll pick you up. Have you decided if you want to stay here?"

"Oh, let's play all that by ear," Isabelle said. "I'll work on my flights today and get back to you."

Something about the past twenty-four hours had turned Jessie into a squealer. She muted her phone and squealed, running in place so fast, her hair came out of its bun. Unmuting her phone, she said, "Great! I can't wait to hear from you. You're going to love it here. Shane, Alvin, and I will show you around. It's a great time of year to visit."

They hung up, and Jessie started the coffee brewing, practically dancing in her kitchen. While she waited, she called Shane.

"Guess what?"

"Do I have to guess?"

In all the years she'd known him, she'd never had this kind of a reaction to his gravely morning voice. Heat pooled between her legs. "No! I'm too excited to make you guess. Guess who just called me."

"I thought you were too excited to make me guess."

Pacing the house, Jessie said, "Oh. Right. Isabelle just called. Just now. She wants to come visit. Guess when?"

"Do I have to guess?"

"Right. No. She wants to come visit in two days."

Silence.

"Shane! Why aren't you saying anything?"

"Hold on."

That's when she realized: he was probably near his dad and didn't want to spoil the surprise. She squealed again. After what felt like a long delay, he said, "Okay. She wants to come visit in two days?"

"Yeah! Can you believe it? She said she's heard Prescott is Arizona's Christmas City, and she wants to see it for herself. Your dad is going to be so excited. Over the moon. Seriously, Shane. We have to tell him."

Another long pause. Then a sigh. Was he *sighing*?

"Shane. What are you thinking?"

"I don't know."

She stopped pacing and stood in the middle of her kitchen, inhaling the nutty scent of the coffee, watching the liquid fall into the pot, creating little ripples in what was already there.

"This is not the reaction I was expecting," she said. "Say something!"

"I don't know," he said again. "I guess I'm just worried."

"What do you *mean*? This is a *great* idea! Your dad *loved* Isabelle. She seems so *nice*. She *wants* to come here and see him."

Another sigh so loud, she could practically feel the air from his exhale. "I know. You're right about all of those things. But like I said before, I don't want him to get hurt."

Jessie dropped her head back and looked at the ceiling. She had to hold in a groan. The coffeemaker gurgled.

"So I totally understand where you're coming from," she said, straightening up. "But they're both adults now. They've already lived their own separate lives. Why do you think he'll get hurt?"

"Oh, I don't know." The edge she heard in his voice made her feel like she needed to move. She retrieved a coffee cup and filled it. He said, "It's just that for all this time, he's probably idolized her. I can tell, from the way he's talked about her for the past week, that he thinks she's like, perfect. You know? What if she comes here and she's not who he thought she was? Just because they're both older doesn't mean they don't have quirks and imperfections."

Shane's comments were putting a damper on Jessie's excitement. She scooped a couple of teaspoonfuls of sugar into her coffee and poured in some cream.

"Right," she said, letting the word draw out slowly. "But —"

"I mean, in all your planning and excitement, did you ever stop and think about what would happen if they get together and don't actually like each other anymore?"

Huh. She hadn't. "I haven't."

"Well, maybe you should, Jess. I mean, I love that you're feeling so romantic about this. And I love that you're planning it with my dad in mind. I know you're coming from a good place. But I'm just worried, that's all."

"Okay," she said, drawing out that word, too, her stomach in knots. "But what are you saying? Should I tell her she can't come? I mean, we already invited her, Shane. She was calling today to say she's organized everything so she can visit. And now am I supposed to call her back and tell her we've changed our minds?"

Yet another heavy sigh came through her earpiece. While she

waited for him to speak, she sipped her coffee, then winced because it was still too hot.

"I don't know. I mean, you're right. We drove one thousand miles to ask her to come. I guess it would be pretty lame if we suddenly changed our minds."

"So I can tell her she can come?"

"Maybe we should talk to Dad, first. Gauge his reaction to the idea."

At that point, it was Jessie who gave a heavy sigh. "All right. Do you want to talk to him together?"

"Of course. If he hates the idea, I want him to know it was mostly yours."

The humor Jessie heard in his voice gave her some relief. "Sounds like a plan. Should I get dressed and come over?"

"Sure."

"That sounded very curt."

"I know. Sorry. See you in what? An hour?"

She scoffed. "Thirty minutes."

Before she could knock on Alvin's door a half-hour later, it opened, and Shane emerged. She assumed he'd come out to greet her and give her a good-morning kiss, and she opened her arms. He did hug her, but it wasn't the sweet, affectionate embrace she expected.

"Good morning?" she tried.

"Morning," he said, stuffing his hands into his pockets.

"Are we going to go inside? It's freezing out here." She pointed at the puffs of steam visible as she spoke.

"Yes," he said. "But first, I wanted to make sure we're on the same page about what to tell Dad."

Jessie nodded. "Okay. What do you want to tell him?"

"We tell him that after he brought up Isabelle the other night, you took it upon yourself to look her up and plan a trip to see her and invite her to come visit."

"Sounds great. Let's go." She didn't understand why he was behaving so strangely about all this.

"Fine."

Despite his obvious aggravation, he opened the door for her and let her walk in first. When Alvin saw her, he stood up from his recliner and gave her a hug. She winked at Shane as if to say, *See? He loves me. This will all be fine.* Shane rolled his eyes, but she could see a smile tugging at the corners of his mouth.

"We have a surprise for you," Jessie told Alvin, who stepped back and raised his eyebrows.

"For me? Well. This is exciting."

Shane shifted his weight from one foot to the other and crossed his arms. He blew out another breath. Paced to the other end of the room.

"Should we sit?" Jessie asked, giving Shane a stern look.

He sat. She sat. Alvin sat. Shane gestured at Jessie to go ahead.

She cleared her throat, surprised at the butterflies fluttering in her stomach. "Remember how, the other night, you were talking to us about your old colleague, Isabelle Sorensen Budgie?"

"I do," Alvin said, his eyes going dreamy. "The one who got away."

"We —" Shane elbowed her, and she course corrected. "*I* thought it would be a fun idea to look her up, see what she's up to now, where she is."

On Alvin's sharp inhale, Jessie glanced at Shane. He stared hard at his dad, anticipating his response.

"And?" Alvin said.

"And we found her," Jessie said. "She's in Buffalo, Wyoming."

Alvin exhaled. "Well, I'll be. Wyoming, you say? Wonder what she's been doing there."

Jessie glanced at Shane again, but he continued staring at his dad. His silence was making her nervous. But Alvin's eyes showed a spark of interest, so she plowed ahead, telling him everything they'd discovered about his old flame — starting with the fact that she'd been divorced for years.

"Well, I'll be," he said again.

This time when she looked at Shane, he gave her a single nod, and she proceeded to tell him about how they'd gone to visit Isabelle in her hometown.

Another sharp inhale and then, "How is she?"

Finally, Shane decided to participate. "She's great, Dad. She seems really happy, very settled. We invited her to come visit."

"You did?" Alvin's eyebrows shot up.

"We did," Jessie said. "And she called this morning to say she's got everything organized. If you give me the go ahead, she'll be here in two days."

"Two days?" His eyes glistened with tears.

"Two days," Jessie said.

"Well. I guess I'd better get a haircut and a shave." He picked up his phone and dialed. A minute later, he hung up and told them, "All right, you two. I've got to get dressed. I have an appointment in thirty minutes."

Once he'd left the room, Jessie jumped up and raised her arms in triumph. "See? I told you he'd be excited!"

Shane remained on the couch, an uncertain smile on his lips.

"What's wrong?" she asked. "I thought you'd be happier."

Elbows on his knees, Shane said, "I *am* happy. It's just that we don't know how it's going to go once she gets here. What if he gets all excited, gets the haircut and the shave, and she comes here, only for the two of them to realize they have nothing in common anymore?"

Jessie nodded. His concerns were reasonable. "I see what you're saying. But what if we didn't try? What if we knew she was alive, knew she was divorced, and never gave him the opportunity to see her again?"

Shane scrubbed his face with his hands. "I see what you're saying. But if he'd really, truly wanted to see her, don't you think he would have reached out to her on his own?"

Jessie hadn't thought of that. "Maybe," she said, chewing her lower lip. "But maybe not. I mean, he probably figured she'd stay married to Jack Budgie ... and, you know, he's older. Older people don't think like us young guns. Not when it comes to technology. Maybe it didn't even occur to him to get on the Internet and find her."

Nodding, Shane said, "I guess you're right. I hadn't thought of it that way."

She grabbed his hands and pulled him to standing, then wrapped her arms around his waist. "Can you at least *try* not to worry? I don't want you to miss out on enjoying the potential excitement here."

She felt his chest rise and fall with another sigh, and she laughed.

"I guess I can try," he said.

She kissed him on the corner of his mouth. "Good."

They heard Alvin coming back down the hall before they saw him — his whistling announced his entrance. She couldn't resist elbowing Shane, whose expression acknowledged that she'd been right.

Alvin said he'd see them in a while, and when the door closed behind him, Jessie said, "See? He's so happy."

"Yeah," Shane said. "For now, anyway."

"I don't understand why you're being so doom and gloom about this," Jessie said. "But I'm going home to enjoy the excitement on my own. Anyway, I have to plan our second date."

"Fine," Shane said. "You do that." He gave her a brief kiss. "Can we go on our second date tomorrow night, before Isabelle comes? That way, we can spend time with her and my dad, run interference if we have to."

"Sure," Jessie said. "But I have a feeling we're not going to need to run interference."

"Maybe not. But I want to be available in case we do."

Jessie hugged Shane again and tipped her head back for a kiss. When he tried to get away with another perfunctory peck, she took his face in her hands and took the kiss deeper. "You'll thank me later."

"I sure hope so."

With that, she returned to her house to begin planning. Not just her next date with Shane, but Isabelle's visit, too.

19

———

When his dad returned from his haircut and shave, he still had quite a pep in his step.

"Can I talk to you, Dad?" Shane said as he sat down in his recliner.

"Of course, son. What's up?"

Shane sat on the couch. "I just want to make sure you're really okay with Isabelle coming to visit. You know how Jessie can be. She gets an idea in her head and just sticks with it."

"Oh, Shane," Alvin said, his eyes softening. "I love your concern for me. But I'm a grown man. I am very much looking forward to seeing Isabelle."

"I'm just worried, that's all. I don't want you to get hurt."

"I promise, I can handle this," Alvin said. "I'd rather have the chance to see her again than lock myself away for fear of being hurt."

Oh. Shane realized with a start that his dad's sentiments echoed Jessie's. Maybe she *was* right.

"Okay," Shane said. "If you're sure."

"I'm sure," Alvin said. "Just relax, would you? Anyway, you're supposed to be focusing on your own romance. Aren't you and Jessie going on another date soon?"

"We are. Tomorrow night, in fact."

Alvin nodded, satisfied. "Okay, then. You focus on that, and I'll focus on reacquainting myself with Isabelle. Then we'll huddle up and discuss. You know, like they do in a football game."

"Fine."

The next day when he went out to Jessie's Jeep at three p.m., she was wearing the biggest grin he'd ever seen on her.

"Wow," he said. "You look like it's Christmas morning already."

"This is going to be fun," she said.

He became increasingly intrigued as they drove further and further from Prescott, down the steep, curvy road toward Phoenix. Pine trees gave way to oak shrubs, which gave way to saguaro cacti. That's when she exited the freeway and pulled into the dirt lot for a trailhead. Right away, Shane noticed tons of pickup trucks with trailers attached.

"Are we going for a Jeep ride?" he asked.

"*You're* taking *me* for a ride," she said. "You're driving."

His heart leapt.

"Are you serious?! You know how much I've wanted to drive it since you bought it."

"I'm serious."

He couldn't believe she was planning this. "Really? Or are you pulling my leg?"

She shrugged. "Really."

They stared at each other across the console, Shane feeling absolutely giddy. It was all he could do to stop himself from giggling like a maniac.

"Want to take the top down?"

"I sure do," Shane said.

They did, and Jessie handed him a handkerchief to cover his nose and mouth in case they got behind another vehicle on the trails.

"Before we go," Jessie said, "what music do you want me to put on?"

"Eighties rock!"

The first beats of *Eye of the Tiger* came on and they were off. Shane pulled onto the main trail.

"Give it some gas!"

He did, and the tires spit gravel against the Jeep's fenders. Shane let out a bellow, and headed up the trail and into the mountains. With the wind in his hair and the music turned up, Shane felt freer than he ever had. Hollering, he whipped around a turn, making the tires skid. Jessie whooped and held onto the grab handle for dear life.

"Maybe this was a mistake," she yelled, and he was happy to see her smiling when he looked over at her.

Still, he slowed down, just a little. At each intersection, she pointed in the direction she wanted him to go. They climbed higher and higher as the trails wrapped around the mountain. In what felt like the blink of an eye, they'd reached the top and Jessie motioned for Shane to stop.

After turning down the music, she gestured at the space around them. "Check it out."

His arms still vibrating from the tight grip he kept on the steering wheel on the rough road, Shane forced himself to relax and look around. "This is certainly a breathtaking view."

The mountain fell away from them on all sides, providing a wide vista where more mountains and tableaus were dark against the bright blue sky. Wispy clouds stretched across the expanse.

"It is," Jessie said. "And we'll get to enjoy it for a while longer, because I brought a picnic."

They worked together to lay out the picnic blanket and she pulled a big basket out of the Jeep's cargo area. Shane whistled when she opened it and he saw its contents.

"You feeding an army?"

"I might have gotten carried away."

When they sat down to eat, she said, "I talked to Isabelle earlier. She reserved her flight and she'll be here tomorrow morning."

Shane's stomach lurched and his throat tightened. He smiled around the mouthful of sandwich and gave her a thumbs up, hoping they didn't have to talk any more about it. He wasn't a fool. He knew he was nervous about Isabelle's visit because her relationship with his dad paralleled his with Jessie. His fear of Alvin getting hurt paralleled his fear of getting hurt. But he couldn't say any of that to Jessie. Not yet.

Fortunately, they enjoyed the rest of their lunch in near silence as the breeze blew and the engines of other Jeeps and 4x4s buzzed below them.

"Let's put the top up before we head up the hill," Jessie said. "It's getting chilly."

Once they were back in the Jeep, she rubbed her hands together in anticipation. "And now for the second part of our date."

Shane grinned. "I'm not sure I like the sound of this. You seem strangely excited."

"What do you mean?" She blinked at him, all innocence, and turned the key in the ignition. The engine rumbled to life.

"The light in your eyes is reminiscent of the time you wanted to sneak into the Alvarez pool."

"What?" Hands on her chest and eyes wide, she shook her head. "This is nothing like that." After a pause during which he stared at her she said, "Okay. It might be something like that. But there is one key difference. No one will be coming home to catch us."

Half nervous and half excited, Shane watched as she tapped her phone screen for a few seconds. Christmas music blared through the speakers. Jessie shifted into drive and they headed for the highway.

"Where are you taking us?"

"You'll see."

They drove north, away from Phoenix and back toward Prescott.

"You know it's getting late, right?" he said to her as they merged onto the interstate.

"Yep," she said, offering him a brief grin before facing the windshield again.

About twenty minutes before they would have reached home, Jessie pulled off the highway. She made a few turns and parked in a dirt lot on a side street. "Ready? This is the part where we need our warm clothes."

The sudden silence made Shane's ears ring. They got out of the car and Jessie said, "Bundle up."

"Where are we going?" Shane wanted to know.

Grinning, Jessie said, "Let's go." They'd walked a few steps when she froze and held up a hand. "Wait."

She got her phone out of her pocket, tapped the screen a few more times, and Christmas music blared from its speaker. "That's better," she said.

They walked about a block along the side street, Christmas music with all its jingling bells playing, before Jessie motioned for them to turn left. That's when Shane guessed her destination.

"Are we *walking* through the Valley of Lights?" He could see the giant light displays in the valley below them.

"We are."

"Really?! That's awesome! I thought the only way through was to drive."

"A few years ago, they started opening it up for walking, just one night per year. That night has come and gone this year, but I thought it would be fun to do tonight as part of our date."

"But will cars be driving through? That seems dangerous."

"No, silly. It's closed."

"Wait. So we're walking through when it's closed?"

Jessie halted. "Yes!"

"I'm sure that's against the rules."

"Maybe, but it's *fun*. Come on."

She grabbed his hand and tugged, and they made their way down the winding hill that led to the park where the displays were set up. Shane's face stung from the cold. After a few more minutes, Jessie stopped again. "Close your eyes. I'll lead you."

He made a show of looking nervous but did as she said and let her take his arm. Eyes closed, Christmas music playing, his body up against Jessie's, the mood was pleasantly festive. Shane told himself to relax and enjoy the moment, despite his rule-following instincts.

Jessie said, "Okay. Open," and when he did, a giant tunnel of illuminated snowflakes greeted him. He felt his eyes go round and his mouth drop open.

"Isn't this amazing up close?"

It was. "I'll admit, it's cooler than I was thinking it would be. I've driven through so many times, but I've never seen it like this."

And suddenly, he was giddy with excitement over the fact that she'd planned this, for him. Strolling through an illuminated park was romantic. Jessie took his hand and they made their way through the tunnel. When they emerged, real, sparkling snowflakes fell from the sky, just visible from the lights on display.

"Oh, my gosh," Jessie said, lifting her arms and turning in a circle. "This is amazing!"

"It is," Shane said, finally letting himself relax and enjoy the illicit activity Jessie had chosen. Watching her enjoy the snowfall, everything illuminated in the glow, was magical, too. Tiny ice crystals stuck in her eyelashes.

"You look like an ice princess," he told her.

She laughed and grabbed his hand. "We'd better pick up the pace or we're going to freeze."

Moving at an accelerated rate while being careful not to slip, they made their way past lit-up Christmas trees and cartoon characters, an old Western town and a tribute to the United States. Meanwhile, the snow continued to fall, twirling silently from the sky.

"Okay," Shane said as they approached the final display, a tunnel made of crisscrossing candy canes. "This was a pretty cool idea."

"I know," Jessie said, adorably smug. "I couldn't have planned it any better, with this snow."

"Yeah," Shane said. "That made it pretty spectacular."

She hugged his waist and he put his arm around her shoulders. They remained like that until the end of the road, where they made a left and headed back to the Jeep.

"Now that we're nice and chilled, I think we should go for hot chocolate," Jessie said.

"We should."

Ice crunching beneath the tires, Jessie pulled out of the parking spot. "Rita's?"

Shane didn't bother holding in his groan. "Do we have to?"

"Shane West! Don't you love Rita?"

"Of course," Shane said. "I'll always love Rita. But every time we go in there together, she's all hearts and butterflies, talking about how romance is born there and to be sure to put Rita's Diner on the wedding invitations."

Jessie snickered. "You're right. Isn't that part of the charm?"

"I mean, maybe. But can we go somewhere else?"

They settled on a little coffeeshop around the corner from Rita's and ordered their hot chocolates with extra whipped cream. When Jessie took the first drink of hers, she got whipped cream on her nose. Shane brushed it off. They smiled at each other across the table. The moment, and the whole evening, were exactly what he'd always wished for with Jessie.

Then she started the conversation he'd been dreading and his sense of wonder deflated like a balloon shriveling. "I think we need to get on the same page about Isabelle's visit."

This time, he stifled his groan. "Can we just not talk about it? Just for tonight?" *This night is supposed to be about us.*

"But I want you to help me make plans for them."

"Don't you think they can make plans for themselves?" he said.

"Yes, but I want it to be *fun*."

"I'm sure it will be," Shane said, "if you consider watching basketball or going to the roller rink fun."

"Testy."

Shane sipped his hot chocolate. "Just realistic. What plans did you have in mind?"

"Oh, I don't know." Jessie looked down at her drink.

Guilt swamped him. "Look. I'm sorry. I didn't mean to shut you down. I'll help you plan."

She looked at him through her eyelashes. "But will you help me plan enthusiastically?"

He sighed. She laughed.

He said, "I'll do my best."

Perking right up, she said, "Great! What should we plan for them to do?"

"Wait," he said, holding up a hand. "Why don't we ask if he has any ideas? I mean, we don't even know Isabelle. What if she has strong preferences, you know? What if she hates Christmas?"

"She doesn't hate Christmas," Jessie said, her voice full of more vitriol than he'd heard from her before. "In fact, she mentioned that she was looking forward to visiting Arizona's Christmas City."

"Fine." The hot chocolate suddenly tasted powdery and bitter on his tongue.

"Listen."

"Uh oh," Shane said, his lips twitching. "You just pulled out the 'Listen.'"

"I did. Hear me out. Your dad is *excited*. He went and got a haircut."

"That's the problem. What if he gets excited, gets the haircut, spends time with Isabelle, and finds it completely disappointing?"

"You can 'what if' all day long," Jessie said. "Anyway. Let's go talk to him. But can we finish our date, first?"

"I guess so." Shane did his best to push thoughts of his dad's potential romance — or heartbreak — out of his mind and focus on the beautiful woman in front of him.

"Shall we?" Jessie said after they'd both used spoons to scoop the remaining whipped cream out of the bottoms of their cups. "Are you ready?"

"As ready as I'll ever be."

Less than ten minutes later, they stood outside his dad's house.

"Back already?" Alvin called from the living room.

Jessie's shoulders shook with silent laughter.

"We're both here, Dad," Shane called.

The old recliner creaked as Alvin stood up. His footsteps sounded pretty spry as he approached, and he grinned as he came toward them. "What a nice surprise!" He hugged Jessie and clapped Shane on the back. "Come on in, you two. I can make some popcorn."

"Actually," Jessie said, looking at Shane. "I think we're both stuffed. We actually came by to talk to you."

Before his dad could respond, Shane held up a hand. "Wait.

Before you get your hopes up, we're not going to tell you we're getting married."

Alvin's laugh in response was way too loud, way too boisterous. Shane looked at Jessie with one eyebrow raised. *He thought that's what we were going to tell him.*

She shook her head. "Let's sit."

They all settled in the living room, Alvin with his elbows on his knees, looking from Shane to Jessie and back again. Shane gave Jessie a nod, and she opened the conversation. While the two of them talked, Shane observed Jessie. Her enthusiasm was palpable, visible in her raised eyebrows and wide smile and the cant of her body toward his dad, who, for his part, mirrored her enthusiasm.

Resentment. That's what he was feeling. He and Jessie had been on a date, and she'd been thinking about his dad's romance. Yes, he appreciated that she'd taken an interest in his dad's love life, but also, he wanted her to be so swept up in him, and their romance, that she couldn't think of anything else.

Just when that resentment started to build to the point where he considered excusing himself to get some fresh air though, she looked over at him and grinned, pulling him back in. A rush of affection hit him, and he tuned back into what they were actually saying.

"So, let me recap," Jessie said. "You and Shane will wait here while I pick up Isabelle, and then we'll all meet at Rita's for lunch. After that, we'll leave you on your own for the afternoon. You wanted to go check out the gingerbread village and do something else spontaneous, and then we'll all meet for dinner downtown, after which you'll walk around the square and look at the Christmas lights. Sound about right?"

Shane held in his laughter. The plan left hardly any room for spontaneity. Jessie was really planning this down to the minute. His dad winked at him and said to Jessie, "Yep. Sounds about right. The Christmas lights — you think that'll be romantic?"

"Absolutely," Jessie said, beaming at him and then at Shane. "It's a great idea."

With the plan in place, Jessie went home. Shane tried not to be annoyed that she left when their business concluded.

After the door closed behind her, Alvin said, "Everything okay, son?"

"Everything's fine, Dad," he said.

Everything *was* fine. Shane could acknowledge, to himself, that his feelings for Jessie were complicated, especially as they became wrapped up in the unfolding of Alvin and Isabelle's love story. He couldn't put a finger on why, exactly, that was, but he would feel better after Isabelle came. He was almost certain of it.

20

———

Jessie stood in the arrivals area at the Prescott airport. Only when she looked down did she realize she was wringing her hands as she waited for Isabelle to come around the corner from where the planes landed. She shook out her arms and took yet another deep breath.

Watching others greet their arriving friends and family members, Jessie ran over her mental to-do list one more time. Clean and vacuum the Jeep. Check. Clean the kitchen. Check. Clean the bathroom. Check. Put fresh sheets on the bed in the guest bedroom. Check. Go grocery shopping. Check. She nodded. Realized she was wringing her hands again. Her heart was actually racing, and a bead of sweat trickled down her back even though the airport was cool.

Ah, there she was. Jessie went from wringing her hands to waving wildly. "Isabelle!"

The older woman's eyes lit up when she spotted Jessie. And, if Jessie wasn't mistaken, Isabelle had spruced herself up for the visit. She pulled her steel gray hair into a high bun, showing off silver highlights. She'd chosen a sweater that brought out the green in her eyes, and she wore lipstick. They walked toward each other, Jessie's heart thumping against her rib cage. Jessie reached for Isabelle's hands, but Isabelle gave a little shake of her head and pulled Jessie in for a big hug. The scent of her perfume, spicy with a hint of vanilla, enveloped Jessie, and all her nerves faded away. "Welcome to Prescott!"

Isabelle gave her a little squeeze before stepping back. "Thank you so much. I'm so happy to be here."

"Did you check a bag?"

Isabelle's high, breathy laugh revealed she might be suffering from nerves, too. "Oh, yes. Absolutely. I thought I could do with a carry-on, but I just couldn't decide on what to bring. So I brought way too much. My suitcase barely passed the weight check."

"A woman after my own heart."

They headed for the baggage claim.

"How was your flight?"

"Fine, fine," Isabelle said. "Everything went very smoothly. I have to tell you." She looked at Jessie sideways, a conspiratorial gleam in her eye. "I'm quite nervous. If it weren't for my jitters, the trip out here would have been a perfectly pleasant experience." There was that laugh again.

"I think Alvin might be nervous, too," Jessie said. "I don't know if that makes you feel any better. He went and got a haircut and a shave, and Shane texted me he's been pacing the house since he saw me leave to pick you up."

Isabelle put a hand on Jessie's arm. "That does make me feel better, actually," she said. "Thank you. Although," she added as they reached the baggage claim carousel, "I don't know why I'm nervous. Alvin and I always had the best time together. We never fell short on things to talk about. I guess it's just that it's been so long since I've seen him."

"I'm sure you'll fall right back into the swing of things."

Although Shane said something about the rumor mill when they talked about meeting at Rita's, Jessie pointed out that Isabelle should experience their favorite hometown diner — and its owners. When Jessie pulled up, she saw Shane and Alvin were already there.

"Are you ready?" she asked Isabelle, who lifted her shoulders and scrunched up her face. "I think so."

Shane raised an arm in greeting when they walked into the

diner. Time seemed to slow down then, as Alvin stood up and Isabelle's gaze locked on him. They moved together like a pair of magnets. As soon as they reached each other, they embraced. Jessie's eyes prickled with tears. She managed to tear her gaze away from Alvin and Isabelle to look at Shane, whose smile reflected the joy she was feeling.

"Let me look at you," Isabelle said to Alvin, taking half a step back and holding onto his elbows. The two of them stood there smiling, examining one another.

"Amazing," Isabelle said. "You haven't aged a day."

Alvin threw his head back and laughed. "You're a liar. But I'm not. And what I'll say to you is that you are as beautiful as ever."

"Aren't you sweet?"

They hugged again, and then Rita was there, smacking her gum, her smile wide. "Well, well, well." She put a hand on her hip and pointed from Alvin to Isabelle and back again. "I'd say I can't believe my eyes, but as you know, Rita's is the birthplace for many a romance. Is this our latest?"

Jessie didn't miss the glare Shane shot at her. She knew what he was thinking. What if Isabelle and his dad were destined for friendship, not romance, and Rita started talking about them to everyone else in town? But the two of them were so wrapped up in each other, they didn't seem to hear what Rita said.

"Can I take your drink orders?"

Shane cleared his throat. "I'll take a beer."

"In that case, I'll take a Bloody Mary," Isabelle said.

"Make that two," Alvin said.

"Make it three." Jessie beamed.

She slid into the booth across from Shane, and Alvin and Isabelle finally let go of each other and did the same.

"It's so wonderful to see you, Al," Isabelle said, her eyes shining.

"You're a sight for these old eyes, that's for sure," Alvin said.

They stared at each other, their menus flat on the table. Jessie looked at Shane and was happy to see amusement playing around his eyes and mouth.

He cleared his throat again. "The French toast is really good," he said.

Isabelle gave a little start. "Oh! That's right. We're here for breakfast. The French toast, you say?"

Shane threw Jessie a look she couldn't read. "Yes. The French toast."

From Jessie's perspective, lunch went spectacularly. Isabelle and Alvin talked and laughed like they'd spent no time apart. Her own happiness bubbled over as she watched them, and she became completely wrapped up in their reunion.

Until Shane nudged her foot with his under the table, she'd almost forgotten they were sharing the meal, too ... she felt for a few moments like she was watching a movie, and Alvin and Isabelle were the main characters.

She jumped when his foot hit hers, and then smiled a "you-caught-me" smile. Only, he wasn't smiling back. Lifting an eyebrow, she waited for him to speak, but he shook his head, his eyebrows drawn together in a frown. A heavy, sick feeling took hold in her stomach, replacing the fizzy, floaty feeling in her chest.

Alvin and Isabelle kept right on talking, oblivious to what was happening between Shane and Jessie. Although Jessie's appetite all but disappeared, she finished her sandwich and fries before Rita brought the check. Shane scooped it up and went to the register to pay.

Jessie faked a bright smile at Isabelle and Alvin. "How did you like Rita's?"

"Loved it," Isabelle said. "I can see why you insisted we come here."

Had she insisted? Jessie thought back to the conversations about lunch. She'd suggested it, certainly. And Shane ... he had been worried about starting rumors. And while maybe she had dismissed his concerns, she wasn't sure she *insisted* on eating there.

"Well," Shane said, returning to the table. "I guess you two are on to the second phase of this reunion. I'll have Jessie take me home so you guys can get going."

They said their good-byes and went their separate ways. In the

Jeep, Shane was quiet as he buckled his seatbelt. He stared straight ahead, even though Jessie turned in her seat, making it clear she intended to talk to him.

"What's up?" she asked.

He rubbed his forehead with one hand. "Oh, I don't know," he said. "I don't really want to talk about it."

"Okay," Jessie said. "But clearly something is bothering you."

"Clearly."

She started the Jeep. "You don't want to tell me what it is?"

"Not really."

"Huh. Okay."

They drove the ten minutes back to their neighborhood in unusual silence, and when she parked in her driveway, he wasted no time unbuckling his seatbelt and opening the door. She put a hand on his arm to stop him from getting out, and he jerked his arm away like her touch burned him.

"Shane," she said, her voice coming out more sharply than she intended. "What's going on?"

He paused, and she felt a little start when her gaze met his steely one. "I feel like you should know. But, since you're apparently completely oblivious, I'll tell you. You're so wrapped up in planning this romantic reunion that it's all you can think about. You can't think about my dad, and what will happen if things don't go as perfectly as you imagine, and you can't think about me, and how I'll feel if things don't go as perfectly as you imagine. And, worst of all —" he opened the door and extended his leg, ready to bail — "you're not even interested in *me*."

Speechless, Jessie licked her lips. She expected him to get out of the car then, but he stopped his momentum and said, "And I know how childish that sounds, coming from a grown man. But it is what it is."

With that, he did get out. He didn't quite slam the door, but she definitely felt the Jeep rock when he closed it. Still unable to process a response, she watched in her sideview mirror as he walked across her yard to his dad's house, his hands in his pockets and his shoulders slouched. Stunned didn't even cover what Jessie felt. She couldn't believe Shane felt like she didn't care about his dad's feelings, or his. Obviously she cared about his dad's feelings, she thought as she unbuckled her seatbelt and got out of the car, taking care to shut the door more gently than Shane had a moment before. She shivered as she walked up her front walkway. The air was cold on her legs, even through her jeans. She flinched at the sting of the cold doorknob on her palm as she turned it.

Her movements jerky, a lump forming in her throat, she once again considered Shane's words. Everything she'd done, she'd done for Alvin. She pulled off her coat and hung it on the hall tree. Shane was just being oversensitive, she told herself. He was worried about his dad and was thinking of him as a frail old man with frail feelings.

Maybe she could explain to Shane that Alvin was a living, breathing man with the potential for youthful love. His need for a little more help around the house didn't mean he didn't have other wants and desires, or that he couldn't fulfill those wants and desires.

Jessie sat down on the bench in her entryway and pulled off her boots. Hands on her knees, she nodded. Yes. All she had to do was explain her thoughts to Shane. Surely he would see things the same way she did. They'd planned to ride to dinner together, so she decided she would go over a little early so they could talk this out. Meanwhile, she would bake cookies for the four of them. She could bring them to the restaurant and they could eat them after dinner. She put on some Christmas music and cranked it up so she couldn't help but feel festive. Then she got out her bowls, measuring spoons, and mixer.

Despite her best efforts, thoughts of Shane kept popping into her consciousness. Usually when he was upset with her, she could see a little humor at the corners of his eyes, or the slight upturn of his mouth — just like she had earlier at Rita's. She used a spoon to scoop flour into a measuring cup. But this time? He didn't seem amused at all. There wasn't even a smidgen of his typical smile.

She dug around in her cabinet for the baking powder. Why could she never find that when she needed it? She discovered it behind the canister of salt and measured out a teaspoon.

How could Shane misread her intentions so badly? From the

beginning, she'd said she wanted to give Alvin a chance at love. Puzzled, Jessie measured out the salt while she thought back to everything she'd done since coming up with the reunion idea.

To protect Alvin's feelings, she hadn't even told him she was looking for Isabelle or thinking of contacting her. When she did tell him, she asked him if he wanted to see her. He said he did. She spent so much time planning the visit, trying to make it easy on Alvin. She picked up Isabelle at the airport and planned for Shane to drive Alvin to Rita's, so the four of them could eat together, minimizing the awkwardness that could happen if it was just Alvin and Isabelle at lunch.

She started on the wet ingredients, tossing a stick of butter into a bowl and measuring white and brown sugars on top of it. The longer she beat, the more affronted she became. Who did Shane think he was, misconstruing her intentions? They were best friends. He was supposed to know her better than anyone. (Although, she acknowledged, they had grown apart since he moved away.) Taylor and Rose wouldn't misconstrue her feelings and villainize her. Come to think of it, maybe she should get their opinions on this topic. She mixed the dry ingredients into the wet and shaped the dough into a ball before putting it in the refrigerator to chill. She had an hour before she could roll and cut the cookies.

After setting a timer and grabbing a sparkling water out of the fridge, she plopped down on the couch, opened her drink, and propped her feet up on the coffee table. She put on a recording of her favorite reality TV show — one where a man interviewed three women without seeing them and then chose one of them to date.

Then she opened her text thread with Rose and Taylor and typed: *Help a sister out. I need your opinion.*

Their responses came through right away.

Rose: *Celeste and I are in the middle of a baking extravaganza. I'll text you back when we're done getting messy.*

Taylor: *Sorry, Jess. I'm about to go into a barrel racing lesson. I'll text you back when it's over.*

Jessie felt her body slump. She sighed and pressed play on her TV remote. She let herself get so caught up in the episode that she actually jumped when her alarm went off, reminding her the cookie dough was ready to roll and cut.

She decided to make buffalos, cacti, and snowflakes, to represent Isabelle's hometown, Alvin's hometown, and the Christmas season. The process of rolling out the dough, cutting the cookies and placing them on baking sheets, and then doing it all again, was so meditative, Jessie's thoughts didn't wander from what she was doing.

She'd doubled the recipe but was still surprised when she had all the cookies laid out to cool and they covered most of her countertop. For a moment, she considered giving some to Rose and Celeste — Celeste never turned down a cookie. But then she remembered Rose had said they were baking, so she probably wouldn't appreciate a bunch more cookies.

Shrugging, Jessie carried on, mixing up batches of colored icing. While the cookies cooled she changed into her dinner outfit, and then returned to the kitchen to put the icing to use.

Dinnertime came around quickly, and she barely had time to package up the cookies before she and Shane met. She'd almost forgotten he was annoyed with her. Almost. The thought occurred to her just as she made it to the sidewalk and saw him approaching, his mouth set in a straight line and his expression cool.

What was it he'd said to her earlier, just as he was getting out of the car?

"You're not even interested in *me*."

How was it possible he felt that way?

Jessie looked so darn happy coming out of her house, Shane almost forgot he was mad at her. Almost. Then he saw she was carrying a platter of Christmas cookies, and he remembered. Of course she'd made cookies. She couldn't help but meddle in the reunion between his dad and Isabelle.

He'd spent most of the afternoon trying to do things to take his mind off her ... because he was *irritated*. But during his weights workout, he thought about how her fingers felt when they wrapped around his bicep. During his shower, he thought about their shower together in Buffalo. When he was choosing his outfit for dinner, he put on the sweater she had complimented for the way it showed off his chest. He immediately discarded it and chose a sweater she hadn't seen before. He couldn't get her out of his mind.

And then, there she was, looking beautiful and radiant and carrying a platter of cookies. Why in the world they needed a platter of cookies when they were going out to dinner, he didn't know. He told her as much when they finally stood face to face next to her Jeep. She looked stricken, almost as if he had taken her precious cookies and thrown them on the ground. Guilt crept in.

She found her voice. "You don't have to eat them if you don't want to."

He shrugged. "I don't."

"I just thought it would be fun to bring them for your dad and Isabelle. See? I made buffalos, like Buffalo, Wyoming. And I made cacti, like, for Arizona. And snowflakes. Because it's Christmas time and we might get more snow."

"I get it," he said, noticing his tone bordered on cruel and hating himself for that.

She pressed her lips together and he knew she was trying not to cry. "Should we go?" Her voice actually trembled.

"Fine."

She made what Shane considered a pretty dramatic show of taking her platter to the back of the Jeep, opening the tailgate, and situating the platter so it wouldn't slide around.

While Jessie drove, Shane crossed his arms and leaned his head against the headrest.

"I feel like I should apologize for making the cookies," Jessie said after a few minutes. "But it was a gesture of goodwill."

Shane heard the derision in his laugh. "No apology necessary. You're quite the goodwill ambassador."

Jessie pressed the button to turn on the radio, and Christmas music blared through the speakers, the cheer and good tidings in direct contrast with Shane's mood. He reached up and turned off the music. Out of the corner of his eye, he could see her glare at him.

He shrugged it off. "Frankly, I'm getting tired of Christmas music."

"But you love Christmas music." He heard the desperation in her voice.

She wanted to make things all right before they showed up at dinner. But, he figured, she probably wanted to make things all right only so Alvin and Isabelle didn't sense anything amiss.

"Don't you?" she asked, reminding him he hadn't responded.

He shrugged. "Usually."

He half expected Jessie to say something to acknowledge the fact that she was the cause of his bad mood. But she didn't. She just twisted her hands on the steering wheel and became extra attentive to the road. Come to think of it, she had almost always been pretty oblivious. Or, if she wasn't oblivious, she had a proclivity for wanting to brush her feelings under the rug. The connection struck him.

She had done the same thing with their plant-growing science experiment as she was doing now. Their teacher, Mrs. Wellington, said everyone would work in pairs, and they immediately agreed to be partners. Mrs. Wellington gave them a list of possible science experiments. The following day, each pair would sign up for one of the experiments on the list.

Shane had a doctor appointment and wouldn't be in class, so he and Jessie spent an entire afternoon discussing which projects they wanted to do. Shane wanted to do a social experiment, and the list included one where researchers kept track of how many people returned a wave or smile and broke those people down into groups by age and gender. Jessie wanted to do the plant experiment.

The discussion was heated. In the end, Jessie promised she would try for the social experiment. When he got home from his appointment the next afternoon, he called her to see if she'd succeeded.

"I'm sorry, Shane," she said, her voice sincere. "Mikey Ramirez and Joe Pacheco chose the social experiment before it was my turn. So we ended up with the plant experiment."

Naturally, he believed her. He had no reason to think she'd lie. But when the science fair rolled around and they won first place, a kid came running up to Shane and said, "Congratulations. It's an awesome experiment. Actually, I wish I could have gotten it. I planned on signing up for it, but you know how Jessie is. She made sure to be the first one done with her test that day so she could sign up first. And of course, she picked the coolest experiment."

Shane remembered a searing heat running through his body, ending up at his ears. Later, he'd identify it as rage. Just momentary, but an emotion strong enough to surprise him. He looked over at Jessie, who was explaining their project to some adults, a smug smile on her face. She'd lied to him. Which meant she had disregarded not only his feelings, but also her promise.

By the time he'd finished replaying that scenario in his mind, they'd reached the restaurant and Jessie had presented the cookies to his dad and Isabelle, who—naturally—made a giant deal of them. Shane smiled and nodded along with their exclamations. He figured keeping the peace was more important than this temporary aggravation.

Still, he could tell his dad sensed something was off. He stole a couple of sideways glances at Shane while they all looked over their menus, and inclined his head and lifted one shoulder when Shane ordered a shot of bourbon as if to ask, "What's up?"

As far as Jessie was concerned, nothing was amiss. Elbows on the table, chin in her hands, she listened, rapt, as his dad and Isabelle talked about the gingerbread village.

"I might have to start one of those up in Buffalo," Isabelle said, and Jessie gushed, "That's a *wonderful* idea! It's a big fundraiser every year."

Not for the first time, Shane wondered why such a beautiful woman had to also be so aggravating.

"One gingerbread house was made to look like a giant spaceship," his dad said. He held out his hands to illustrate its size, and Jessie gasped. "Wow! I'll bet that was difficult to make."

As everyone ate and drank and was merry, Shane's frustration grew. How could none of them see anything was wrong? He had enough self awareness to know he risked ruining the evening if he spoke up, so he soldiered on, smiling and laughing in all the appropriate places, commenting on the food, and paying for the dinner like he didn't have a giant ball of lead in his stomach.

Outside in the parking lot, Shane suggested, with great merriment, that they ride home just as they'd driven to the restaurant, with Alvin and Isabelle in one car and him and Jessie in another.

Alvin and Isabelle smiled at each other like a couple of adoring lovebirds, and Jessie looked up at him like they were seeing the most magical moment. It took all of Shane's self control to not roll his eyes. His dad and Isabelle walked off, hand in hand, and he spun on his heel and stalked to Jessie's Jeep.

Once they were both inside, Jessie turned up the heat and the fan and rubbed her hands together. "Well, I'd say that went great, wouldn't you?"

"It did," he said. "I'd call it a smashing success."

Completely wrapped up in what she'd probably call the romance of it all, Jessie didn't even notice his dry tone.

"Want to put on some music?" she asked, adding, "It doesn't have to be Christmas music."

Well, at least she'd heard him on that point. He turned on the stereo and she turned up the volume as she pulled out of the parking lot. He turned it down. She looked at him across the cab, her forehead wrinkled in confusion.

"Everything okay?"

"Not really, no. I turned down the music so we could talk."

"Oh," she said, so casually, Shane wanted to scream.

"You really have no idea."

Jessie stopped at the stop light where they'd turn onto the highway and looked at him again. "No idea about what?"

"Jessie. Throughout our entire friendship, you've been like a steamroller. There have been so many times when we've talked about something and you've asked my opinion and then done whatever you want, anyway, even when it's completely different from what I said I wanted to do."

Her mouth dropped open. The light turned green. She accelerated. "Like what?"

Shane drew in a breath. He *should* feel relieved. She was giving him the chance to air his grievances. Instead, he felt sick. What if, by sharing these things, he lost her? That ball of lead still heavy in his stomach, he swallowed, clenched his teeth, and exhaled. "That time with the science experiment, when I had to leave school early and you were in charge of signing us up. We talked about it ahead of time and you agreed to choose the social experiment. Later, you told me someone else chose that one, but a few days after that, another kid told me you were first in line and had first pick. You chose the plant experiment and then lied about it."

He kept his gaze fixed on the cars in front of them, but he could see the muscles in her jaw clenching as he spoke.

"I did."

The admission was something, but it didn't make Shane feel any better. "Why?"

He turned toward her. She shrugged. "Because I wanted to do the plant experiment. And I didn't think it was that big of a deal to you. And we won the science fair, didn't we?" Her grimace-like attempt at a smile made it obvious she knew she'd messed up.

"We did," Shane said. "But that's not really the point."

"Right."

They were about halfway home, and Shane thought he'd better get everything off his chest before they made it there, because he suspected Jessie would want to get out of this uncomfortable, feelings-laden conversation as soon as possible.

"Then there was that time we did that Christmas angel thing with your parents. Do you remember that? We got to choose a child to shop for. I wanted to choose a boy and you wanted to choose a girl. Which I get. And I probably wouldn't have cared that much. But I went to the bathroom and when I came out, you and your parents were waiting for me, angel in hand ... and you'd selected one with a girl on it."

In the light from the street lamps, Shane could see Jessie press her lips together.

"You told me all the boy angels were gone."

She nodded.

"But they weren't. A while later when we were shopping, I asked if I could run back to the food court and get a lemonade. I looked at the tree and there were plenty of boy angels on there."

"That's true."

"And then there was the time —"

She held up a hand. "I get the picture."

"And you're doing it again with my dad."

"I'm doing it with your dad because the potential payoff is greater than the risk," she said. "All you're concerned with is playing it safe."

"That's not true," he said. "Anyway, how does that apply to the Christmas angel thing?"

She waved him off and he said, "You can use the playing-it-safe idea all you want, but the problem is that you're in the habit of making decisions for me without a second thought."

By then, she'd pulled into her driveway.

"Listen," he said, turning to face her. "I really, really enjoyed our little dating experiment. We definitely had the chance to explore our chemistry, and that's been great."

She opened her mouth and inhaled, about to interrupt him.

"But. We can't be together long-term. I can't have you making decisions for me all the time. I think the success of my business proves that I can make good choices without you. In fact, that's part of why I moved away — so I could separate myself from you, do things on my own. And I think I've done a pretty damn good job."

So many emotions were visible in her expression: surprise, hurt, uncertainty.

"Shane."

He shook his head. "I don't think there's any more to say right now. I'd like to go back to being friends, but I may need a couple of days to reset. My dad would never forgive me if we stopped talking and you stopped coming over."

Before she could say anything else, he got out of the car. He should have felt light and free and unburdened, but he didn't. His body was coiled tight with heavy, negative energy and his throat ached with emotion.

As he walked across her lawn to his dad's house, he listened for her to get out of the car, but she didn't. He hated himself for wondering how long she'd sit there, and how cold she'd get, before she came to her senses and went in the house.

The front door was unlocked and when he opened it, he heard his dad and Isabelle talking and laughing.

"Hey, guys," Alvin called.

"It's just me," Shane said, certain the two of them could hear the sullenness in his voice.

A short silence followed as he walked into the kitchen, where his dad and Isabelle stood at the counter, cocktail glasses and a few bottles in front of them. As soon as his dad saw him, his eyes lit up — maybe a little too much — and he said, "Come on in! We were just making some post-dinner cocktails. Let me get you a glass."

"Oh, that's okay," Shane said, doing his best impression of a happy smile. "I'm beat. I was just going to head to bed."

Isabelle and his dad had been reunited for exactly ten hours and they were already exchanging the kind of look a long-together couple would.

"Everything okay?" his dad said.

Shane shrugged, wanting to avoid a conversation. He would have walked right through the kitchen if Isabelle wasn't there ... or maybe even if she was.

But then she said, "What happened with you and Jessie?"

Caught.

He cleared his throat. "Nothing."

Isabelle leaned against the counter and pinned him with her gaze. In that moment, he could see why his dad had been attracted to her. Her eyes were the most startling shade of green, and he felt like she could see his actual soul. Not only that, but with that stare she compelled him to tell her what had happened.

Laughing a little (a completely unexpected reaction), he said, "We had a bit of a disagreement."

Another look passed between his dad and Isabelle.

"Might I ask what it was about?" she said.

"It's sort of a long story," Shane started.

"Oh, nonsense," Alvin said. "We've got all night. We're making you a drink." He pointed at the barstool across from him. "Sit."

Sighing so long and loud, he made them both laugh, Shane obeyed. He placed all his focus on his dad and Isabelle, watching as they worked together to make the drinks. She put ice in the glasses, and he measured out the ingredients. She stirred and added a sprig of rosemary to each glass.

Once the drinks were ready, Isabelle slid one across the counter so it ended up between Shane's hands. "Cheers," she said, holding up her own glass. "To lifelong friendships."

Shane tried his best to smile while he tapped his glass to theirs. "Cheers," he said.

"Now, spill," Isabelle said.

Figuring the situation couldn't really get any worse, Shane did. He explained that he and Jessie had always been the best of friends, and that only recently they'd decided to experiment with taking things to the next level. Things went swimmingly at first, until he started to feel like she was disregarding his opinion, just as she had numerous times throughout their years-long friendship.

"She doesn't realize I'm capable of making good decisions on my own. I can't be with someone like that. So, I think it's better if we just stay friends."

What he didn't say was that he worried they could never go back to being friends in the same way they had been. And he'd miss the hell out of her, as his girlfriend. Their time together, as short as it had been, was *special*.

"Should we toast to that?" he said. A lump formed in his throat. Mortified that he might actually cry in front of a stranger, Shane took a long gulp of his drink.

"I think this requires a conversation in a more comfortable setting," Isabelle said.

His dad nodded as if he knew just what she meant, and somehow the two of them got Shane to standing, herded him to the living room, and got him to sit.

"When the two of you came to visit," Isabelle said, "you seemed totally smitten with each other."

Miserable, Shane nodded. "We were. But that's because I'd agreed to do things her way."

"And what way was that?" his dad asked.

Shane felt his eyes go round. He couldn't answer that. Not in front of Isabelle.

"I can see what you're thinking," Isabelle said.

Shane wondered if she were some kind of a mind-reading magician.

"You're thinking that you can't disclose what, exactly, you were doing in Buffalo," she said. "But I think your dad and I already have a pretty good idea. Don't we, Alvin?"

She smiled at him and patted his knee. He smiled back and put his hand on hers. Shane's mind, as tired as it was from everything that had transpired in the past week, couldn't quite keep up, but he could swear they were acting like a couple.

"We do," his dad said. "I'm guessing, based on Jessie's romantic notions, that she believed Isabelle and I were in love at one time, and she thought she could help us rekindle that."

Shane's focus snapped to Isabelle. In Buffalo, Jessie had tried to make it sound like she wanted Isabelle and Alvin to reconnect as friends ... but Alvin's take was more accurate.

"That's so sweet," Isabelle said.

Shane couldn't quite read the look she gave Alvin.

"The problem is," he said, "she's like a bull in a china shop. She'll do whatever's necessary to get what she wants. She's been that way since we were kids."

His dad and Isabelle exchanged yet another look.

"I feel like the two of you keep having these unspoken conversations," Shane said. "You know what? It's been a long day. I'm going to go to bed. The two of you can have these conversations out loud once I'm gone."

If he wasn't mistaken, he heard Isabelle's tittering laugh, a girlish giggle, as he made his way to his bedroom. And yes, maybe his lips twitched at that, because it confirmed what he'd said was true. Their silent conversations proved that two of them really did have quite the connection. Maybe Jessie was right about that, but she didn't have to be such a bulldozer.

THE SUN HADN'T YET RISEN when Shane left the house the next morning. He'd thought leaving at this hour would make his mind too fuzzy to function — to think about Jessie. But he'd been wrong, he thought as he took the long, straight road away from Prescott.

His mind conjured up images of their time together, alternating between surreal, passion-filled moments and those when she drove him crazy with her bossiness and wacky ideas.

Each time, he did his best to clear the image from his consciousness and focus on the road. He could see the edge of the sun cresting the horizon, a sliver of flame. If there was one thing he could count on, it was that the sun would continue to rise and set, no matter what happened between him and Jessie. The gentle morning light illuminated the rolling hills and sweeping meadows.

Could they still be friends if they put an end to their romance? Shane didn't think so. Every time they saw each other, his heart would ache for what he couldn't have. The sun was now a disc, hanging suspended just above the land. The sky had lightened, turning a pale pink. Shane cursed himself. Maybe things would be different if he'd actually had the courage to tell her how he felt. Instead, he let her do the very thing he was so mad at her for: he let her take the lead, dictate the terms of their relationship, set the tone.

Shane got to Jump Zone's office before Roman did and just after the coffeemaker finished its auto-brew cycle. He let himself in, inhaling the scent of coffee and fresh paint. The place had served as a haven when Shane first left Prescott, searching for a way to move past his heartbreak. Come to think of it, maybe coming to the office hadn't been the best idea. It brought back that old pain, layering it onto the new.

In the early days of the business, Shane poured every ounce of himself into the books, marketing, and business plan. He spent most of his time with Roman, and all they talked about was skydiving. Planes, schedules, parachute photography, anything and everything to make their business successful.

The whole thing served as a great distraction, but the problem was that Shane knew it was a distraction. Just like now. He was back at his business seeking solace. And while he loved being there, he didn't think it could heal him. He turned on the lights and booted up the computer, unsure of what else to do with himself. If he'd been here the night before, he would have checked the schedule for the day and he could start checking parachutes and getting organized. He heard Roman's car pull up outside and exhaled. The door swung open, and Roman's massive shoulders filled the frame as he came in. His friend glanced around to make sure Shane was alone. "Back again? I hate to say it, man, but this doesn't seem like good news. I take it there's trouble in paradise?"

"I don't know. I mean, there's trouble, but I'm not sure it was ever paradise. I thought it was going to be, but now I'm thinking I was wrong."

Roman came in and stowed his backpack under the counter. Standing next to Shane, he looked at the computer screen. "Did you check the schedule for today?"

Shane shook his head. "I just finished booting up the computer. I figured you probably already have everything ready to go, but I thought I'd look things over, just to kill time 'til you got here."

Roman gave a little shrug. "Actually, that's cool. I left early last night. I had a date."

Thrilled at the prospect of having something other than his failed relationship with Jessie to focus on, Shane jumped at the chance to talk about Roman's date. "Yeah? With whom?"

Roman's eye contact was brief, fleeting. "A girl."

"Oh, yeah?"

Finally, Roman stood up straight and tore his gaze away from the computer screen. "Five jumps today. Want to help me check the equipment?"

They walked over to the wall where the parachutes hung.

"So," Shane said, "is this a new girl?"

"Yeah."

When Roman didn't immediately offer additional details and buried himself in checking a parachute bag, Shane let out a bark of laughter. "You must like this one. I don't think I've ever seen you so tightlipped over a chick."

Shane knew better. He shouldn't have called Roman's date a chick while they stood in such close proximity. Roman's elbow made contact with his rib cage, causing Shane to erupt in a fit of giggles. Holding his hands up in surrender he said, "Sorry. Sorry, man. Couldn't resist."

Smiling at that point, Roman said, "If you must know, her name is Kelly. She also runs her own business. Landscaping."

Shane quirked an eyebrow at that and hung up the bag he'd just checked. "Interesting. What's she like?"

"You know. She has all the same positive qualities I do. Smart. Funny. A hot body."

Shane shook his head. "Nice, bro."

"I invited her on a second date. Tonight."

"Well," Shane said. "Moving fast."

"Nah," Roman said. "I just want to get to know her. I want to be friends, first. You know, when you and your girl — Jessie, right?"

Shane was about to point out that she wasn't his girl when Roman went on. "The two of you have been friends forever, right? It got me thinking, a friendship is a great foundation for a romantic relationship. You already know each other so well. All the quirks that take time to reveal themselves — you know about those. You know what you're getting into. I don't know about you, but I've found relationships go bad when someone's expectations aren't being met. But if you guys already know each other really well, then it seems like you'd know what to expect."

"Right," Shane said. "Or you realize those quirks you knew about our fine when you're just friends, but they might be less manageable in a romantic setting."

"Is that why you're here?"

Shane shrugged. "Pretty much." They'd finished checking the parachutes and Roman gestured for Shane to follow him back to the counter. Roman sat on the stool in front of the computer and Shane sat down across from him.

"Tell me more," Roman said.

As he started talking, Shane felt his shoulders slump. "One of Jessie's *quirks*," he said, using air quotes, "is that she gets an idea in her head and will stop at nothing to see it through. She's done it since we were kids. This time, she wanted to reunite my dad with the woman he had a workplace crush on years ago."

"And did your dad want that?"

"He was open to it, yeah. We drove up to Wyoming to meet this woman, and she decided to come visit."

Eyebrows raised, Roman said, "That's cool. Right?"

Shane shrugged again. "I mean, it is. But she gets here, and Jessie wants to commandeer practically every minute of the visit."

"What's your beef?"

Shane stood, stretched, and started making a lap around the room. "I don't know. I guess I'm just afraid that if my dad gets his hopes up, and this Isabelle woman doesn't feel the same way he does, he's going to wind up hurt."

"Maybe," Roman said. "But at this point, wouldn't that risk exist whether Jessie was commandeering the visit or not?"

Shane stopped walking, scrubbed his head, and started walking again. "I don't know. I guess I feel like she's influencing the dynamic. If we left my dad and Isabelle to their own devices, the relationship could unfold naturally. But with Jessie meddling, her fingers stirring the pot, they might believe they love each other but soon realize they don't."

"So," Roman said, the word coming out long and slow, "kind of how you're feeling about Jessie right now."

That stopped him in his tracks. "Well, when you put it like that."

Roman smiled the smile of someone who'd just received vindication. "Just calling it like I see it." When Shane didn't answer right away Roman said, "I mean, your dad is an adult. Theoretically, I assume Jessie at least had the emotional intelligence to ask him if he wanted this Isabelle woman to come visit?"

Shane nodded. "She did. And he said he was up for it."

Roman shrugged. "Then I feel like the rest is on him and Isabelle. Yes, maybe Jessie's idea of helping feels overbearing to you, but it sounds like she's just trying to be a good hostess. And from what you said, it sounds like she knows your dad pretty well. And cares about him. So I don't see her doing anything to hurt him."

"Not intentionally."

Putting a massive hand on Shane's shoulder, Roman said, "I get it, bro. But I think things will turn out just fine. Your dad's been fine before this reunion, and however things unfold, I'm sure he'll be fine afterwards, too."

"I hope so."

"He will. I assume you didn't come here to shoot the breeze. I think I heard Pete the Pilot pull in. Want to get in a couple of jumps before our clients get here?"

"I sure do."

22

———————

Shane's revelations left Jessie reeling. Twelve hours had passed since he'd unloaded on her, and she'd thought of almost nothing else since then. After they had dinner with Isabelle and Alvin, they'd gone their separate ways. Jessie was relieved Isabelle went to Alvin's house too, so she had alone time to process what he'd said.

Only, she found that she couldn't process his criticism. Her brain was on repeat: "Does not compute."

By the time Isabelle came home well after eleven p.m., Jessie felt so fried she said goodnight and went to bed.

In the morning, Isabelle was up and gone before Jessie even made it to the living room. She left a note on the kitchen counter: *Alvin's taking me to breakfast. Be back soon.*

"Looks like the two of them are fine on their own," she said to the empty house.

And there she sat, in her pajamas at the kitchen counter, drinking her coffee and forcing herself to consider Shane's words.

That's part of why I moved away — so I could separate myself from you, and do things on my own.

I can't have you making decisions for me all the time.

I really, really enjoyed our little experiment.

She didn't know which phrase hurt the most. She twirled her coffee cup on the surface in front of her.

He wanted to separate himself from her? But why? They'd been inseparable ever since he moved to Prescott. He felt like she made decisions for him? Did she do that? Maybe she did. And he'd called their time together — the time she'd cherished and considered wonderful — a *little experiment* ...

Her throat tightened at that thought, and the image of her coffee cup blurred before her. The front door opened and then closed quietly, and Jessie heard Isabelle's soft footsteps coming toward the kitchen. Sniffling, she brushed the tears off her cheeks and turned around with a smile on her face.

"Oh, good morning, honey," Isabelle said as she came into the kitchen. She slowed when she got a good look at Jessie's face, but Jessie noticed she didn't look surprised. "What's the matter?"

"Oh, you know," Jessie said, her voice wobbling. "Just that I messed up everything between Shane and me, and I'm in danger of losing my best friend."

Almost as if she'd expected this conversation, Isabelle nodded, walked across the kitchen, and retrieved a coffee cup. She took her time pouring herself a cup and adding sugar and milk.

"Shane mentioned the two of you talked last night."

Jessie scoffed. "He did most of the talking, actually."

"And?"

On a sigh, Jessie said, "I guess I can see where he's coming from. But I feel a little like he doesn't recognize that everything I do, everything I've ever done, comes from a place of love. Since the moment we met, I felt like it was my job to care for him, to make his life easier, to be there for him. But when I hear him say I'm like a bull in a China shop, I think maybe I've gone overboard. I just don't know how to get back to where we were ... or if we even can."

Kindness shone in Isabelle's eyes. "Alvin mentioned that you took Shane under your wing almost the instant he adopted him."

"That's sweet." *And maybe it's why I've become a steamroller.* Seven-year-old Shane was timid and shy, afraid of disappointing people by making the wrong decisions.

"Tell me about the time you spent *together* together," Isabelle said.

"It was wonderful." Jessie sipped her coffee. "We had the best time. At least, *I* thought we did. You know, we've always had fun together, and when he came back to town this time, it was like *wow*, you know? If I were a cartoon character, my eyes would have popped out of my head. I think he felt it, too. And when we, you know," she said, a blush rushing up her neck and into her cheeks, "it was amazing. Like, better than I've had with anyone else. But then last night, he called it a little experiment and said that while we got to explore our chemistry, that experiment failed, basically."

"Hmm."

Jessie didn't know Isabelle well enough to ask her what "Hmm" meant, so she stared into her coffee and waited.

"Do you think it failed?" Isabelle said, finally.

"Obviously it did," Jessie said, hearing the immaturity in her voice but not caring. "If one of us thinks it did, then it did."

"But how did you feel when you were *together* together? If you hadn't been thinking of it as an experiment …"

"I mean, it was wonderful," Jessie said again.

Isabelle held up a hand. "How did you *feel*?"

Huh.

"Have I stumped you?" Isabelle asked.

Jessie looked at her, shrugged. "I don't love talking about how I feel."

"I'm getting that sense. I used to be a lot like you: all action. I made plans and carried them out and never paused for a moment to think about *feelings*."

Jessie laughed. "Sounds about right."

"You go a million miles an hour, don't you?"

"I do."

"Which explains how you have the time and energy to work full-time and help out Alvin." Isabelle straightened up on her barstool. "Would you be willing to try something for me? A little experiment?" She winked, and Jessie smiled.

"Sure. What is it?"

"Would you be willing to sit here for maybe five minutes, or maybe three, and just explore your feelings about Shane?"

"Just sit here and *think*?"

Isabelle's contagious laugh echoed through the house. "Yes. Pretty much."

Jessie put a hand on her chest, feigning shock. "I don't know if I'm capable of that."

Reaching across the space between them, Isabelle took Jessie's hand and squeezed it. "I felt the same way, once. But learning to slow down and really think things through has changed my life. I'd love for you to try it."

"Okay," Jessie said, taking a deep breath. "I'll try it."

"Close your eyes, if you want," Isabelle said. "I find that reduces the distractions."

Jessie did, and when she realized she was fiddling with the handle of her coffee mug, she clasped her hands together in her lap.

"That's it," Isabelle said. "Now, just *think*."

At first, Jessie found her mind wandering. Should she make more coffee? Would the car wash be crowded that day?

"Your mind is like a pinball machine," Isabelle said.

Jessie could picture her smile. "You can tell?"

"I can tell. Just let all those thoughts fall away and think only of Shane."

Shane. Finally, her muscles relaxed. Memories came flooding back to her. The way he'd looked at her the first time they met, like he worshipped her and feared her, simultaneously. How he'd unconsciously moved toward her so their arms touched when they walked into school together on his first day. How she vowed in that moment to protect him, to help him, to make him feel at ease in his new world. That time she was sick in fifth grade, and he made her chicken noodle soup ... he looked so proud when he hand-delivered it to her bedroom on a tray.

During the long summer days between sixth and seventh grade, the two of them spent every spare moment together. They watched four entire seasons of a kids' baking show and whiled away many afternoons attempting to replicate the creations they saw.

When she beat her own high-jump record junior year, it was Shane she looked for in the stands, and Shane who gave her a thumbs up and a big grin because he knew how much it meant to her. Every time she liked a new boy, she sought Shane's approval. And she never broke their standing Friday-afternoon visits to Scoops — except for a couple of months when she was dating some boy whose name she couldn't even remember now. She cringed, remembering the way Shane looked the first time she told him, "Maybe we can go tomorrow?"

Even throughout college, his presence was a constant. They met in the quad every Tuesday to read between classes and went home together most weekends. When they graduated, they celebrated together.

Then he left town, and Jessie floundered. Even then, she didn't realize she'd taken him for granted. She simply noticed and hated his absence.

Shane was the first person she thought of when she woke up each day. She'd reach for her phone to text him about his plans, and then remember he wasn't next door anymore. When she did text him to check in, his responses were short and final ... like he didn't want to talk.

By then, she'd already made friends with Rose and Taylor and she clung to their trio like lifeline. Slowly, over the months, she stopped thinking of Shane every time she saw the Scoops sign, every morning when she woke up, and every time she looked at the porch swing in front of his house. She noticed that his visits home coincided with her trips away, but chalked it up to bad timing.

She craved information about Shane, and listened intently to every story Alvin told and every one of Shane's phone calls home if she happened to be there.

And then he came home ... and for more than a week, he stayed.

Seeing him — the new him — at Rita's Diner threw Jessie for a loop. Her mouth actually watered as she remembered getting that first look at the muscled-up version of this man she'd known most of her life. And, okay, because she didn't love thinking about or talking about or even really considering her feelings, she jumped at the chance to explore her new attraction for him, feelings be damned.

That week and a half they spent *together* together — it was wonderful. They fit so well. They had so much fun. And the sex? Off the charts.

She hadn't even realized she'd fallen in love with him.

Fallen in love?

Yes. She felt herself nodding. Fallen in love. She was in love with Shane West.

"I'm in love with Shane West."

Her eyelids fluttered open and she was almost surprised to see Isabelle there, beaming at her like she'd just solved a tough math problem. "Yes, you are."

"Wait," Jessie said. "Why are you saying that?"

"It's so obvious, isn't it?" Isabelle said.

"Is it?" Was it?

"When the two of you came to Buffalo, I could see it, clear as day," Isabelle said. She stood up and went to the coffeemaker. Finding the pot empty, she rinsed it and set to work making more.

Jessie sat, mute, on her stool. "You could?"

Pausing to look over her shoulder at Jessie, Isabelle said, "Of course. And do you know what else I could see?"

"No, what?"

Her back to Jessie again, she said, "I could see that you didn't even realize you were in love with him. But the way you two move together, the way you watch each other, the way you finish each other's sentences — yes, I know that's cliché, but it's true. You were oblivious, but Shane? He knew. He's been guarding his heart because he's afraid your feelings aren't as strong as his, or that they'll change."

"You got all that from a couple of hours with us?"

Isabelle turned around and shrugged. "It's a gift." After a beat she asked, "Have you ever considered that while Shane may have benefitted from you taking him under your wing as a child, what he needs from you now is different?"

"Only just now."

Isabelle nodded.

"This is a lot to take in."

After pressing the button to start the coffee brewing, Isabelle returned to her stool and smiled. "It is. But more importantly, what are you going to do about it?"

Jessie's heart thudded in her ribcage. "What am I going to do about it?"

"Right," Isabelle said.

"Nothing."

"Nothing?"

"There's nothing I can do," Jessie said. "Shane made it perfectly clear that my bull-in-a-china-shop mentality is what caused the failure of our little experiment."

"Did he?"

Jessie sighed. "He did."

"Well, I'll tell you what. Not once in my lifetime have I let a man determine my fate. And you shouldn't, either. If you're in love with him, then I'd encourage you not to take 'no' for an answer. Which," Isabelle added, her lips quirking, "it sounds like you do anyway."

But this was different. Wasn't it? Shane had made it very clear that he didn't want her to bulldoze his feelings anymore, and his feelings were that their experiment failed. If she tried to convince him they were meant to be together, wouldn't she be doing the very thing he hated.

"I'm afraid I may have wrecked things permanently," Jessie told Isabelle. "I'm going to have to think about this."

"Fair enough," Isabelle said. "I'm going to have another cup of coffee. And then let's find something to do in town. Alvin said he had an errand to run, but he'd catch up with me later this afternoon."

While she showered, Jessie tried to keep her mind blank. Like meditating. Only, she couldn't stop thinking about life without Shane. It was true that they'd drifted apart over the past several years, she thought as she poured shampoo into her palm and then rubbed it into her scalp. But he'd always been there. Since they were seven years old, he was a constant in her life. Her eyes prickled. She rinsed out the shampoo, put in conditioner, and picked up the soap. They might not talk every day, but he was always the first person she texted when something exciting happened. How many times had she sent him a picture of something funny or strange she encountered during an otherwise mundane day? How many times had he sent her something? They were at the front of each other's minds, constantly.

What would life be like if she couldn't reach out, just for fun?

The realizations hit her fast and hard. She could almost physically feel their impact as she rinsed the conditioner from her hair and the soap from her body.

When they'd made love, she'd never considered things would change.

She didn't even consider that they'd go back to being friends.

And she considered *even less* that they might come out of the whole thing not being friends at all.

But ... what if?

Losing Shane forever was a real possibility.

The shower floor tilted under Jessie's feet. Her head spun. Bracing herself against the wall with one hand, she used her other hand to turn off the shower and grab her towel. She pressed the soft cotton to her chest, which rose and fell dramatically with her breaths.

A knock sounded at the door.

"Jessie? Everything okay?"

She sucked in oxygen and responded (in her best impression of a calm voice), "Everything's fine."

"All right. Just checking because you've been in there a while."

How long?

When she finally emerged, Isabelle looked her over as if she was checking her for wounds. "While you were gone," she said, "I got the notion to get pedicures. I haven't had one in forever. What do you say?"

With that decided, Jessie invited Taylor, Rose, and Celeste to join them. The hot water felt heavenly on Jessie's feet, and she could have fallen asleep in the heated massage chair if it weren't for Taylor's memory.

"Hey, Jess, what did you want advice about the other night?" Her eyes were closed, her head back against the headrest.

"Oh, nothing," Jessie said. "After I texted you both, I realized it wasn't as big of a deal as I thought."

Celeste, never one to miss a tell, pointed at Jessie. "You're lying, Aunt Jessie. You always do this weird thing with your mouth when you're not telling the truth."

Isabelle's laugh rang through the nail salon as Jessie's face went a million degrees hotter and as many shades redder.

"So," Rose said, "it's a big deal. I'm sorry neither of us could text right then — and apparently I completely forgot to get back to you."

Jessie didn't bother trying to stick with her lie. Instead, she told them everything that had happened with Shane, including what he'd said about her being a bulldozing bull in a china shop, emotionally.

"Do you guys think that's true? I mean, can you see where he's coming from?"

A nail technician came to sit at Jessie's feet, and the conversation paused while he scrubbed. Her body relaxed, and she almost forgot the question she'd asked.

"I think it's true," Celeste said.

Jessie's eyelids flew open. "You do?"

Again, Isabelle laughed out loud. "This girl tells it like it is."

Rose rolled her eyes. "Sometimes it's better not to," she said to Celeste. Then she turned to Jessie and said, "You do bulldoze. And when it comes to Shane … you've always been the leader in that relationship."

"Is 'leader' synonymous with 'bossy britches'?" Jessie wanted to know.

Rose looked at Taylor who said, "Maybe?"

"That's not necessarily a bad thing," Isabelle said.

"But the dynamic shifted," Rose said, sighing into the pleasure of the woman massaging her feet. "I mean, especially with the romantic shenanigans at the wedding, maybe he was thinking longer-term ... he was imagining the two of them being *together* together, like, indefinitely."

"No," Jessie said. "There's no way. Shane doesn't think of me like that."

"Doesn't he?" Isabelle said.

Crickets.

The technicians continued to massage and scrub and rinse while Jessie considered.

"He does," Celeste finally said, her voice breathy with the romance of it all. "I saw him at the wedding, Aunt Jessie. You know how I love watching those princess movies, where the couples fall in love and get married?"

Jessie repressed a groan. "Yes, I know how you love watching those movies."

"Well, whenever I watch those movies, I think about weddings, too. I mean, I know I'm only five, almost six, but I still think about stuff like flowers. Like, I love the flowers in that movie about Princess Jasmine, but not the ones in the movie about Princess Lucy." Her tone was so matter of fact, Jessie wondered if she was five, almost six, or five, almost twenty. "You know how I was the flower girl at Auntie Tay's wedding, right?"

"Right," Jessie said, looking over to see Rose trying not to smile.

"Well, I could see Shane's face the whole time. He was looking right at you. And he was definitely thinking about weddings."

23

———————

Business done for the day, Roman stretched his arms above his head and rubbed his six-pack. "I think I'm gonna hit the gym. You heading home to face the trouble in non-paradise?"

"I don't want to go home."

Roman laughed. "You sound like a pouty little kid."

"Maybe I am. Still, I'll join you for some gym time."

Roman shrugged. "Suit yourself. I'm just going to show you up. I've been lifting hard while you've been gone."

"Always gotta make it a competition."

"That's right." Roman punched him in the shoulder.

Fifteen minutes later, they were in the gym's weight room, the clank of metal on metal a balm to Shane's nerves. He did a particularly difficult set of bicep curls and felt the sweat start popping out of his pores. After a break, he did a set of squats that had his quads and glutes burning.

Roman, grunting his way through a set of overhead presses, said, "Burns so good, right?"

"Right," Shane said. He grabbed a towel and wiped the sweat from his face and chest.

Roman came over to stand next to him, twisting the cap off his water bottle. "So, did you ever tell Jessie how you feel?"

"Nope."

That earned him another punch on the arm.

"Shit, man." Shane rubbed his shoulder. "I'm walking out of here with bruises."

"You deserve it, bro. You've got to tell her. If you don't, you're an idiot. You're going to have more than bruises. You're going to have a broken heart."

"That was poetic, dude."

Roman punched his other arm. "I know. But I'm serious. If you don't tell Jessie you've been in love with her for as long as you can remember, she might never know."

Shane returned to the weight rack to do another set of bicep curls. He hissed through his teeth on the first couple, but when Roman gave him a raised eyebrow, he laughed and said, "Even if she knows, that's not going to change anything. She's proven over the past several days that my feelings don't matter."

A long-suffering sigh came out of Roman's mouth as he stepped over the weight bench to sit down for his chest press. "I don't believe that's the case. Sounds to me like she's used to doing things a certain way when the two of you were friends. Maybe you wouldn't have minded if you hadn't switched things up ... but you did switch things up, and nobody wants their old lady bossing them around."

He had a point, and Shane told him so as he lowered and raised the weights. "But that doesn't make me want to run home and talk to her."

Roman finished his chest press reps and sat up. "Okay, bro. But imagine where you'll be in five years. Even if you're right here, running a thriving business, and we're making bank and showing people the best time of their lives. Tell me you won't be thinking about Jessie and what could have been, if only you'd had the balls to speak up."

"First it's poetry, and now it's deep shit," Shane said, rubbing his forehead.

Roman stood up, straddling the bench. He swung his arms back to stretch his chest muscles, and then stepped over the bench and grabbed the bar for another round of overhead presses. "If I don't say it to you, who's going to?"

"I guess I am."

Shane's head whipped around at the sound of his dad's voice. "What are you doing here?"

"That's no way to greet your old man," Alvin said, his eyes twinkling through the reprimand.

Properly chastised, Shane said, "You're right. Sorry. I just wasn't expecting you. Is everything okay?"

"Everything's great," Alvin said. "In fact, it's better than great. Isabelle and I had a lovely breakfast this morning, and we have plans for a nice hike this afternoon. But I wanted to talk some sense into you, first. Buy you a beer?"

"You can't buy me a beer and then drive all the way back to Prescott."

Alvin gave him what he could describe only as a withering glare. "Son, I've been drinking beer since before you were a twinkle in anybody's eye. I can drink a beer, have a conversation, and drive my own old ass home."

A beat of silence followed, and Roman broke it with a loud guffaw. "Guess he told you. Workout's over, good buddy."

He clapped Shane on the shoulder, making him wince, again. "I hear they're having a two-for-one special over at Traffic Control."

Alvin grinned and Shane told him, "That doesn't mean you get two beers."

Traffic Control was bustling — that two-for-one special really brought people in. Shane found them a corner table while Alvin went to the bar. He shouldn't have been surprised when Alvin turned around with four beers — one in each hand and one tucked under each arm.

"How'd you know I'd be at the gym?" he asked after watching his dad carefully set the beers down.

"Oh, I don't know." Alvin took a sip of his beer, and then another. "You looked like hell when you came in last night. Weren't there when I woke up this morning. I figured you'd either gone to Jessie's or gone to work. Since, strangely, jumping out of planes seems to have a calming effect on you."

Shane shrugged, sipped his beer.

"I went to Jump Zone, but when I didn't see your truck, I figured if you'd worn out skydiving, you were probably punishing yourself in the gym, lifting heavy things."

"You know me well."

"Just about as well as anybody could know a guy."

"I'm afraid you've wasted your time coming here," Shane told him.

Alvin didn't speak for a moment. His attention was on the bar, and Shane watched as the bartender tossed a spinning glass into the air, catching it and setting it down before twirling a bottle of liquor and pouring some into the glass.

"Why do you think I'm here, son?" his dad asked, his gaze piercing.

"I don't know. I figured you probably wanted to convince me to come home now, talk to Jessie, make things right. Tell her about my feelings."

"Nah," Alvin said. "I just wanted to thank you for helping me reconnect with Isabelle."

"You came all the way over here to thank me?" Shane asked. He could feel his eyebrows make their way toward his hairline.

"So what if I did?" Alvin took another gulp of his beer, the movements exaggerated.

"I don't believe you."

"Fine by me."

A group of guys came in and surrounded the pool table. One of them racked up the balls and the rest of them selected cues from the bracket on the wall.

"Anyway," Alvin said after they watched the first guy break, sending a couple of stripes into the corner pockets. "Why don't you come on home?"

"Aha!" Shane pointed at his dad, lifting his beer and almost sloshing it out of the bottle. "I knew it! You're here to try to get me to talk to Jessie."

"Be right back. I've got to go to the bathroom. This old bladder doesn't hold up like it used to."

"Thanks for letting me know."

While his dad was gone, Shane watched the pool game. The guy who'd gotten the stripes in on the break had obviously had his one lucky shot. Solids were falling left and right, while stripes rolled around the table, bouncing off the bumpers.

"Well, son," his dad said, sliding back onto his stool, "if you don't want to go home, I think I'll hang out for a while. Why don't we get some snacks? It's been forever since I had good, greasy bar food." He checked his watch. "Plus, the Cardinals are playing in a little while. I'm sure they'll put on the game."

"All right," Shane said. "I can't think of a time we've ever hung out in a bar and watched football while eating greasy bar food. You're on."

24

———

After Celeste shared her wedding observation with the women, Jessie fell into a trance while her technician massaged and oiled and scrubbed and filed. She thought of Shane and the wedding and all the shenanigans afterward. When she finished thinking about those things, she thought about their relationship before their *relationship*. She'd chosen a fluorescent pink nail polish, and while the tech painted it on, she realized: every step of the way, Shane had proven he cared for her. She'd always thought it was because they were friends, but now, in hindsight, she could see that he loved her. He'd loved her for years.

How could she have been so stupid?

Whenever she'd talk to him about guys she had crushes on or guys she was dating, he'd change the subject. She'd always thought it was because he was trying to cheer her up, but could those conversations have hurt him all along? He was always there for her. When she got her tonsils out at twenty, he showed up with a box of popsicles and watched movies with her until she felt better — even though his guy friends invited him to a Cardinals game. A Cardinals game! Tickets to those games were like gold. She'd been so oblivious, she hadn't realized at the time what a big deal that was. When he moved away and decreased the frequency of their contact, she

figured it was just because he was so busy with his new business. But
—

"Ma'am?" The technician was patting the side of her knee. "Ma'am? Are you all right? We're all done here."

"Oh! Right!" Jessie forced herself out of her daze. "Sorry about that. I was just thinking about ..."

"It's fine, it's fine," the technician said. "It happens more often than you might think. Let me help you up."

Pedicures done, Jessie and her friends gathered to say their goodbyes before going their separate ways.

"Where did you go?" Taylor asked.

"What do you mean?" Jessie tried to play dumb even though she knew it wouldn't work.

"You disappeared," Rose said. "Your eyes glazed over and you missed out on us telling Isabelle all about Sugar Pine Barn."

Wow. She really had been in a trance.

"I feel like there's something you're not telling us," Rose said.

Eyes sparkling with mischief, Isabelle said, "She realized right before this that she's in love with Shane. Only, she doesn't know what she's going to do about it."

Jessie's jaw dropped. "Isabelle!"

"Just saying it like it is."

Celeste started bouncing, giggling like a little maniac, singing "Aunt Jessie's in love with Shane" on repeat.

"Is this true?" Taylor asked. "Not to say I doubt Isabelle's sincerity. But I need to hear the words from your lips!"

"Same," Rose said, placing a hand on Celeste's head in an unsuccessful attempt to calm her down (and, Jessie suspected, get her to stop singing, "Aunt Jessie's in love with Shane").

Not for the first time that day, Jessie's heart thundered. Why was she so nervous? These girls were her best friends. They'd understand. Wouldn't they? Or would they? Maybe they'd think she was an idiot for not seeing Shane's true feelings this whole time. Or maybe they'd think this whole thing was a terrible idea.

"Whooaaa," Taylor said, and Rose giggled. "Your wheels are turning a million miles an hour."

"It's true," she blurted out. "I love him."

Taylor's eyes widened, and Rose gasped. "You do?" they both said.

Isabelle's smiled. "She does."

"And I think, in some misguided way, I always felt like I'd taken him under my wing and had to take care of him and protect him. Which was fine when we were seven, eight, ten, but now that we're adults, he doesn't need that. He just needs me to love him."

Both of her friends — and Isabelle — nodded along with her words.

"So, what are you going to do about it?" Taylor asked.

Jessie threw up her hands. "I don't know." Her voice may have come out in a wail, but she didn't care. "I've already ruined every-thing. There's no point in saying anything to him now. He's already made it perfectly clear he's no longer interested in our *little experi-ment*." The last two words tasted bitter.

"Can't you just talk to him?" Celeste asked. She had a grip on Rose's hand, and was hanging from it, head tilted up to look at Jessie, knees almost on the ground.

"If only it were that simple," Jessie said.

"Isn't it?" Rose said.

"I just can't," Jessie said. She hooked her arm through Isabelle's and added, "Thanks for coming, you guys. We've got to go. Isabelle and Alvin have plans."

With that, the two of them walked out of the nail salon. Jessie almost laughed as she pictured her friends standing there looking at each other, wondering what to do. Shivering through the parking lot, Jessie and Isabelle didn't speak until they reached the Jeep.

"Should I take you back to Alvin's? What time were you supposed to meet up?"

Isabelle broke eye contact, suddenly becoming very interested in the cloudy sky. "Well, I hate to ask," she said, facing the window, "but Alvin's at a sports bar and he asked me to meet him there. I guess there's a football game on. Would you mind?"

"No problem at all," Jessie said. "I know how much Alvin loves his football."

"The thing is," Isabelle said, "he told me he's at ... um, let's see..." she pulled her phone out of her purse and tapped on the text icon. "He says he's at Traffic Control? In Cottonwood?"

Jessie wondered why Alvin was in Cottonwood when Shane was in Prescott, but she figured maybe he had something special planned for Isabelle. So she shrugged, said, "Okay," and started the hour-long drive.

"I hope you didn't have plans for this afternoon," Isabelle said as they came through town.

Jessie sighed. "I don't. I mean, maybe some nice self-pity at home in front of the TV. But driving you to Cottonwood is probably healthier than gorging on baked goods and wine."

Isabelle made a dismissive gesture. "Oh, honey. You can indulge in self pity after you drop me off. Whoever said anything was wrong with one afternoon gorging on sweets and wine was out of his mind. And I just know it was a man."

"If I haven't made it clear enough already, honey," Isabelle said once her laughter died down, "I so appreciate you and Shane coming to Wyoming to meet me, and to help me reconnect with Alvin. I don't know what will come of it, but it's been so lovely spending time with him again."

Another round of tears flooded Jessie's eyes, and she swiped at them with one hand. "You're welcome. I knew it was a good idea."

25

As much as Shane enjoyed hanging out with his dad in a bar with beers and snacks and the Cardinals game on, he found he didn't feel quite as festive as he should. The first quarter was in full swing, and Alvin pushed the plate of nachos across the table so Shane could get better access. Shane picked up a wedge of chips smothered in beans and cheese, the crumbled meat still sizzling on top, and shoved it into his mouth.

Alvin smirked at Shane's giant mouthful and pushed his beer a little closer to his hand. "You're gonna need a swig of this to wash down that humongous bite."

Smiling despite his overstuffed mouth, Shane nodded and took a swig.

"Are you okay, son?"

"Of course," Shane said. "Aren't I always?"

Shaking his head, Alvin said, "Not always, no. And I don't expect you to be. I'm real sorry things didn't go well with Jessie."

Ah. So his dad was here to babysit him, he thought. Here to sit with him while he pouted. Which was really sweet. Shane felt the unexpected tightening of his throat. Even if he didn't have Jessie, he'd always have his dad. And hadn't his dad been there for him since before he even adopted him?

Yes, whispered a small, mean voice at the back of his mind. *He has ... and Jessie's been there almost as long.*

"Thanks, Dad."

Alvin's eyes softened. He speared a boneless wing with a fork and offered it to Shane.

He took the fork and bit off half the wing, chewing and swallowing to give himself a little time. His voice cracked when he said, "I just don't think I can bear to see her, Dad. Maybe ever. I thought I could handle it if we dated, or slept together, or whatever, and went back to being friends. But I don't think I can."

"I can understand that."

He used his teeth to pull the other half of the boneless wing off the fork tines.

"The worst part is that I got a taste of what things could be like when we were *together* together," Shane said. He hated that he sounded like a whiny baby, and was grateful for all the noise in the bar. Cheers erupted as the Cardinals made a touchdown. "We were great, Dad. We had so much fun. We had real conversations. And — well, never mind. But I think you get the picture."

His dad's eyes twinkled. "I was a young man too once, you know."

To save himself from having to respond, Shane took another gulp of beer. "I know. I didn't mean to take things quite that far during this conversation, though. Anyway. Just saying, I could have done that forever. With her."

The bar's door opened then, and a shaft of blinding light came through, making Shane wince. For a moment, he thought he recognized the silhouette there ... but certainly he was kidding himself. Hadn't someone written a song about seeing his ex-lover everywhere? That's what would happen to Shane. For years, probably. For the rest of his life, maybe. It already was.

But then his dad's face lit up and he lifted an arm in greeting. How did she find them here? He'd come back to Cottonwood believing he and Jessie wouldn't cross paths until he was ready. As the door shut, his eyes readjusted to the dim light. He saw Jessie, looking stricken and surprised, her body freezing as she saw him. Behind her, Isabelle, her lips in an uncertain smile as her eyes focused in on his. That's when he realized: his dad and Isabelle had set them up.

His dad, wiley old guy that he was, motioned for the two women to come over. "Plenty of room, plenty of room," he was saying, pretending he was surprised to see them there.

Shane started to get up so he could move to the stool closest to the wall. That's what he'd do under normal circumstances. But then, midway to standing, he realized these weren't normal circumstances and he had to stop going out of his way to be a prince to Jessie's princess. She didn't want a prince, anyway, he thought, his blood running hot. She wanted a floor mat.

Even though she offered him an apologetic smile before she squeezed behind him to get to the vacant stool, all he felt was resentment that she had let Isabelle dupe her into driving all the way into Cottonwood.

She surprised him by asking, smile still frozen in place, molars stuck together, "What are we doing here, Isabelle?"

"You know, I think I'd like a beer," Isabelle said.

Jessie actually groaned, and Shane, realizing she was as much of a victim in this as she was, had to hold in his laughter.

"I'll get it," Shane said. "What would you like?"

"I'll take an IPA," she said, winking at Shane.

He turned to Jessie, feeling his grim expression loosening, just a little. "Want anything?"

"Oh. Um. Sure. Whatever you're having. Thanks."

When he returned from the bar, beers in his hands, he slid the IPA to Isabelle and the porter to Jessie. She looked from her frosty glass to his half-empty bottle, and then at him, understanding showing in her face. He was drinking a beer she hated, and even though she said she'd have what he was having, he'd chosen one she loved.

Her "Thank you" was barely audible.

Isabelle took a drink of her beer and dabbed at her upper lip with a napkin. "Now that we have beverages, I think it's time we have a little chat."

Shane was relieved to see fear and uncertainty in Jessie's eyes, mirroring his own, when they looked at each other. She had no idea what was about to happen.

"Do you want to start, Alvin, or should I?" Isabelle asked.

Shane didn't know how she always managed to look bemused, but she did. If he wasn't the object of her laser focus at the moment, he'd find her expression charming.

His dad cleared his throat. "You can start."

His tone was so deferential, Shane imagined he would have bowed to her if they weren't seated. Isabelle beamed back at him. Shane braced himself. He had a pretty good idea of what the little chat was going to be about, and he wasn't sure he wanted to have it.

Isabelle looked at him then, for so long he started to squirm on his stool. She did the same to Jessie. Probably this intimidation tactic was designed to make them feel aligned — like they were under scrutiny, together.

He felt Jessie glance at him, saw the movement out of the corner of his eye, but didn't return the glance. He stared straight ahead, feigning calm even though his body had started to tremor.

"You know? I think you should start, Al."

His dad laughed out loud as if that was the funniest thing he'd heard in ages. He cleared his throat. "Son. Just like you wouldn't stand by and let me live the rest of my life without reuniting with Isabelle, I won't stand by and let you live the rest of yours without telling Jessie how you feel. How you've always felt."

Although the sounds of the football game on TV, balls hitting each other on the pool table, and people cheering, talking, and laughing should have drowned out the sound of Shane swallowing to ease the tension in his throat, he could have sworn everyone at the table heard it.

"Go ahead," Isabelle said, nodding toward Jessie as if Shane didn't know where to direct his message.

This can't be happening. A strangled noise came out of his mouth. He cursed himself and his lost ability to speak. Under any other circumstances, Jessie would turn toward him, smiling, and say something like, "Yes, tell me, Shane. Tell me how you've always felt."

She loved putting him on the spot. But something was different at the moment. She remained still, staring at the beer she held between her hands. Was she as uncomfortable as he was?

A bolt of heat, lava, rose up in Shane's torso. Turning toward his dad, he growled, "I can't believe you're doing this."

His dad's eyes widened — Shane rarely spoke like that to anyone, least of all his dad. But then he pulled himself together (Shane could tell by the straightening of his spine and the adjustment of his shoulders) and said, "You're right. We'll give you some privacy. But I won't stand by any longer and watch you hurt, Shane. You deserve to tell Jessie how you feel, and she deserves to know."

He dad grabbed his beer, then Isabelle's, and she followed him across the bar to a booth in the opposite corner. They sat down, and then, apparently having had a revelation, his dad was back, taking the platter of nachos.

When Shane finally dared to look at Jessie, she was smiling. "Your dad is really full of it this evening."

"He is."

"I know this is *so* awkward," she said. "But what is he talking about?"

Shane sighed, yet again, and put his head in his hands. "I can't believe they schemed this up."

"Oh, come on. We schemed their reunion."

"Yeah, but that was all you."

He recognized his own stall tactics, and wanting this moment to be over, he forged ahead. Sitting up straight, looking Jessie right in the beautiful eyes, he said, "I'm in love with you, Jess."

Her mouth formed an *O* and she snapped it shut. She inhaled, preparing to speak, but he held up a finger to stop her.

"Just let me finish. This is a long time coming."

She nodded.

"I'm in love with you. I've been in love with you for fifteen years, since that day you came out of your house with that new hairstyle. When we're together, I feel like everything is right with the world, like we can conquer everything, like nothing can stop us. And when we're apart, I feel like I'm missing an actual body part. Whenever I get a text, I wonder if it's you, and what funny thing you've sent me this time. Whenever I see a Jeep, I think of you. Whenever I'm deciding what to eat for dinner, I consider what you'd want to eat. Since I moved to Prescott at seven years old, you've been a huge part of my life. The only thing that changed is that I realized I love you. Not like a friend loves another friend, but like a man loves a woman."

He paused, and Jessie breathed, "Wow." The noise swirled around them, but silence filled the space at their table. "Why didn't you tell me?"

His laugh carried derision, and all the pain of the past decade and a half. "Oh, I don't know. It seemed like you always had your eye on someone else, I guess. And I was your trusty confidant, the victim of countless acts of torture, having to hear about every boy you liked, what kind of kisser you thought he'd be, what kind of kisser he *was*. It was obvious you didn't see me like that — like a prospective romantic partner. You never talked to me about what kind of kisser I'd be."

"How could I have known?" her voice rose in pitch and intensity. "I'm not a mind reader."

He reached out and covered her hand with his. "I'm not blaming you. At all. If anyone's to blame, it's *me*. For not saying anything before this."

Her body relaxed and she left her hand under his.

"When you announced that you suspected Mitch Williams was going to propose," he said, "I was devastated."

"That's why you moved away."

"No," Shane said, "not *just* that. I decided that night I was going to wait for him to leave your house and I was going to tell you how I felt. Before you made the mistake of marrying that good-for-nothing — sorry."

"No," Jessie said. "Carry on. He did end up being a good-for-nothing scoundrel."

Despite the tension in his shoulders and neck, Shane felt himself smile. "I would have called him worse than that."

"But when I got there, the two of you were saying goodbye. He wasn't even supposed to be there." All that old anger, that long-held hurt, exploded in his body, a hot, electric shock. "You were supposed to be home alone that night. And then I saw you, wrapped in his arms. He'd obviously surprised you — back then, you wouldn't be caught dead in that onesie pajama with the flying pigs on it."

Jessie snorted, but her eyes shone with pity. Which Shane hated.

"Anyway. I'd pined after you for so long, Jess. My dad finally convinced me to talk to you. Said I'd regret it if I didn't. I wrote a *script*. Practiced it alone in my bedroom, and then in front of my dad. I memorized it. I gave myself the biggest pep talk. I was certain that if I just told you how I felt, you'd change your mind. You'd see me differently, and you'd want to be with me. But I didn't get the chance."

Jessie didn't speak, but her expression said enough.

"Of course, when I saw you and Mitch kissing so passionately, I took it as a sign from the universe. I tucked tail and ran. All I could think to do was separate myself from you. As certain as I once was that I could convince you to love me, I was equally certain you didn't notice that I talked to you way less than I had before."

"I noticed," she whispered.

"And, some time after I moved away, I heard the two of you broke things off. I should have been sad for you, Jess, but in my childish, vindictive way, I was happy for *me*. I knew he was a good-for-nothing scoundrel all along and the thought of you being with him forever broke me."

Jessie sniffled and reached for his hand, but he wasn't ready to receive comfort from her just yet. He tipped back his beer bottle, found it empty, and set it back down.

"Like I said, I figured the universe was trying to tell me you would never love me. I didn't figure I'd ever have a chance with you — well, not in the way I wanted. And then, that night at Rita's, something had changed. You looked at me differently."

She nodded. "'Cause you were *hot* all of a sudden."

That made him laugh. "Thanks. I probably had some twisted sense of confidence, too, since I was no longer pining after you."

"Were you really pining, all that time?"

"I was."

She sighed.

"Anyway," he said. "Even though the time we spent together was better than I could have imagined, I felt myself holding back a little. I think because I couldn't believe my good fortune, couldn't believe it would last. And we were talking about it like it was an experiment ... not like it was a real relationship — the kind I always wanted. So when I felt like you were disregarding my feelings, it sucked."

"Shane," Jessie said. "I'm so sorry."

He shook his head. "You don't have to apologize. You didn't know how I felt. And I never told you. So that's on me."

Like always when she was nervous, Jessie spun her beer bottle on the table in front of her. "I have another apology and I'll get to it in a minute. But the week and a half we spent doing romantic shenanigans? It was hands-down the best week and a half of my life."

"You don't have to say that."

She held up a hand. "I *do* have to say it. You're right. I've always thought of you as a friend. My best friend. My confidant. I could share anything with you and I wanted to share everything with you. But I also took you for granted. I assumed you'd always be there. And I'm sorry for that."

"Thank you," he said.

"I did notice when you stopped talking to me. And it hurt. I dealt with it by throwing myself into new friendships and my job ... and never slowed down to think about what I might have done to cause that."

He nodded, something inside his chest releasing as she spoke.

"You're also right that when you came into town earlier this month, I suddenly saw you differently." She reached out and caressed his bicep. "I can't even say what changed things. Maybe it was the confidence, like you said. You were standing there in Rita's, the angels were singing, and the image of you as a sex god hit me out of nowhere."

His voice cracked when he said, "I could see that. And you don't know how good it felt."

"Here's where my second apology comes in," she said. "When we decided to date, experimentally, the thought that I might hurt you never crossed my mind. Maybe because you'd never hurt me before. Even if I didn't know how you'd felt all those years, I should have taken more care with your heart. I was excited, caught up in that mind-blowing chemistry. Taking our friendship for granted. Again. And, as usual, I was moving too fast. I jumped in, headfirst."

"Which was great," Shane said.

Another sad smile. "I was having so much fun. I totally did the bulldozer thing. And I hurt you, again. But I hurt myself, too. When you said you thought our experiment failed — and I don't blame you — it tore my world apart."

When he quirked an eyebrow at her, she laughed. "Okay, not at first. At first I thought you'd lost your mind. But after reality set in and I lived with it for a couple of hours, a day — and Isabelle convinced me to slow down and actually think about things — I realized that although I *can* live without you, I don't want to. I messed up. And when I did, I put myself in danger of losing my best friend, one of the absolute best parts of my life."

He started to speak, about to tell her she'd never be able to cut him out of her life completely, but she cut him off.

"That was my ton of bricks moment. I realized that I want to be with you. Not just experimentally, but for good. Living without you is like living without oxygen. I can't do it. When I thought things were over, my chest literally ached. It burned, like I was missing an essential element. And that's because I was. You are an essential element for me, Shane."

A cheer went up in the bar, and Shane glanced at the TV to see the Cardinals running back celebrating a touchdown. When he looked back at Jessie, her gaze was on his face.

"You wouldn't believe how long I've waited to hear you say that," he said.

She cupped the side of his face, sliding her hand around the back of his head, bringing it to rest on his neck. "I love you, Shane West."

Before he could respond, she brought her mouth to his, tender and affectionate. This time, the kiss wasn't firecrackers or explosions.

It was love, strong and sweet and sure. When it ended, Shane rested his forehead against Jessie's. "I love you too, Jessie Monroe."

"What do you say we get out of here?"

"That sounds like a great idea."

When Shane went to the bar to pay their tab, the bartender told him, "It's already taken care of, bro. And, your dad left this for you."

The note, written on a bar napkin, said, *We're getting out of here. We'll leave you two lovebirds to it. I told you that if you'd just tell her, she'd understand. See you at home. But take your time. These two old lovebirds wouldn't mind a little space.*

Jessie couldn't stop smiling. It was Unofficial Christmas — the day she, Shane, Alvin, and Isabelle had decided to celebrate before Isabelle went back to Wyoming. The men were set to come over in an hour and she and Isabelle were in the kitchen making cinnamon rolls.

Christmas music played from the speaker on the counter and the tree twinkled in the living room.

"So you'll be back for New Year's Eve, right?" Jessie asked as she sprinkled brown sugar and cinnamon on the dough.

"Right," Isabelle said. "To tell you the truth, I would love to spend Christmas here too, but I think my kids might have a fit if I wasn't home."

"I know I gave my parents a hard time when I found out they decided to go to the Bahamas for Christmas this year," Jessie said.

She stopped herself from saying she hoped she and Shane would have their own place, their own tree, and their own traditions the following year.

Isabelle smiled. "Maybe next year, Alvin and I will go to the Bahamas for Christmas."

"Ooh, if you do, I'm getting in on that," Jessie said.

Together, they rolled up the dough and Isabelle held its shape while Jessie sliced it.

"Can I ask you something?" she said as they began placing the rolls into a baking sheet.

"Of course, dear," Isabelle said. "I'm an open book."

Jessie sprinkled more cinnamon and sugar on the rolls, then opened the oven and put in the pan. "You said that when Shane and I came to Buffalo, you could see that he was in love with me, and I didn't know it yet."

Expression thoughtful, Isabelle nodded. "I did, yes."

"How could you see those things? I mean, what did we do?"

Another tinkling laugh from Isabelle had a smile tugging at the corners of Jessie's mouth.

"Honestly, honey, I can't believe you couldn't see it, yourself."

Jessie rolled her eyes. "Apparently, I'm completely oblivious."

"I'd say you're hyper focused, not oblivious."

"Well, that's a nice way of putting it," Jessie said.

"You came to Buffalo on a mission, right? To get me to come to Prescott so Alvin and I could reunite."

"Right, but according to Shane, he's loved me for years and I've been oblivious the entire time."

"Chin up." Isabelle leaned gently against Jessie. "Let's have another cup of coffee and go sit down."

Once they were seated on the couch, coffee cups in hand, Isabelle said, "You asked me how I could see that Shane was in love with you."

"And that I was oblivious."

Eyes crinkling at the corners, Isabelle said, "Right. And that you were oblivious. When you meet someone for the first time, you kind of get into observation mode, don't you?"

Jessie nodded, sipped her coffee. The scent of the cinnamon rolls baking drifted into the living room, sweet and spicy.

"So that's what I did," Isabelle said. "These two young people — strangers — show up at my door, of course I'm going to observe, learn as much as I can. You know what I saw? That young man hangs on your every word. He watches you carefully, anticipates your needs, and steps in to fill them before you even ask. When we sat down to eat at my place, he handed you the salt without you saying anything. But not the pepper. When it was time for you to go, he got your jacket first and helped you into it. Opened the door for you. Deferred to you during conversations — and don't say it's just because you're bossy, because it's not."

Isabelle picked up her coffee mug and took a drink.

Hearing all of this from someone else's point of view made a rush of shivers run over Jessie's skin.

"How could I have been so oblivious?" she said.

"Because he's always treated you that way. Tell me this. Have you had other relationships?"

"I've dated a handful of people," Jessie said. "Only one I thought was really serious."

"And did you find yourself comparing them to Shane?"

Hands wrapped around her mug, Jessie considered. Did she? "I guess I did. I never put two and two together, until now, but most of the guys I dated didn't measure up to my standards. Now that I'm thinking about it, I realize I based those standards on Shane. How I felt around him, how he treated me, how polite he's always been."

"Well. Isn't that something?" Isabel said nothing else. She simply raised her eyebrows and held eye contact while Jessie let that idea sink in. The oven timer went off.

"I'll get it," Jessie said, almost withering under Isabelle's gaze. A blast of hot, cinnamony air hit her when she opened the oven. "These look perfect!" she called to Isabelle.

"They smell perfect, too," Isabelle called back.

Jessie was still frosting the rolls when a knock sounded at the door.

"Come in," she hollered, and looked up from her work to see Shane and Alvin, their arms full, each carrying a big cardboard box stuffed with gifts.

"Santa's here!" Shane said.

"Come on in and set down those boxes," Isabelle said. "Shane,

Jessie could use your help in the kitchen. Alvin and I can arrange the presents."

Jessie started to object, to say she didn't really need help in the kitchen, but then she realized she was being oblivious yet again. And why would she turn down any time with the man whose smile made her heart jump around in her chest like it was doing right now? Compelled, almost as if she didn't have control over her body, she set down the spatula and moved around the counter to wrap her arms around Shane's waist. "Merry Unofficial Christmas," she said to him, inhaling his freshly showered sent.

"Merry Unofficial Christmas to you," he said. He used one hand to tip her head back, and then his lips were on hers in what she'd consider a very merry way. Joyful champagne bubbles burst inside her body as she wrapped her hands around the back of his head and kissed him even more deeply. One of his hands moved to her breast and the other cupped her butt. She moaned with pleasure. "If you're not careful, this is going to get you on the naughty list. You're keeping me from finishing the cinnamon rolls."

She felt his lips curve into a smile. "Totally worth it."

After a few more minutes of toe-curling kisses, Jessie gave Shane's butt a two-handed squeeze, and then a swat. "We'll get back to this later. Isabelle and your dad are really looking forward to these cinnamon rolls. If we're not careful, we're going to have a mutiny on our hands."

He gripped her hips and pulled them against him so she could feel his erection. "Fine. But we'd better come back to this."

He gave her one more kiss and she peeled herself away to finish icing.

"You know I'm going to need a taste of that frosting, right?" He came toward the bowl with his pointer finger extended. They'd been through this interaction countless times throughout their lives. Like she always did, she smacked his hand before his finger came in contact with the icing.

"At least use a spoon."

As always, he said, "Why dirty a spoon for just one taste?"

He took a swipe of the frosting and instead of sticking his finger in his mouth like always, he rubbed a little of the icing on her lower lip and then swiped his finger into her mouth. She gave a surprised yelp, but nearly melted when he said, "Go ahead. Taste it."

Smoothing her tongue along the bottom of his finger, she sucked off the icing while fire burned in his eyes and heat shot between her legs.

"Delicious, right?" he said.

Almost too turned on to function, she said, "Delicious."

Grinning broadly, he used his other pointer finger to take a second swipe at the icing. This time, he tasted it himself. He gave her a single nod, and said, "Delicious." He flashed her a wicked smile. "I'm going to go see if my dad and Isabelle need any help with the presents. Why don't you finish frosting those, huh?"

Sexual energy still zinging around inside her body, Jessie smiled, rolled her eyes. No sooner had Shane left the kitchen than he came back in, eyebrows raised and a completely different kind of smile on his face. He hooked a thumb toward the living room and stage whispered, "Isabelle must have had her own ideas about what to do while I helped you with the icing."

"Are they in there making out?" Jessie stage whispered back.

A blush had made its way up Shane's neck and into his cheeks. "They are. I don't know whether to be delighted or grossed out."

Then he was snickering, as amused as a little kid would be.

"Too bad we don't have any mistletoe," he said in a booming voice, and a second later, Isabelle's laugh reached them in the kitchen.

Shane helped Jessie carry plates and forks to the table, where the four of them gathered to eat the cinnamon rolls.

"I have to say, this trip turned out to be a dream," Isabelle said. "I was so excited to spend time with Alvin, and I didn't even realize what a special treat it would be to spend time with the two of you."

Alvin's eyes shone at Isabelle across the table. "I'm so glad you took a chance on their crazy idea and came to see an old friend."

Isabelle reached out and took his hand. "I am, too."

"Well, for the record," Jessie said, "so am I. If you guys hadn't set us straight, I don't know what would've happened."

"Or not happened," Shane said. "Thank you for helping me find the courage to tell Jessie how I feel."

"You're welcome, dear. I just think it's so funny how you two came looking for love — for Alvin and me. And we ended up helping you find it, as well." She lifted her orange juice glass. "Cheers. To finding love, right in front of your face."

"Cheers," they all said, touching their glasses together.

Under the table, Shane put a hand on Jessie's thigh and squeezed. She looked over at him and the love she saw in his eyes made her breath catch.

After breakfast, the four of them opened gifts and then put on a Christmas movie.

As the end credits rolled, Isabelle stretched. "Merry Unofficial Christmas, everyone. I have a special gift for Alvin, so we'll go over to his house for now."

Isabelle winked at Jessie. Jessie looked at Shane. Shane shrugged.

Alvin said, "Well, let's go then, shall we?"

Once they said their goodbyes at the front door, Shane pulled Jessie close. "This might be the best Unofficial Christmas ever," he told her. "I can't believe you scored Cardinals tickets for my dad and me."

"It has been a very nice morning so far." Jessie agreed. "But I have an idea of how we can make it even better."

She took his hand and led him to the bedroom. Pointing at the chair in the corner she said, "Sit."

She walked into her closet and shut the door behind her.

When she emerged a moment later, she could practically see the anticipation thrumming through Shane's veins. He stood when he saw her, and took a step toward her.

"Well hello, Santa," he said, letting his eyes roam over the lingerie set she'd bought just for that day. He took in the tiny swatches of fur-lined red fabric that covered her breasts and the opaque material that draped over her stomach. Watching him look at her, seeing the desire in his eyes, Jessie felt her own body heating up. He made a twirling motion with his pointer finger, and she turned a slow revolution, showing off the red g-string that completed the outfit.

"Do I get to unwrap you?" he asked.

She took a step toward him. "I would love that."

Shane had spent many a New Year's Eve with Jessie, but never one as special as this. In previous years, all the fun had been in going outside at midnight and banging pots and pans with wooden spoons to welcome in the next year. The past several years, he'd gone out with buddies and closed down the bars. But now, sitting around the table playing cards with Jessie, his dad, and Isabelle, the highlight for Shane was the newfound love swirling around the house.

A fire burned in the fireplace, casting a merry glow throughout the living room. The Christmas tree remained in the corner, its colorful lights shining and its tinsel sparkling.

"I think we should go around and share our New Year's resolutions," Jessie said.

"Yes!" Isabelle said. "That sounds like fun. Alvin, why don't you go first?"

Shane's dad sat up a little straighter. He looked into Isabelle's eyes as he said, "My New Year's resolution is to make sure I have no regrets when it comes to showing the people I love exactly how much I care about them."

Isabelle's smile broadcast affection.

"Shane?" his dad said.

Looking at Jessie and linking his fingers with hers, Shane said, "Mine is to be more open and honest with the people I love."

"It's about damn time," Alvin said. "What about you, Isabelle?"

"I'm glad you asked," she said. "I plan to spend a little more time in Arizona, near the people I love."

"Aww," Jessie said. "I can't wait."

Shane, Isabelle, and Alvin looked at Jessie.

"Mine is to slow down and enjoy the people I love."

"I love that one," Isabelle said. "And now, it's almost midnight. Let's put on the ball drop and pour ourselves some champagne."

They gathered in front of the TV, watching the festivities in Times Square. "We're just one minute away from midnight," the announcer said.

The screen showed an image of the giant, sparkling ball atop its pole. The timer appeared in the bottom corner.

"Everyone have their champagne ready?" Alvin asked.

Shane, Jessie, and Isabelle held up their glasses. The countdown had reached ten seconds, and the announcer, along with the crowd, chanted out the single digit numbers. Shane and Jessie joined in at five seconds remaining, and once they reached zero, the four of them called out, "Happy New Year," and touched their glasses together.

After they all sipped their champagne, Shane pulled Jessie in for a New Year's kiss. Her hands on his chest and her hips against his, she kissed him back, gently at first, and then with increasing intensity.

"Get a room, you two," his dad said, guffawing and smiling at the same time.

"I think we will," Shane said, keeping an arm around Jessie's waist. "If you two will kindly excuse yourselves."

Giggling, Jessie swatted his shoulder. "You can't kick them out so we can —"

"Stop right there," Alvin said. "Just because you're adults doesn't mean I want to hear about what you're planning to do when we leave. Give us a minute to gather our things."

After they left, Shane pulled Jessie in again. "Now, where were we?"

The pleased sound she made when their lips met drove him wild. Her lips parted, and he plundered her mouth. He couldn't believe that after all this time, they were finally together. Not as friends, not as experiment, not just for fun, but for real. He finally had the chance to explore her body as he'd always dreamed about, and tonight he'd take full advantage of that (again).

His hands ran down her arms, from shoulder to wrist, and found their way to her waist and up to her breasts. When he brushed his thumbs over her nipples, she moaned again, and he repeated the movement. Pressing against him, she trailed her fingertips down his torso and used her palm to caress him through his pants.

"Why are you wearing so many clothes?" he murmured against her mouth.

"Why are *you*?" she asked, her lips quirking into a smile as she unbuckled his belt. "I think we need to remedy this."

She unbuttoned his pants and slid them down, along with his boxers, so he could step out of them. He pulled her sweater over her head and tossed it onto the couch, immediately pulling down the cup of her bra to put his mouth on her breast. He gasped when she grasped him and began to stroke him, the movements urgent.

"Careful," he told her.

Her throaty laugh made him throb against her palm, and she wrapped her hand around the back of her neck as she kissed him again. "Let's get started, then."

Desperate for release, he yanked down her leggings and flung them aside. They moved together, kissing, stroking, and sighing, to the couch.

"Sit," she said, reminding him of the week before when she'd gone into the closet to change into her Santa lingerie. He might lose it then and there, but he obeyed.

Kneeling in front of him, she took him into her mouth and wrapped one hand around the base of his dick. He slid his fingers through her hair, holding onto the back of her head while she moved over him.

"Jess," he said after a few glorious moments.

She paused and looked up at him, her hand still wrapped around him and her mouth just next to his dick, and he almost blew his load.

"Yes?" she said, eyes wide with innocence.

"I need to be inside you. Now."

She laughed and straddled him. They both gasped as she sank down onto him, and he gripped her hips as she started to move. Within a few seconds, he felt her shuddering release and allowed himself to go over the edge with her as they held on, their bodies quaking.

They were both out of breath when he said, "That didn't take long."

"You're right," she said. "I don't think I've ever been that turned on from a little kissing. And I've definitely never come that fast."

"Good," he said. "Just shows how amazing I am."

"You are," she said. "I'll get us a towel."

She kissed him on the nose and climbed off him. He swatted her bare ass and watched her walk into the bathroom. He felt like he was living his dream, after all this time.

The next morning, Shane once again left home before sunrise — this time with Jessie in the passenger seat and a song in his heart.

"I can't believe we're up in the dark on New Year's Day," Jessie said.

"We're hitting the new year hard — it's a sign of things to come."

"I like your thinking," she told him.

"Admittedly," he said, "this was a crazy idea. But it's going to be worth it."

They pulled up at Jump Zone, and Jessie squealed. "I'm so nervous!"

"It gets easier every time," he promised.

Roman met them at the shop door. "First customers of the new year! Welcome! This is quite a way to kick things off."

"Damn straight," Shane said.

Roman helped Jessie suit up and checked all her equipment and then checked Shane's.

He glanced out the window. "Plane's here. You guys ready?"

On the short walk out to the plane, Shane noticed the sky was just starting to lighten. "By the way," he told Jessie. "You look smokin' hot in that jumpsuit."

"Same to you," she said.

The pilot, Pete, stepped into the plane's doorway, waving. "We'd better get going if we're going to time this right," he hollered.

Shane, Jessie, and Roman broke into a jog and climbed the stairs. Inside the cabin, Jessie gripped Shane's hand so hard, he worried she might break his bones. As they taxied to the runway, the sky became even lighter and the sun, a fiery disc, peeked over the horizon.

"Beautiful sunrise," Jessie said, her words echoing Shane's thoughts. Her grip on his hand loosened, just a bit, and he leaned his shoulder against hers.

"It's a great symbol for new beginnings," he told her. "Sunrise on the first day of a new year, and we're about to have a special adventure together."

"Ready for takeoff?" Pete called from the cockpit.

Shane and Roman gave him a thumbs up, and Jessie offered a grimace. Shane felt the shift of gravity as the plane lifted off and gratitude washed over him. They were airborne, the plane moving from ground to sky as the sky brightened into a bold watercolor painting, smoky gray clouds streaking peach-and-purple sorbet.

"We've reached altitude," Pete said.

Jessie squealed again. "I'm so nervous!"

"I think you already said that," Shane said.

He strapped her body to his, and felt a thrill knowing she'd come to Jump Zone to share this experience with him. They moved to the door while Roman opened it.

"Ready?" he said.

Jessie shook her head wildly, and Roman glanced at Shane, concerned.

"I'm fine," Jessie yelled. "Really. I'm just nervous."

"Are you sure?" Roman said. "It's go time."

"I'm sure."

"All right," Roman said. "I'll go first. Give me a few seconds, and then take your turn."

Jessie nodded. Licked her lips. Roman saluted them and grinning, fell backwards out the door. Jessie's eyes were so round, Shane couldn't help but laugh out loud.

"Okay," he said. "We'll count down from three, and then we'll jump. Okay?"

She nodded.

Shane counted down, and when he reached one, the two of them leapt from the plane. They couldn't speak — the wind rushing past them on their descent was so loud, it prevented that. But her body pressed against his, Shane could feel Jessie's excitement, her thrill. She turned her head to grin at him.

Shane pulled the cord and pointed at Roman, who had his camera raised as they passed him. They drifted down and he could feel her laughing. He knew she was experiencing the unimaginable exhilaration he felt on every jump.

He warned her before they landed and they ran to a stop on the landing pad. After he disconnected her from his body, she spun around and hugged him hard. "That was amazing!"

Roman jogged up then and she threw her arms around him, too.

"Thank you!" she hollered, and laughing, he said, "Pretty awesome, right?"

"I can see why you guys are addicted," she said.

"And now you're gonna be addicted, too," Roman told her. "Oh, I forgot something. I'll be right back."

Still breathless, Jessie turned to face Shane again. "Shane," she said.

"I take it you liked that."

"I *loved* it! But that's not what I was going to say. I've thought of you like a best friend for so long and I took you for granted. You've always been there for me. And without either one of us even realizing it, you became the standard by which I measured all other men. It's no wonder none of them measured up. You're perfect for me. You're kind and smart and funny. And great in bed," she added, almost as an aside.

"Thanks," Shane said. "But —"

Jessie held up a hand. "I'm not done yet. I'm so sorry that I took you for granted for so long. I'm sorry I didn't even recognize my own feelings for you until recently. I'm sorry I made you feel like your feelings didn't matter. I want you to know I'm going to try my hardest to be the best possible partner I can be."

Shane nodded, his throat too tight for him to speak at that moment.

"I love you, Shane. Not like a brother. Not like a best friend. But like a lover. A husband."

When he saw her unzip the pocket on her jumpsuit and reach into it, he thought he must be mistaken. His eyes must be deceiving him. But no. When she brought her hand out of her pocket, her fingers were wrapped around a black velvet box. She opened it to reveal a gleaming gold band. When she made eye contact again, he could see a little fear, a little uncertainty, in her eyes. "I know this isn't really traditional," she said. "But I'd like to ask you — will you marry me?"

For Shane, time ceased. The world stopped turning. He was conscious of the desire to freeze this moment so he could remember it forever. The bright colors of the sunrise fading into pastels as the sun made its ascent. The woman he loved standing there, asking him to be with her forever. The feeling in his chest: love, tenderness, affection.

He realized he hadn't answered. Crushing her body against his, he said, "Of course I'll marry you. Of course I will."

She tilted her head back and he brought his mouth to hers, pouring every ounce of love into that kiss. When it ended she stepped back, took the ring out of the box, and held it up for him to slip his finger through.

"Perfect fit," she said.

"Perfect fit," he said.

Only then did Shane realize Roman had reappeared, camera in hand. "Captured every second of that moment," he said.

Punching him on the shoulder, Shane said, "Did you know all along that was her plan?"

"I did."

"Surprised you, didn't we?" Jessie said.

"You did. And it was the best surprise ever."

28

———————

"And that is the story of how I proposed to Shane," Jessie said, having scrolled through all the photos from their skydiving date and the proposal, which they'd cast onto the TV in her living room.

Their friends — Taylor and Judd and Rose, Mac, and Celeste — clapped. The men gave handshakes all around and the women hugged. Celeste tugged on Jessie's hand. "Does this mean I get to call Shane *Uncle* Shane now?"

Shane tousled her hair. "It sure does."

Celeste bounced off to the snack table, where she'd spent most of the afternoon grazing while everyone else celebrated Shane and Jessie's engagement.

"So when are you two going to tie the knot?" Rose wanted to know. Before either of them could answer, she rushed to add, "No rush! I was just curious. We all had so much fun at Judd and Taylor's wedding. Mac and I are planning ours, but it's less stressful to go to someone else's."

"Looks like we might have two weddings to work around," Shane said. "My dad proposed to Isabelle, too. In fact, they should be here any minute to celebrate with us. They're just coming in from Wyoming."

As if on cue, Jessie heard a knock at the door. Alvin and Isabelle let themselves in and everyone greeted them with congratulations, more hugs and handshakes, and fresh glasses of champagne. While the other happy couple shared the details of their news, Shane pulled Jessie into the kitchen.

"Nice party," he said. He refilled her champagne and then his.

"It is." She sipped from her flute. "But if we keep drinking champagne like it's water, I'm going to be sleeping through the end of it."

"Don't do that." He took her glass and set it on the counter. He took her hands in his. "I wanted to get you away from all those people."

Laughing, she playfully swatted his shoulder. "Stop it! We can't make out while we have company."

"We can't?" He kissed her, and she kissed him right back despite her protests. After a few good, solid kisses that left her toes curling, he stepped away from her. "I know this isn't really traditional," he started. "But I can't have my girl going around without an engagement ring."

Jessie's hand flew to her mouth. His eyes sparkled at her. He opened the box he'd taken from his pocket and a dazzling diamond glittered up at her.

"Shane," she breathed. "It's beautiful."

He smiled that smile, the one that turned her insides to the warm and gooey cinnamon-roll center. "A beautiful ring for a beautiful woman." He took the ring from the box and slid it onto her finger.

"Perfect fit," she said.

"Perfect fit."

After turning her hand this way and that, admiring the way her diamond twinkled, even under the kitchen lights, she wrapped her arms around him.

"Thank you," she said. "I love the ring, and I love you."

"You're welcome. Just for the record, I've always loved you. And I always will."

Jessie noticed then that the living room had gone almost silent. Celeste's voice came through the house, singsongy.

"What's going on?" Jessie said. She walked into the living room to see that it had been transformed.

Against the wall perpendicular to the TV, someone had placed an arch made of glittering pine boughs, pine cones, and cranberries. A small podium stood in its center, and Jessie's kitchen chairs and an assortment of others sat in rows facing the scene.

Behind the chairs, an easel held a sign that read: Welcome to the Monroe-West Wedding.

Jessie looked around — at her friends, Alvin and Isabelle, and Shane, and felt her eyes tearing up.

"You guys!" she said. "Did you plan this without telling me?"

"You're always moving so fast," Taylor said. "You're a step ahead of the rest of us. We rarely get to surprise you. But I'd say we did pretty good this time."

"You did!" Tears fell freely now, and Jessie swiped at them before taking Shane's hand.

"We have one more surprise for you," Shane said.

"You do? How could you possibly? This is all so magical."

He walked to the front door and opened it, and there stood her parents, smiling, arms open for hugs. She ran at them, sobbing as they embraced.

"We're here for the wedding," her dad said. "I hope you saved us a seat."

"Did we?" Jessie asked, looking around the room at her friends, whose smiles held as much excitement as she felt.

"We did," Rose said. "And we bought you a dress."

"You bought me a dress?"

"Upstairs," Celeste said, pointing.

Jessie led the way, and Taylor, Isabelle, her mom, and Celeste followed. Rose came up a minute later, a dress hung over her arm.

"Taylor, Celeste, and I picked this out for you," Rose said. "I'm positive it's going to fit. It looks just right."

She held it up, and a fresh round of tears threatened. The bodice would fit close to her body, and the skirt's ivory fabric would trail behind her.

"It's perfect," she said. "It's exactly what I've always wanted."

"They know," Celeste said. "You've been talking about it forever. They found it at a big bridal shop in Phoenix. We were there for hours. But the nice lady there fed me snacks."

Jessie's mom put an arm around her shoulders. "It's beautiful, Jess," she said. "Why don't you put it on?"

She did, and after a few minutes of fussing over her hair, Jessie's crew went downstairs to where the men waited. From the bedroom, Jessie heard the first notes of the bridal march, and Celeste hollered, "Okay, Aunt Jessie! It's time to come down."

Jessie descended the stairs. She came around the corner and saw Shane standing under the arch. When he saw her, his eyes lit up. Their gazes held, and love welled up in Jessie's chest. Isabelle stood at the podium, her gaze switching from Jessie to Shane and back again, her grin wide.

Jessie's parents sat in the first row of chairs, with Alvin beside them. Rose, Celeste, Mac, Taylor, and Judd sat in the next row. They'd all turned to watch Jessie walk into the room, and she nearly burst with love for them ... her family. Shane reached for her as she approached, and when he took her hands, she felt a connection she'd never experienced before: it was like pure light radiating through her body.

Someone turned off the music and Isabelle started to speak.

"We are gathered here today to celebrate the marriage of Jessie Monroe and Shane West. Although it was a surprise gathering, in a way, I think most of us would agree it was a long time coming."

Someone whistled — Jessie guessed it was Mac — and a few laughs ensued. Although Jessie heard what Isabelle said, and repeated her vows with solemn sincerity, she found that all she could think about was spending the rest of her life with Shane. In that moment, she could see their whole future. A house, a couple of pets, a handful of kids, maybe even a minivan. Dinners around the table, bedtime stories, sporting events on Saturdays, and visits from Santa. And eventually, retirement vacations to the beach.

When Isabelle pronounced them husband and wife, the little crowd cheered. Shane took Jessie's face in his hands and kissed her. The kiss went on and on, delighting Jessie's senses and making her realize there was one thing she hadn't pictured a moment before: hers and Shane's wedding night.

Everyone cheered when they ended the kiss and faced the audience, hand in hand.

They walked back down the makeshift aisle to applause, and just like he had before, Shane pulled Jessie into the kitchen.

"I wanted to get you away from all those people," he said again.

"We'd better hang out with them for a while at least," she said. "They're here for our wedding. But after this, you'll have me to yourself for the rest of our lives."

~

The End

ABOUT THE AUTHOR

Hilary Dartt loves great adventures, whether she's writing, reading, or living them. The author of twelve novels, Hilary lives in Arizona's high desert with her husband, their three children, and her Weimaraner, Leia. She loves camping, exploring in the Jeep, and dance parties with her kids. Learn more and sign up for her newsletter at www.hilarydartt.com.

www.ingramcontent.com/pod-product-compliance
Lightning Source LLC
Chambersburg PA
CBHW061800190726
48289CB00007B/2009